An Affair with Beauty

An Affair with Beauty

THE MYSTIQUE OF HOWARD CHANDLER CHRISTY

THE MAGIC OF YOUTH

JAMES PHILIP HEAD

NORTHLOOP
BOOKS

For my wife, Rita,

my daughter, Christianna . . .

and for Holly, Jocelyn, Elsie, Collette, Maxine, Marilyn, Melodie, Mitzi, Olga, Jane, Jennie, Joyce, Helen, Diane, Elaine, Ellen, Jan, Linda, Lyn, Phyllis, Laura, Barbara, Marguerite . . .

and all of the other remarkable women whose strong voices, unwavering spirits, and incomparable perseverance have transformed my dream of writing this epic story into a reality.

Forever they will be . . . my Christy Girls.

TO DISCOVER AN UNKNOWN LAW OF HUMAN LIFE

Intellectual energy, like every other of which we have knowledge, is the product of antecedents. A great genius never comes by chance. It always bursts upon the world, as the new star in Auriga burst upon us, unexpectedly, but only because we have not explored the depths out of which it has come. Every man at birth is an epitome of his primogenitors. He starts out with the elements of his character drawn from the widest sources, but so mixed in him that he differs necessarily from every other individual of his race. Here is the problem of life. Not the dome of St. Peter's, but how the hand rounded it acquired skill; not the play of "Hamlet," but how the mind that gave it its wondrous birth was developed—these are our chief concerns.

—Edwin Reed (1835–1908)

CONTENTS

Introduction   *xiii*

PROLOGUE

An Affair with Beauty   *1*

BOOK ONE: THE MAGIC OF YOUTH

CHAPTER ONE

Homeward Bound   *9*

CHAPTER TWO

Fanfare for a Common Man   *27*

CHAPTER THREE

Moments of Pleasure   *53*

CHAPTER FOUR

A Lovely Place to Be   *69*

CHAPTER FIVE

Of Youth and the Magnificent River   *109*

CHAPTER SIX

A Glimpse of Heaven   *139*

CHAPTER SEVEN

An Unexpected Visitor   *155*

CHAPTER EIGHT

The Gift of Immortality   *189*

*A List of Selected Books Illustrated
by Howard Chandler Christy*   *213*

Author's Note   *221*

Notes   *235*

Endnotes   *267*

About the Author   *270*

Stylistic Note

ALL QUOTATIONS contained in this book originate from words either spoken or written by the person to whom they are ascribed. The quotations are taken verbatim and, therefore, may contain grammatical errors. All italicized portions of the narrative are based upon words either spoken or written by the person to whom they are ascribed, or are expressly devised to fit the context of the particular scene in which they are used. All references to "Howard" mean Howard Chandler Christy, and all references to "Nancy" mean Nancy Palmer Christy.

Howard Chandler Christy, as he appeared in February 1918, in front of the lens of Arnold Genthe (Arnold Genthe Collection, Library of Congress, Washington, DC)

Introduction

*D*URING THE JAZZ AGE, the most celebrated artist in America, if not Europe, was not Grant Wood, Edward Hopper, or Georgia O'Keefe. It was also not Henri Matisse, Edvard Munch, or Pablo Picasso. Norman Rockwell? No, it was not even the great Rockwell.

This artist was a once-blind illustrator-turned-portrait-painter who, until his dying day, was referred to by many as the "Barefoot Boy from the Blue Muskingum." By 1938, *Time* magazine proclaimed him "the most commercially successful U.S. artist." He typified the quintessential American dream, and his achievements captured, illuminated, and influenced the extraordinary times in which he lived—an era that spanned the Gilded Age, the Spanish-American War, World War I, the Roaring '20s, the Great Depression, the Golden Age of Hollywood, World War II, and the post-war boom of the late 1940s and early 1950s.

His name, now forgotten to many, was Howard Chandler Christy.

In this day and age, it is difficult to comprehend thoroughly the true extent of the tremendous success and popularity that Christy achieved during his eighty years of life. This is primarily true because he was an artist not of today, but of an uncommon epoch that extended from the late nineteenth century through the first half of the twentieth century. It was a time of exceptional growth in population, industry, technology, and culture in which one could witness the birth of the automobile, airplane, and luxury liner, all within a few short years of each other. This exciting chapter in history also saw the rise of the modern news media and mass advertising, both extremely powerful tools that would forever sway and motivate the general public's sentiments in politics, commerce, fashion, and even warfare. In the first part of this remarkable era, the public's informational and entertainment needs focused on newspapers and magazines, while during the latter part, radio and motion pictures dominated the scene. In every medium, Christy's artistic influence was present, if not profound.

Advancements in science, medicine, and architecture also contributed to the flourishing expansion of the time, giving rise to the dawn of a new social order, one marked by fabulous wealth, glamour, and elegance but set against a backdrop of intense political, economic, and racial turmoil. Out of this unprecedented phase of America's development emerged a new culture, one consisting of ambitious business tycoons, charismatic political leaders, fearless military heroes, and sultry matinee idols, the likes of which the world had never seen before and will likely never see again. Many of these luminaries, like Christy, sprouted from humble beginnings to be eventually hailed as living deities. Even today, some of them, long since departed, are instantly recognized by their names or faces, icons forever etched in the minds of millions as being legends in their time. Yet only a select few were honored by having Christy's masterful hand immortalize their figures on canvas, preserving their best traits, their youthfulness, and their beauty for future generations to admire and venerate.

In viewing the essence of Christy's life, one can say that it was primarily centered upon beauty—specifically physical beauty—mostly of people but also of nature. In the same vein, he was fascinated with portraying the deeper inner beauty found within God's creations, an attribute that distinguished him from almost every other artist of his time. Christy did not merely look at his subject and then apply paint to canvas in an attempt to mimic in color what he saw in flesh. To the contrary, he would observe, study, and oftentimes research his subject. In most cases, he would spend hours, if not a few days, first conversing with and enjoying the pleasure of his benefactor before beginning a commission. The time that Christy spent absorbing the internal beauty of his sitter permitted him to convey in oil paint the person's true character and personality, a subtlety that photography could never reproduce.

In 1924, one perceptive interviewer succinctly characterized Christy's unique talent of depicting his subject's inner spirit in this way: "It is undoubtedly Mr. Christy's ability to thus comprehend and present to others through the medium of brush and canvas the inner self of the men and women whom he paints that makes his portraits stand out from those of other artists, until today he is known as America's foremost portrait painter."

In rendering portraits, Christy would delight in depicting his subjects' most impressive attributes with such an exquisite charm and tenderness that, upon completion of his work, they would invariably be stunned. On closer inspection, they would remark that they never knew how strikingly handsome or beautiful they were. This was his passion. He adored all things beautiful, and he painted them "in the grand manner" like that of Thomas Gainsborough, Joshua Reynolds, and John Singer Sargent. This was how he was instructed as a young student, and in his opinion, like that of his distinguished clientele, this was the best style for the highest form of art he knew—portrait painting.

More important, Christy's graceful painting style reflected the refined and genteel tastes of his patrons and the distinctive times in which they lived.

The measure of Christy's greatness, however, is not just found in the splendor of his art or his mysterious ability to seize on canvas a person's inner and outer beauty. It can be seen in his life story—an incomparable journey of how he rose from poor Midwestern beginnings, much like that of Mark Twain, to become the most successful and famous painter of his time, acquiring a celebrity status akin to that of a modern-day rock star. Unlike most artists—whose lives were generally replete with frustration, loneliness, despair, poverty, and the inevitable untimely ending—his life was so charmed with energy, excitement, opulence, and fame that it reads like a script for an epic motion picture.

Born in a log cabin in Morgan County, Ohio, during the winter of 1872, Christy lived as a young boy on an Ohio farm overlooking the Muskingum River Valley. There, from high among the bluffs under cloudless skies, he watched whistling steamboats ferrying worldly passengers to exciting unknown destinations. As he viewed the steady streams of smoke trailing off in the horizon, he vowed that he too would travel far one day, even farther than the steamboats, and would learn to "paint big pictures of big things." He made good on that promise.

At the age of eighteen, Christy ventured to New York City with two hundred dollars in his pocket and a dream of becoming a distinguished artist. He studied under various artists of the Art Students League in New York City and, a year later, under William Merritt Chase, the foremost American impressionist painter of that era. Within only a few months under Chase's direction, Chase declared Christy to be the most brilliant student he had ever taught. A few years later, at the age of twenty-three, Christy got his big break and began drawing illustrations, first for *Century* magazine and then for *Harper's Weekly, Scribner's Magazine*, and *Leslie's Weekly*.

With the advent of the Spanish-American War in 1898, Christy traveled alongside the United States Army in Cuba to record in visual form the encampments, the battles, and the horrors of warfare. On his way there, he met then Colonel Theodore Roosevelt and witnessed firsthand the bravery of Roosevelt and his Rough Riders. Christy's sketches, many of which were published in weekly magazines as large two-page centerfolds, became the focal point for tens of thousands of American readers whose only glimpse of the crossfire would come not from photographs but from these works. By August 1898, Christy's pictorials became so popular that *Leslie's Weekly* published Christy's own personal account of the war in six separate installments. The critical acclaim that Christy received from his stories about the war helped him convince Roosevelt to commit his own story of the conflict to Charles Scribner's Sons. Roosevelt listened, and his account, titled *Rough Riders*, became an instant best-seller upon its 1899 release. The relationships that Christy forged and the images that he produced during this war guaranteed his future success as an artist whom America would adore.

Upon returning to New York City, Christy became a noted illustrator of books and magazines. He would typically earn between four hundred and a thousand dollars—a phenomenal sum for that time—to produce four to six illustrations per week.

Ever enterprising, Christy ventured away from merely making storybook pictures, the usual fare of illustrators of that day, and instead concentrated on portraying a new figure emerging in society, one that was liberated, wise, youthful, zestful, and self-reliant. It was the modern American woman.

Motivated by his friend and colleague, Charles Dana Gibson, Christy invented the "Christy Girl," an idealized portrayal of feminine perfection intermixed with independence and confidence. With some of the most beautiful women in America as his models, Christy borrowed upon their best qualities to create a romanticized, statuesque goddess who would redefine the concept of feminine beauty in the early twentieth century and influence fashion for decades to come. The Christy Girl was virtuous, athletic, secure, graceful, and determined. But above all, she was undeniably beautiful, and America could not get enough of her. Countless books, calendars, and prints with her face and figure were sold. Shoes, hats, and dresses—and even dances and an entire musical—were named after her. People would frame pictures of the Christy Girl and place them throughout their homes. Men would write letters proposing marriage to her. Newspapers held contests in the hope of finding her living personification. She became an American icon of beauty.

By April 1917, Christy's fame and dexterity for painting glamorous women catapulted him from the ranks of celebrity painter to that of a superstar. As World War I escalated, the United States government capitalized on Christy's success and his ability to influence American tastes. To build morale, the government recruited him to paint alluring women for posters that would compel thousands of young men to join the military and others to help the war effort. Everywhere one went, a captivating Christy Girl would beckon him to join the Army, Navy and Marines or to "Fight or Buy Bonds!" Christy generously donated his time and talent during World War I and, on numerous later occasions, painted posters for patriotic and humanitarian causes.

After portraying captivating women for two decades, whether for commercial illustrations or for war posters, Christy became renowned as the premier authority on feminine beauty. When the Atlantic City Businessmen's League wanted to produce a fall beauty pageant as part of an effort to entice summer tourists to remain in the New Jersey seaside town after Labor Day, it was only natural that Christy would be selected as judge. This two-day pageant, first held on September 7, 1921, eventually became known as the Miss America Pageant. Christy was the only famous artist serving as judge in that first pageant. He was the chairman of the judges' panel and would remain in that role for another three years, serving alongside his close friends and colleagues James Montgomery Flagg, Coles Phillips, Charles Chambers, and Norman Rockwell.

In the fall of 1921, at the insistence of Nancy Palmer Christy, his former model and new bride, Christy abandoned illustration in favor of portrait painting, which he considered to be a far superior art form. With commissions coming in daily, he soon became the preferred painter for presidents, generals, movie stars, socialites, and famous personalities of the era. He would go on to paint the faces of countless notables, including presidents Warren Harding, Calvin Coolidge, Herbert Hoover, Franklin Delano Roosevelt and Harry S. Truman; aviators Amelia Earhart and Eddie Rickenbacker; humorist Will Rogers; publishing magnate William Randolph Hearst; and Allied General Douglas MacArthur.

Indeed, the "Barefoot Boy from the Blue Muskingum" had arrived, and America received him as its foremost painter and portraitist.

As his rare talent became in exceeding demand, Christy's fame and achievements also transcended international boundaries. He was asked to paint Europe's royalty, nobility, and principal leaders, including the Prince of Wales, Benito Mussolini, Prince Phillip of Hesse, and Crown Prince Umberto of Italy.

In between the important portrait sittings, Christy always seemed to have time to entertain his favorite pastime. He loved painting beautiful young women, specifically the best America had to offer. And, because of his exceptional talent, they all came to him to be painted. In a June 1935 *Movie Classic* article titled "Who Are the Beauties of Today?" journalist B. F. Wilson remarked, "Howard Chandler Christy has been painting beautiful women ever since he began his famous career as an illustrator and portrait painter. He has seen all the great beauties of the past forty years. He has known them all. He has painted them all. And today he stands alone as an authority on beauty." With America's most gorgeous women at his call, Christy indulged his passion for immortalizing the feminine physique in all its glory. A select few of these curvaceous beauties, particularly those who were the most vibrant, graceful, and charming, he invited to pose for his special paintings—the nudes.

Not surprisingly, wherever Christy went, he was hounded by press reporters, columnists, and radio personalities. Each hoped to be the first to land a story that would detail Christy's latest travels and disclose the warm friendships that Christy developed with his celebrity patrons. Each wanted to be the first to announce to the public the intimate hours Christy would spend observing, conversing with, and capturing in paint his famous subjects. Then, they would invariably inquire about his trade secrets. How did he produce, in a week or less, a masterful likeness of his sitter in the grand styles of Gainsborough and Reynolds? What was his magic? How was this humanly possible? Christy would generally indulge them with a glimpse into his artistic genius and give them a little insight behind his adroit brushstrokes. No doubt, he would also provide a firsthand account of his humble beginnings, his artistic heroes, and his philosophy on fine art. After these interviews, the reporter would leave little, if any, of

Christy's statements on the cutting room floor. People wanted to know everything about him.

In 1939, the United States government commissioned Christy to recreate on canvas the momentous signing of the Constitution of the United States, an accolade that he considered his finest achievement and the crowning glory of his illustrious career. The monumental work became the largest painting on canvas in the United States Capitol—and the largest in America—when unveiled in May 1940. In the twelve years following, he would continue to receive large commissions to paint historically important events and would also paint biblical works inspired by his love of Christ and his devotion to God, whom he credited for miraculously restoring his eyesight from blindness years earlier.

Despite his declining health in the early 1950s, Christy continued to apply his usual vigor to the passion that was his life. Even then, the demand for Christy's work far outstripped his ability to supply it. Yet he continued his usual daily pace of painting from nine in the morning until four in the afternoon, diminishing his routine only after he suffered a heart attack, less than three months before his death on March 3, 1952.

▣

MANY YEARS EARLIER, while interviewing Christy after he had painted President Coolidge's portrait, an unidentified but observant journalist remarked, "You can learn a good deal about a man's work by talking about it with him; but if you want to find out about the man himself, go straight to the headquarters—ask his wife." So the interviewer did just that and was aptly rewarded by his insightful discussions with Nancy Palmer Christy.

Described as having "the softest of real golden-blonde hair, gray-blue eyes, regular features, and the loveliest complexion imaginable," Mrs. Christy was her husband's model, muse, best friend, and true love. The two were inseparable. During that same interview, the journalist then perceptively discovered, "They seem to have a mutual admiration society—these two—and Mrs. Christy's loyalty and affection are reciprocated in overflowing measure by her husband. No wonder they are such a popular couple—wherever they go, they are much sought after, not because of Mr. Christy's reputation, but because they are so attractive and such awfully good company."

It is then fitting that this interpretative biography is written through the eyes of the person who knew the artist best. Fortunately, Mrs. Christy kept fairly detailed records of her life with her husband in the form of letters, diaries, newspaper clippings, scrapbooks, and an unfinished biographical manuscript. Accordingly, the narrative is told through the perspective of Nancy Christy and, when the occasion merits, transitions to the voice of the artist himself.

An Affair with Beauty—The Mystique of Howard Chandler Christy is not a definitive biography. It does not reveal every deep wrinkle or smooth perfection of Christy's life. Rather, its purpose is to distill his essence and character—and to provide a distinct impression of his immense genius and popularity during the time in which he lived.

In short, this is a portrait of the artist in words . . . as his wife, Nancy, remembered him.

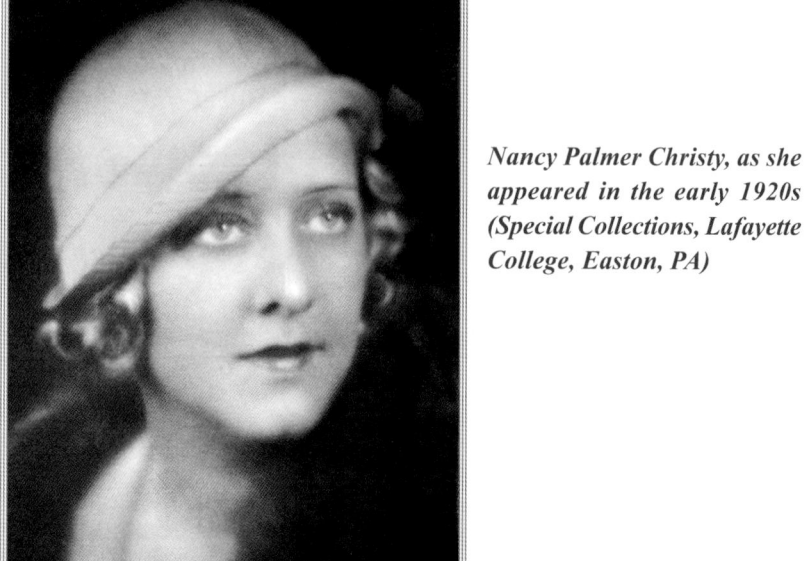

Nancy Palmer Christy, as she appeared in the early 1920s (Special Collections, Lafayette College, Easton, PA)

Nancy, later in life, with her beloved husband, Howard (Special Collections, Lafayette College, Easton, PA)

PROLOGUE

An Affair with Beauty

September 1969—New York City, New York

*I*F I REMEMBER CORRECTLY, it was Sigmund Freud, the great German psychoanalyst, who once said that all artists want in life are three things: fame, money, and beautiful lovers.

It was during the autumn of 1923 that I first heard this aphorism.

As the sun slowly descended behind the city's jagged skyline of concrete and stone, I found myself milling about a crowded art gallery in midtown Manhattan. The main exhibition space swarmed with pearl necklaces and gold pocket-watch chains. For the exhibiting artist, this was absolute splendor; the throng of prospective wealthy patrons meant success—a newfound clientele, new acquaintances, and, of course, old friends. For me, the whole affair became a fantasy of elegance spun of shimmering silk, painted chiffon, and violet georgette.

As I left the main gallery, my attention was drawn to the exotic headdresses adorning two young women. Sheathed in crimson red and rust, they desperately wanted to appear like modern-day Egyptian princesses, perhaps distant cousins from the same royal bloodline as Tutankhamun, the young pharaoh whose tomb was discovered the previous year. But somehow, with their fair complexions, they looked more like showgirls from Grauman's Egyptian Theater in Hollywood. Close by, two tall enchantresses in flowing gowns of iridescent blue and royal purple hastily retreated from the crowd, only to fall victim to the idle plans of a pair of even taller gentlemen. Arms linked, they were off.

In the distance, beyond the din of the celebration, a white ostrich fan darted in and out of the room's darker recesses. Carried by unseen hands, it oscillated to and fro, here and there, from one corner of the room to the next, reminding me of gossamer floating over a sunny meadow I once knew.

Willowy gowns, some lavishly dripping with beads or metallic threads, swirled about that evening. The varied styles, patterns, and hem lengths all seemed lost in an ever-shifting sea of black dinner jackets. Dominating the scene then were high wing collars with a glistening gold button in front and a simple, narrow bow of black satin below. White piqué shirts—as stiff as sign board—and tight black waistcoats transformed even the most modest gentleman into a debonair man of mystery like that of a movie star.

As the people passed, I kept thinking, *There goes Rudolph Valentino!* Or, *Here comes Douglas Fairbanks!*

Wait! Is that Mary Pickford?

Who is that? Harry Houdini? Oh, he knows Howard and me.

They all knew us . . . in fact, they were our close friends.

It was all so difficult to avoid illusion then, when the entire room and its occupants glittered. Beauty reigned everywhere. Or so it seemed. This was the sublime sophistication of American prosperity during the early days of the Coolidge administration. Everything was magical then. The music seemed louder, the buildings seemed taller, and the cars seemed faster than I had ever known. The men and women seemed more daring. After what they had been through, no burden seemed too great. Invincibility filled the air. Diamond dust fell at their feet.

And that is how it was on that October night when I met Emil Fuchs.

Mr. Fuchs was an astute Austrian painter whom Queen Victoria and King Edward VII commissioned to paint the English royal family years earlier. Lean and somewhat gaunt, he had a distinctive, aristocratic accent and a well-trimmed white beard. Knowing who I was and to whom I was married, he edged up beside me in his white tie and tails and furtively uttered those insightful words of Dr. Freud: *"Fame, money, and beautiful lover-r-rs; that is all ar-r-rtists want in life."*

My sudden unrestrained giggling could have stopped all conversation midafternoon in any tearoom in this metropolis but not there, not in that gallery.

Yes, it is true. I have encountered scores of artists. The vast majority certainly fell into this category of unbridled cravings. But I wonder now. If anyone overheard Mr. Fuchs or my reaction, perhaps they thought ill of us. Then again, perhaps they didn't suspect anything at all.

In those days, the profession of an artist was considered a distinguished line of work. And for an artist, the ingredients of fame, money, and beautiful lovers are a certain recipe for tragedy. The exception to this rule of thumb was a painter who possessed an extraordinary gift. With his brush, he could seize beauty and immortalize youth. His observations went well beyond the physical being; the inner beauty he would see. Some say he could capture a person's soul.

This painter was my husband, Howard Chandler Christy.

In Howard's life, he accomplished those three objectives and much more, but along the way, he paid a significant price. Was it all worth it? I will leave that for you to answer.

For me, that is a particularly difficult question, now that over seventeen years have passed since the day he departed this life. What I do know as a certainty is this: Howard turned out far better than anyone could have envisioned. More important, he unearthed something more precious than those ideals. His discovery transformed his life forever. To him, it was all worth it. And for good reason.

Something was uniquely different about Howard. As he became older, he didn't seem to feel the ill effects that old age generally casts upon most. For some unexplained reason, he remained strong to the end.

His memory never faltered.

His eyes never failed.

He still worked constantly, possessing a vitality equal to that of his youth.

Everyone was in awe of him, especially those forever-youthful models of his, the ones with perfect skin and lithe, ivory bodies. They simply adored him.

All of them.

MY JOURNEY WITH HOWARD began many years before that lavish art exhibition.

Now that I am in the winter of my own life, I, on occasion, reflect upon those early days with a bit of nostalgia. It was precisely that way when, on this late September afternoon, I decided to stroll through Central Park, a world-famous pastoral oasis just across the street from where I live. To me, it was a foreign land, but I longed to experience what he had seen those many years earlier.

From the park's dimly lit, tree-framed corridors, I see young couples emerge. Refreshed yet weary, they forge home hand in hand, amid the alluring glow of headlights streaming up and down the busy avenue. I press ahead and see the panorama that I had once envisioned but never took the time to discover.

Oh, yes! It's everything that he said it was.

It's so beautiful.

The sun tumbles through the distant trees. Its last rays guide my path.

The birds that once filled the park's bright pathways prepare to take flight for an evening's slumber.

Within this rare hour of the day, when the soft hues of deep violet, indigo, and amber intersect the sky, I explore the woods and begin to contemplate my life, much like Howard did those many years earlier when he walked the same tree-lined meadows.

Striding the pavement at a rhythmic pace, as he once did, I take notice again of those fleeting years and the rapidity with which they deserted me. When I do, I feel more than a touch of old age and fading beauty. Perhaps that is because when I view my own life, I look not at myself but at the many exceptional individuals, now gone, who have enriched it, who have taught me and comforted me. In doing so, I know that no one impressed me more than he did. And so, when I think of Howard now, my heart returns to his last few hours on this earth. And those melancholy emotions return to haunt me again. With them, a tinge of regret unavoidably follows.

BOOK ONE: THE MAGIC OF YOUTH

Surrounded by fragrant flowers, Howard enjoys the comforts of his pipe and easy chair in the living room of his Hotel des Artistes studio apartment, circa 1927. On the day of his death, the great window was stripped bare, and the Christys' Steinway grand piano sat front and center with a bust of Mussolini on top, a gift of the former dictator. (Underwood & Underwood; Special Collections, Lafayette College, Easton, PA)

CHAPTER ONE

Homeward Bound

March 3, 1952—The Christy Studio, New York City, New York

*A*s I PREPARED TO DEPART ON THAT COOL, cloudless Monday morning of March 3, 1952, Howard was comfortably settled in his favorite chair.

I remember the sunlight filtering through our living room from the great rectangular window, the largest of several within our studio apartment. In its sheer brilliance, the light was quite stunning yet tranquil. For this light was the north light, the best for Howard's work.

Two days earlier, the heaviest snowfall of the season—nearly five inches—crippled the metropolis, but workmen and a temperate sun returned the area to its former self. The lingering cold that had pervaded the city for weeks was silently surrendering to the warmth and hope of a new spring.

Just before dawn, when Howard was asleep, the serenity of the studio was interrupted by a beam of moonlight streaming in from the upper reaches of the huge window. A ghostly aura was cast upon a bust of Benito Mussolini perched upon a fringed Spanish shawl covering our grand piano. The Italian leader gave us that statue when Howard painted him years before. A redemptive shroud cloaked the deposed dictator.

Standing by the window, I noticed two table lamps shining below from a floor of one of the brownstone buildings lining West Sixty-Eighth Street. Someone was awake, perhaps an executive, a musician, or a painter. Then again, perhaps it was a restless woman, like me, who found herself pacing the floor in the dark early hours.

Sleep was never an easy task in this, the largest city in America.

NEW YORK CITY always seems to have an uncompromising effect upon people. It turns many of its denizens into insomniacs. Things move more quickly here; they have to. To the uninitiated, it is forbidding, dark, and cold. But to those who call it home, it is lively and vibrant. Typically, one can become accustomed to the ceaseless humming, honking, and screeching of the endless traffic that floods its thoroughfares and bridges at all hours. The constant noise is the heartbeat of the city, giving it character. A living pulse.

To me, residing in Manhattan was much like attending a fabulous party every night. Yet on some nights, the party was just Howard and me in our apartment with our maid, Callie, and maybe our butler, George, if he stayed late. But the most difficult part was becoming acclimated to the unremitting pressures that surround a metropolis of nearly eight million inhabitants. Everyone came from different backgrounds, cultures, and nationalities, a melting pot to be sure, but the one common denominator in this city was energy. Most people would spend the better part of a day pushing buttons, telephoning orders, writing out requests, delivering parcels, picking up crates, traveling here and there, going up and down, this way and that. It was maddening, or so it seemed.

Everyone was struggling to find a place in this looming yet promising city. They were here because they wanted to achieve the American dream. Howard and I were no different.

We lived in a duplex studio apartment, number 707, located at One West Sixty-Seventh Street, an eighteen-story cooperative known as the Hotel des Artistes. For over thirty years, this was our home.

◫

As the dawning sun grew stronger, the light from the adjacent building slowly faded. Within minutes, the cavernous space of our living room, some twenty-two feet in height, came alive.

From high above, many eyes were watching me. It felt like the eyes of angels. I had seen them so many times before and in so many different moods—the beautiful faces that Howard had painted through the years. As they emerged from their quiet shadows, they reclaimed their regal station. First, human outlines surfaced; then, figures. The soft texture of human flesh came into view. The pallid light intensified. With the brilliance of molten glass, the huge, gilded frames began to smolder in the receding darkness. I was no longer alone.

Directly across from the window was Howard's work area, a small cove nestled underneath the second-floor balcony that ran the length of the studio from the grand fireplace to an angular staircase. A gallery of his full-length and half-length portraits lined the wall of this grand promenade and along the corner walls of the stairs.

Just underneath two large, ornate tapestries, cascading from the center balcony balustrade, was Howard's spot. A platform and tall easel rested there. On any given day, he could be seen in front of his easel but not then.

On that particular Monday, Howard quietly descended the stairs, sporting a blue suit, pressed white shirt, and fashionable tie. He walked across the room to the far right corner and deposited himself in his favorite chair, a large, ornately carved Italian piece that sat before a narrow Italian table flanking the north wall. This table served as his desk.

From this solemn corner, Howard labored on as the light's soft glow fell upon his hunched shoulders and untamed white hair. Once handsome and strong, his face reflected the harsh effects that the passage of time can have on a human body. His jaw, formerly sharp and clean, had developed distinctive jowls and a

The Christys' living room, facing east. Before Howard died on March 3, 1952, he was seated in the large Italian chair (behind the far left flower vase), then positioned farther back at the far left corner, in front of where the baby grand piano is shown here along the east wall. (Underwood & Underwood; Special Collections, Lafayette College, Easton, PA)

double chin that, when his head moved downward in a nodding motion, added a few more layers to it.

His eyes remained the same piercing shade of azure blue that I recall seeing when I first met him, but they were now barely visible. Snowy-white eyebrows hooded them. When he squinted, and his forehead furrowed ever so slightly, his face would exude a regal air, like that of an eagle sizing up its prey. Metaphorically, this stately bird fitted Howard's persona. He saw everything with deep perception and incisiveness.

His five-foot-eight-and-a-half-inch frame, previously straight and limber, had visibly shrunk. Physical frailties, however, never deterred him. Like his stalwart Midwestern forebears, Howard exuded a strong, physical prowess and an industrious work ethic that seemed old-fashioned to most, almost puritanical in scale, but it suited him well. Work dispelled his worries. Perhaps this is because he was always doing what he loved best—painting.

It was within this soft light of the early morning that Howard was diligently applying pen to paper. Unlike his usual custom and practice, he was not sketching out the preliminary details for a great mural or tall portrait. Instead, he was endorsing a small batch of checks that lay on his desk. He wanted them to be deposited later, when the bank opened, and he required my assistance to do so. Howard could not make the trip himself. The effects of time were finally prevailing upon him.

HOWARD WAS EIGHTY YEARS OF AGE, and by the standards of the day, he had exceeded his life expectancy, having outlived many of his contemporaries, a talented generation that had either succumbed to the tragedies of war, the excesses of high living and hard drinking, or the inevitable realities of growing old.

For a person engaged in Howard's specialized line of work, it was this last category—the process of existing well beyond one's prime—that became the most difficult to endure. He persevered through this stage quite well. Most people he knew did not. For them, growing old was a tragic affair filled with melancholy and despair. Youth had slipped through their fingers, much like the fine grains of sand on some long-forgotten beach from childhood.

When youth is gone, beauty is all that is left in this world.

To Howard, beauty was everything. But to understand this, one must first learn the truths about youth, age, and beauty—the triumvirate of life. To do this best, I will use an allegory, an artistic device of ancient origin that Howard often used in his paintings to depict many ideas all at once.

IT IS A WELL-KNOWN TRUTH that no matter what occurs on this earth, that mysterious, silver-winged sprite called Youth always gives way to her silent, distant cousin named Age.

After many years, the attributes that accompany Youth, such as ignorance, indiscretion, frivolity, and folly, eventually leave each of us without warning. They are like the snow castles of our childhood. One day, these white, crystalline palaces appear to be strong and lasting. Yet the next, they are gone. From frosted window, we stare in heartbreak as we learn, during the quiet hours of our slumber, these seemingly impenetrable fortresses had succumbed to the forces of nature.

When the last vestiges of adolescence disappear, and Youth vanishes—and inevitably, she will—our innocence is lost, but we are not left to despair. Nature comforts us. She confers upon us the companionship of a graceful, wise lady known as Age. And along with Age come all of her splendid charms, such as reason, experience, wisdom, and patience. Howard understood this fact of life almost instinctively from his early days of studying people and their personalities. For others, the comprehension of it always seems to arrive much later in life's journey and amid much regret.

Youth—that fanciful, careless nymph who dishes and dashes frolic, whimsy, and invincibility upon us in our formative years.

She seems to cause us mortals the greatest pain and sorrow in our later years, when all else has vanished. For that is when we long for her, but she is not there. We search for her, but we cannot find her. Indeed, she has left us, and despite our most valiant efforts, we do not seem to encounter her; we never will. Youth and all of her charms are as irrecoverable as those white palaces we once built on a snowy winter's day.

In this world, there is no fountain of youth. No immortality. Living forever is simply all a myth.

Or is it?

And so, in our early years, with reckless abandon, Youth makes us look and feel like millions, when all along we are worth nothing—that is, nothing more than that which God had ultimately intended for us to be in this temporal life. Eventually, we discover this, perhaps long after Youth has left us. Yet somehow, many of us become aware of this quiet transition as we begin to see those whom we admire appearing older, more dappled than we had noticed before, and we begin to criticize a younger generation for ideas that we do not fully comprehend. In most cases, it is well before this point that Youth releases us, spreads her wings, and takes flight. But with vice-like grip, Age takes hold and slowly escorts us to our final destination. It is at this precise moment that we find solace in Youth's stunning twin sister, Beauty.

When we were young, we may have ignored Beauty. I know I did. But once we are old, we cannot imagine life without her. Other than God and the people with whom He blesses our world, all that we have left on this earth, in the end, is Age and Beauty.

If *you* do find Beauty, and *you will* many times in life, you must seize and nurture her, or you will risk losing her. For it is these rare moments, when we are with Beauty, that become the most precious. They give us pleasure and make us forget the anguish of the past. Beauty is the antithesis of pain, you see. She knows no destruction or anger. She is perfection and harmony, not discord or chaos. She is there to please and soothe, not puzzle or bewilder. Her spirit enchants and inspires us. We love life, because we love her.

In some respects, Beauty is a two-faced spirit within one. We are struck by her rosy-hued appearances at first—her glamour, luster, and sheen. The elegance of her outer façade is flawless; we are attracted to her like bees to the flower. It is this external side of Beauty, the visual perfection, that we see at first—until our vision widens and our myopia disappears. Then, through the depths of Beauty's ever-changing prismatic eyes, we encounter her splendor.

Inside Beauty, neither falsehood nor deception exists. She is true and pure.

Within the human soul, true beauty dwells. Looking outside our mortal selves, beyond mere physical appearances, we too can view and experience all that is beautiful and good in God's world, and by doing so, we see our own internal glory, instilling in us a hope that we are indeed worth something much more than we ever envisioned.

Youth's untimely departure and Age's sudden appearance can never harm us. Neither one can thwart the strength and endurance that is true beauty. For beauty is truth, and truth is beauty. It survives all, surpasses all.

With true beauty, there is no illusion.

This, Howard understood instinctively, and it became more than just his philosophy and his life. It was his driving force to create and achieve the greatness that became his destiny.

Youth had long since abandoned Howard; no one knows precisely when.

Beauty, on the other hand, had always remained by his side— to his very end—inspiring and feeding his soul and, in turn, his work.

To Howard's distinguished clientele, Youth and Beauty meant everything. They would pay almost any price to seize them—to live forever. And with their extraordinary wealth, it was all easily within their reach, if not for the transitory moment that is known as a lifetime, then perhaps for the eternity that is called the promise of art.

◉

WE HAD BEEN through it all, Howard and I. He was my husband of over thirty-two years. I loved him and was devoted unconditionally. The public also adored him and was in awe of his special gift, which he gave back to them many times over. Through paint and canvas, paper and pen, pastel, watercolor, and sculpture, he created human documents that touched and inspired millions, memorialized an era of elegance, and captured beauty in all of its divine forms—human, natural, and spiritual.

Like most artists, the tools of Howard's trade always seemed to surround him. On that particular morning when he died, they were right there, directly across from him.

Glinting in the sun sat a half-tarnished copper pitcher, swelling to the rim with varying sizes of sable brushes. Inches away, a deplorable metal pie plate, beaten and misshapen, lay in abandon. A white rag, once soaked in thinner but now dry, sat crumbled in a ball. Half-used tubes of paint lay scattered on a table next to a wide painter's palette covered with an impasto kaleidoscope of dried colors. Below the balcony, propped up by the wall, were sizable wooden stretchers that could support a life-size canvas. A half dozen landscapes, each awaiting completion and Howard's signature, flanked the other wall.

Typically, he signed his paintings faintly so as not to distract the viewer's eye because he wanted each to speak for itself rather than to boast of his famous name. Howard considered himself just a plain, everyday American, and being an American was of much greater importance to him than being an artist. Once his work was branded, he often dated it, invariably noting the year and, on rare occasion, the month. Other works, however, such as the portrait of his friend General Douglas MacArthur, would never be blessed with his great signature. It just sat there, languishing, on his easel that morning.

Like Howard, General MacArthur had his own great story of success.

A YEAR EARLIER, following the outbreak of the Korean War, General MacArthur had successfully pushed North Korea's Communist Army past the Thirty-Eighth Parallel, a monumental achievement that crowned his distinguished military career, which began when he graduated at the top of his class from West Point. By World War I, he had become a brigadier general. In 1930, he rose to Army Chief of Staff with a rank of four-star general. During World War II, he was designated Allied Commander of the Philippines. When the Japanese nation surrendered on board the USS *Missouri* in September 1945, ending World War II, he presided over it. It was said that the general's greatest contribution to history may have been when he was appointed Supreme Commander of the Allied Powers in Japan. For five and a half years, he and his staff rebuilt the devastated country, established a democratic government, and mapped out a course transforming it into a global industrial power.

Despite all of his accomplishments and immense popularity, MacArthur remained at odds with the United States foreign policy. He believed that America's frontiers were in Asia and that Communism should be stopped in that hemisphere, whatever the costs may be, but this view was in direct opposition to President Truman's decision not to escalate the war in Korea north of the Thirty-Eighth Parallel. Once the general's views became public in the spring of 1951, President Truman relieved him of his command. MacArthur returned home, the last great general of World War II to do so.

In April 1951, General MacArthur appeared before an overly jubilant Congress, which bestowed upon him thirty ovations as he delivered his farewell address. It was during this famous speech that he declared that "old soldiers never die; they just fade away." The next day, he received a hero's welcome in New York City from almost ten million people in a ticker-tape parade, hailed as "the most stupendous mass tribute in American history."

Following the festivities, General MacArthur's military career ended, but public sentiment for him remained strong, leading many to believe that he would run for the presidency in the 1952 election.

IN THE WARM SECLUSION of the studio, the general's portrait stood on the dark oak floor, awaiting the day when the nation's busy hero could schedule a personal sitting so that the finishing touches could be applied. Mrs. MacArthur had sent her favorite photograph of the general, thinking this would serve as a good composition guide. Howard perched it by the painting, out of courtesy. He never used photographs to paint people who were living and could quite easily sit beside his canvas; he only painted from life or from the fragments he could remember from various social encounters he had with his subjects.

Even at his ripe old age, Howard could still remember the general's towering presence, the jut of his chiseled chin, the distinctive bridge of his Roman nose, and the khaki field marshal's hat that was so often associated with his brave deeds in the South Pacific. As I looked at the portrait in the blazing light, the general became a mythological god descending from the heavens. Unfortunately, Howard never saw the greatness that this painting would later attain.[1]

AGE NEVER HINDERED Howard's work nor slowed his pace. His list of outstanding commissions seemed endless, and in the recent months, more requests continued to pour in. He had a passion for creating that was continually fed by the demand for his work. It pushed him to produce at the same frantic rate at which he had

Unfinished and unsigned, this portrait of General Douglas MacArthur sat on Christy's studio easel on the day of his death, March 3, 1952. (National Portrait Gallery, Smithsonian Institution, Washington, DC, Gift of Henry Ostrow)

been accustomed since he started as a professional artist in the early 1890s, when he worked as a commercial artist or, more specifically, as an illustrator for books and magazines like *Leslie's Weekly*, *Harper's Weekly*, and *Scribner's*.

To Howard, commissioned works of art always had to meet the client's exacting standards, particularly if the artist who produced them wanted to retain his reputation and develop a clientele. Consequently, his work ethic and attention to detail never faltered.

The initial drawings that layered his workspace on that early March morning bore witness to this dedicated artistic life cycle. On his crowded desk lay the initial pencil sketches that were to form the basis for an inspirational painting titled *Christ at the Peace Table*. Over another table, preparatory drawings and composition drafts were scattered. One was for a grand commission of Thomas Jefferson, another for a rendering of Lincoln at Gettysburg.

Amid the preliminary composites and sketches were letters from the Gilcrease Museum Foundation in Tulsa. The last painting the museum received, which many considered to be Howard's finest accomplishment in romantic beauty, was unveiled there the prior November amid an enthusiastic crowd. Inspired by Henry Wadsworth Longfellow's poem, the nine-by-sixteen-foot masterpiece, titled *Hiawatha's Wooing*, depicted the youthful Hiawatha courting his alluring mate, Minnehaha. The museum had devoted an entire gallery to Howard's work, and it wanted more to fill another one. So it was commissioning him to paint four more paintings on Indian subjects and some depicting early America. The Hiawatha canvas would be the last of his great feats.

Howard's time on this earth was quickly waning.

ON DECEMBER SEVENTEENTH OF THE PRIOR YEAR, at two o'clock in the morning, Howard suffered a heart attack. He awoke me from my sleep, whispering, "Don't be alarmed, Nancy, but I need your help."

Days later, he was bedridden. His breathing became more labored.

The news of Howard's illness rapidly traveled throughout the nation. Soon, we received a flood of telegrams, letters, and phone calls. With the advent of Christmas and Howard's eightieth birthday on the tenth of January nearing, our studio apartment looked as if we were newlyweds and had just returned from a month-long honeymoon. Bouquets of flowers, large baskets of fruit, and presents with beautiful bows were placed all throughout our living room. This excitement certainly brightened Howard's spirits, as did the large contour chair that General James Doolittle, the famous World War II aviator, had sent to him. I set a few pillows on it and immediately Howard took to it and humorously remarked, "This is fine. A bed with too many pillows is worse than no bed at all."

As the weeks moved on, Howard's health seemed to improve to the point where he ventured from his bedroom on the second floor to the studio below. Soon, friends stopped in, and Howard graciously received them.

"I'll be painting again before long," he quipped to one of our guests. "Besides, if I don't get back in shape, I don't know what they'll do downstairs when another guest loses her teeth in the swimming pool." His blue eyes twinkled as a wide smile broadened across his face.

Howard had been a strong swimmer since his youthful days of chasing the paddlewheels of tall-stacked steamboats ferrying up the Muskingum River in Ohio. His endurance in rough water followed him throughout his life, and on one occasion, years earlier, it had served him well in a unique rescue effort in the basement swimming pool of our building.

"He was in the middle of portrait painting," I explained to our guest. "He stopped everything, changed into his bathing suit, went downstairs, and rescued the teeth; then came back to the studio to dry off, change clothes, and start painting again."

"I had to do it," chuckled Howard. "Otherwise, they would have had to drain the pool."

Howard was just like that—light-hearted, spontaneous, and heroic. Above all, he had an infectious, cheerful personality that charmed people and made them instantly gravitate to him. This sunny disposition followed him throughout his entire life and gave rise to his boyhood nickname, "Smiley." This nickname still fit him, even decades later. But at that time, he insisted that his close friends call him Poppy. For others, they would simply call him Howard, or to those more distant, Mr. Christy.

Many other artists, especially those who were as well known as Howard, might have possessed a cynical or critical disposition, but not him. He did not resemble the typical conception of an artist or go for those eccentricities of dress and character that are often associated with some artists. The so-called artistic temperament never ventured into his character. Whatever temperament he had, he infused in his painting and not on people. The spirit and conviviality that came with meeting and talking to people fueled his life.

It was the company of people and the many letters that Howard received from his friends that kept his spirits bright, particularly during those long winter weeks of recovery.

One letter of interest came from Dr. Norman Vincent Peale, the esteemed pastor of Fifth Avenue's Marble Collegiate Church and the author of numerous books about faith and optimism, including *The Power of Positive Thinking*. Reverend Peale wrote to him a short birthday greeting, a portion of which reads:

> Just a note to extend to you my best wishes and my affectionate regards on your eightieth birthday. What a glorious thing it is to arrive at four score years and to be famous the world over, known and honored, and respected and loved by thousands of people.
>
> In the course of American history millions of people have lived but only a few of them have risen to your eminence and your name will always abide in the annals of this land as one of the immortals.
>
> I am honored to be included among the circle of your friends. May God bless you and give you health and strength to carry on your wonderful work for many years to come.

Howard was delighted, but I tried not to let the flattering sentiments of the good reverend go to his head. I am kidding, of course. Despite his fame and success, Howard always retained a strong sense of modesty and humility. He shrugged off compliments and always returned the thanks. That was his nature.

This particular letter, however, was striking in that it included me.

"Also I congratulate you," Dr. Peale added, "on being blessed with a wonderful wife. I think that Nancy Christy is one of the finest women I have ever known and her devotion to you is beautiful to behold."

Dr. Peale's letter had raised both of our spirits.

By late February, Howard mustered the strength to walk to the elevator and descend to the ground-floor lobby. Below the dark oaken beams of the lobby's high ceiling, he sat for as long as he could, greeting many friends with a warm smile and quiet conversation.

Sometimes, Howard strolled into the Café des Artistes, the small restaurant to the right of the lobby entrance. He was instantly recognized by everyone who entered. Years earlier, he painted all the murals inside. They are of lithe nymphs, frolicking in a forest, unabashedly naked. The theme was Ponce de León searching for the Fountain of Youth. It is this name, *The Fountain of Youth*, that he gave to the mural above his favorite table. Young, beautiful women, immortalized in all of their God-given glory, bask in a flowing fountain of everlasting life. Howard's murals drew throngs of people there, very few of whom, I should say, would ever be immortalized by his brush. These exquisite murals were the closest that they would ever come to that mythological fountain or the immortality they so desperately wanted.

Those short hours that Howard spent in the lobby, glancing through the glass doors, made him long to go outside and stroll across the street to Central Park, a daily event before his heart attack. On most occasions, regardless of the season or weather, he would greet the dawn with a brisk stride, usually without wearing any overcoat or hat. Sometimes before returning home, he might make a detour to Schneider & Company, an exclusive purveyor of artists' materials at 123 West Sixty-Eighth Street, where he generally purchased his oils and canvas in his later years.

Wherever he went, Howard would talk to everyone in sight—Herman, the doorman; policemen on horseback; taxi drivers; men on garbage trucks; elegantly dressed riders traversing the park trails on saddle; and, of course, children. He so loved children. To them, he would offer a buckeye as a token of his friendship and his native Ohio roots. Sometimes, he might provide a brief sketch.

Mindful of his slow recovery, Howard knew that his customary walk had become too great a journey. So in those fading days of February, he would withdraw from the lobby's doors and return to our apartment.

回

As HOWARD WORKED AT HIS DESK on that splendid March morning, I was planning a brief trip to the bank to deposit those checks he had endorsed. To keep him entertained during my absence, I invited Mrs. William P. Timmon, an old friend of ours, to stay and chat until my return. I did not want to be away long, but I knew that he would be in good company with her and my Negro maid, Callie. So I left them and departed.

Outside, the cool breeze and mellow sunshine welcomed me. The promise of spring was within view, and our neighborhood sensed it. Central Park West bustled with traffic. In the middle was a white-gloved policeman flagellating his arms to keep the oncoming traffic at bay. Well-coiffed women in fashionable hats and long coats strolled along the sidewalk with their children in tow. Nannies pushing baby buggies quickly ambled across the pavement. They too turned into the park's entrance.

At the bank, I fulfilled Howard's request and quickly left. Turning homeward, I stopped momentarily at a sidewalk flower shop to purchase two potted hyacinths that caught my eye. They were Howard's favorite flowers. As I chose them, I could hear in my head his voice distinctly saying, "It's almost spring, Nancy."

The price of the flowers was insignificant, but the time that was lost in selecting them was beyond measure. Upon my return home, I learned that in my brief absence, Howard had died of a heart attack.

In his late years, Christy stops to draw a quick sketch while two boys admire the artist's handiwork. (Special Collections, Lafayette College, Easton, PA)

CHAPTER TWO

Fanfare for a Common Man

$\mathcal{A}$T FIRST, I REFUSED TO BELIEVE THE NEWS. Howard cannot have left me. He still lived; I knew it. I ran to his side. In vain, I tried to revive him but could not. So I did exactly what he would have wanted me to do: seek spiritual guidance.

Upon my request, a Christian Science practitioner was immediately summoned. He arrived and placed his hands over Howard while muttering some prayers. All of it was incomprehensible to me. This went on for a few minutes, but it seemed like an eternity. And then, with a look of complete frustration, the practitioner nodded, opened his eyes and turned with a silent stare.

"It doesn't look good," he remarked. The man said nothing more and left.

A coroner was phoned. After his arrival, my suspicions were confirmed. Howard had departed from this world. If only I had known, I would have been there, next to him, by his side. But I was too late.

AS WORD OF HOWARD'S DEATH blazed across the city, journalists called. They became relentless for the truth. What had happened? Who was there with him?

The report I gave them was short: I had left that morning to run a bank errand, leaving Howard in the company of our Negro maid, and an old friend, Mrs. William P. Timmon. While writing checks at his desk, Howard slumped over in his chair at five minutes before noon and passed away.

I purposely delivered this brief account, because that is how that morning began. But what had happened during the brief period between the moment of my departure and the point of my return was quite different. What occurred was unknown to me then. Only later did I discover the truth from my maid, Callie.

I knew that the true circumstances surrounding Howard's death would become just as spectacular to the public as his life once was; that is, if those last moments were ever revealed. To me, one's public image meant everything.

Thus, I kept silent, and the events, as I had described them to the newspapers, became the official story. It was a modest account—an illusion—that revealed only part of that morning, but it would have to suffice. It did.

WITHIN HOURS OF HOWARD'S PASSING, couriers arrived bearing colorful flowers. Bountiful masses of daylilies, gladioli, irises, and roses spilled over from huge silver vases. The next day, more vases, baskets, and planters appeared, filling every conceivable space in the living room until it looked like the staging grounds for a flower show. Naturally, other homes had to be found for them. Some were given to friends. Others were transported to the funeral home.

Many of my close friends, such as Mrs. Doolittle and Mrs. Rickenbacker, the wives of famous American flying aces, came and stayed for a while. They all tried to cheer me up. But their efforts were of little consequence.

By the early morning of Howard's funeral, the clamor that once echoed throughout the studio for what seemed like days on end had suddenly and rather inexplicably ceased. It was as if an entire city, once thriving with commotion and the commerce of thousands of people, had, without warning or notice, come to a complete and tragic end. This was not some primitive nation, but a great empire, one full of culture and sophistication. How deserted lies this city, once so full of people!

Those poor mortal souls, I thought. Those fearless men and women who once inhabited this great civilization; those geniuses who transformed their dreams and fantasies into reality and perfection. Their golden age was not long ago. Their works were in great demand, coveted by commoners and kings. Yet this once-esteemed legion of creators was nowhere to be found now; all that remained were the physical objects that once defined their daily lives—their tools, sculpture, drawings, paintings, and the written records of their advanced society. The sudden departure of just this one man from my world instilled within me the same sense of utter desolation as would the complete loss of a metropolis of gifted artisans.

During those hushed early hours, I found myself once again before that great sunlit window in the living room. As I viewed the horizon, the aroma of fragrant, young lily buds interrupted my thoughts, along with another familiar smell: the faint honey-sweet scent of pipe tobacco.

He was nearby, I knew.

Howard loved his trusty pipe, but he stopped smoking it just over a decade earlier. I could still envision him, standing in a blue double-breasted painter's smock, the black tip of his pipe tightly clenched between his teeth. In his left hand, he wielded a long sable brush. In his right hand, he balanced a broad palette. Before him would stand a large canvas set upon an easel littered with bent, blackened matches.

When he painted, he would often stand and totter from left to right to get the proper perspective. At other times, he might perch himself on a stool in front. In either case, his sitter was always permitted to view the full canvas as he labored on.

Throughout the day, he would puff away on his pipe. This was his artistic release, a beloved ritual learned decades earlier after transitioning from a stable of thick cigars. In those days, he inhaled those smoke-devils incessantly, to the point where they became a constant distraction from his work. Eventually, he took up a pipe.

Smoking provided a calming effect upon Howard, and oftentimes, perhaps surprisingly, upon those whom he painted. There was a certain poetic syncopation to it all, like a well-timed waltz.

First, he struck a match; the sulfur-tipped end flared. He would place its flame in the pipe's burlwood chamber, a fresh plug of fine tobacco nestled deep inside. The bowl smoldered. Dense clouds of ashen smoke would follow. The pipe would rage and billow. From his fingers, the spent match would descend, landing in the same spot as its predecessors—a wasteland at the easel's base, spotted with a collage of paint droppings.

Howard would smile and his eyes glimmer. He would give the pipe a few more puffs. Then, thin, long ribbons of white would slowly ascend to the heavens like holy incense. The ethereal trails twisted and turned upon each other. Around and around, they gently moved, intertwining, encircling and gliding upward in a graceful dance. As they spiraled to the far reaches of the ceiling, the ghostly strands would slowly fade, like a fog lifting from a distant pasture on an early morning.

The dance was complete.

Every ten minutes or so Howard's pipe would burn out. In his right hand, already saddled with a palette, he palmed a pad of matches. Like clockwork, he would pull it out, strike a match, and the process would repeat.

In the midst of this seemingly futile exercise, Howard's graceful model might become impatient, relax a bit, shift positions, and take a time out. He wouldn't mind. "I take too much time out myself, lighting this old pipe of mine," he would say. A hearty laugh would surely follow.

I could almost hear his voice as I looked out at the tall buildings and water towers stretching far off into the distance.

The subtle smell of embers, along with the fragrant bouquets that saturated the air, gave this place a warm and comfortable feeling, like that of a fine library within a private New York club.

Howard once eloquently described our living room as a "[s]alon, equal of years ago in Europe, but virtually American in spirit, in which men and women of arts and letters and social prominence find themselves at home." Endowed with an eclectic mix of Old World antiquities, it was steeped in a late-Edwardian style décor and outfitted with plush chairs and sofas, bold Italian Renaissance furniture, and sleek, contoured lamps hooded with wide fringed lampshades of the type popular in the late 1920s. Heavy drapes once shrouded the large north window years earlier, but they acted like a camera aperture, reducing the light that Howard so needed for his work, and were taken down. Since then, light had flooded the entire room every morning.

At the far end of the studio was a large, intricately carved fireplace, over which hung a portrait that Howard had completed in 1928 of me in an elegant pink and blue dress with my white Russian wolfhound, Brassie. In front lay a white bear-skin rug. The once noble head protruded in a silent but defiant growl. Nearby were tall, seventeenth-century turned candelabra; a polychrome Madonna and child; large, intricately carved oak library tables; Italian Renaissance objets d'art; Chinoiserie; books; statuary; and armor. Many of these treasures we had purchased as souvenirs of our trips abroad and were used as props for his paintings. Howard called them his "relics."

On a nearby table lay a copy of *The New York Times*. Each morning, Howard would regularly thumb through its pages as he sat for breakfast, his favorite being bacon and eggs with a cup of hot coffee laced with modest amounts of cream and sugar.

On occasion, when the mood struck him, he would jot a brief note to *The New York Times* editors, thanking them for printing something of interest to him or commenting on an article he admired. When this happened, and it often did, the editors would print in the following day's paper Howard's precise words. Thus, it wasn't at all unexpected that *The New York Times* published a flattering obituary, hailing him as "an artist of tireless energy, a veritable journalist of the easel and brush."

The *New York Herald Tribune* contained an editorial of a similar nature. It said:

If popularity is a hallmark of artistic success (and thousands have striven for it in all eras), Mr. Christy was one of the most successful of all artists, for his illustrations appeared in scores of periodicals and books, his portraits were eagerly sought after, and his famous painting of the signing of the Constitution still is an object of admiration in the Capitol. Medals came to him in profusion, as did friendships, and he had a substantial influence as a teacher. Perhaps his greatest achievement was in winning acclaim both as a popular illustrator and as a serious painter. It is for posterity to determine in which field he will be remembered longer, but certainly in his own lifetime he found renown and satisfaction in both.

From New York to New Mexico, South Carolina to Iowa, Howard's passing made front-page news. In death, he was afforded just as much publicity as he experienced so readily throughout much of his life.

For over half a century, Howard had commanded great press. His persona seemed to be tailor-made for the public and, therefore, the newspapers. For instance, during the 1922 Miss America contest, fellow illustrator Norman Rockwell experienced firsthand the public's insatiable infatuation with Howard for three straight days when they served together as judges. Norman discovered that Howard, the chief judge of the pageant, stole the show. Some judges who had tasted fame were envious at Howard's uncanny ability to entrance the masses. But Norman admitted he wasn't. Publicity and Howard were "right for each other," Norman observed, "like pearls and duchesses or coleslaw and church suppers."

Howard never had to grandstand or orchestrate a publicity campaign. He naturally attracted public interest. His extraordinary talent, exciting life, and approachable personality did all but guarantee this.

Much of what was written about him in the days following his death could not fully explain his varied accomplishments, his influence on the art world, his impact on the nation, or the dramatic events he encountered as he scaled the heights of success to achieve the American dream. Only summaries and small glimpses were given.

One newspaper from Zanesville, Ohio, a city not far from where Howard once lived, called him "the Ohio artist whose magic brush captured the pageant of American history." Another newspaper from the same city imparted this message: "[f]rom a barefoot boy, Mr. Christy rose to [be] one of the world's most famous artists." There was an editorial that praised him for his sincerity and "honest, straight-forward personality." Another editorial, from a Helena, Montana, newspaper unequivocally declared his art "seldom equaled" and further emphasized that Howard, unlike most artists of the time, had become a veritable institution well before his death, because he "influenced and reflected the customs and tastes of the changing decades."

Some accounts of Howard's life were more anecdotal in nature.

The Lethbridge Herald, a Canadian newspaper, thought it appropriate to end a pithy three-paragraph obituary of Howard by disclosing that the walls of our studio apartment were plastered with his paintings of girls, "some of them nudes." "He was proud of them," the article continued, "and delighted in pointing them out to favored visitors."

Perhaps the most poignant of all the commentaries on Howard's life was a brief editorial printed in the evening edition of a small-town Maryland newspaper. It said this: "If it were given to all men to see with the eyes of a Howard Chandler Christy and to depict with his hand what had been seen, there could be a wealth of beauty now denied to those who see distortion and ugliness and reflect nothing better."

Had he been alive to see all the nice comments written about him, he would have shrugged off the accolades with his usual modesty and gratitude, because that was just the way he was.

Howard considered himself a common man whose hands had been blessed with an extraordinary gift.

◳

THE FUNERAL SERVICE was set to begin promptly at one o'clock. It was a Christian Scientist service, just as Howard would have wanted it, for he was a devout member of that denomination. I was of the Methodist faith myself, but I ensured that everything was in place. The Walter B. Cook Funeral Home on 117 West Seventy-Second Street did the rest.

Early that morning, a young, blue-eyed girl named Jocelyn Johnston stopped by the studio. She had posed as a model for one of Howard's more demure works, a portrait of Mary Baker Eddy, the founder of the Christian Science religion. Jocelyn's mother, Ruth Johnston, lived next door to me in Apartment 712 and was one of my very best friends. Through the years, Ruth had become my trusted friend and confidante, someone I could turn to in difficult times. But she had left to go to Chicago on business two days before Howard died. Her daughter, Jocelyn, was the next best thing.

With a clear complexion and her shoulder-length auburn hair pulled back and curled, Jocelyn was the epitome of the girl next door. Her infectious smile, bordered in bright red lipstick, provided comfort to me during this difficult period.

Upon her arrival, I gingerly placed in her hands a small fragrant gardenia, with the request that she hurry to the funeral home before the others arrived. Howard must have a fresh flower in his lapel. She willingly agreed.

I also asked one more favor of Jocelyn: to oversee the guest book. Hundreds of people were traveling from across the United States to give Howard the same befitting honor in death that he received in life. The list of his honorary pallbearers, some forty-five men strong, was a veritable *Who's Who in America*. Howard had personally known each and had painted virtually all of them.

JAMES PHILIP HEAD (35

Other notables would also be there. It was important that their presence be recorded for posterity.

Standing before the mahogany casket, Jocelyn struggled to find the courage to pin a gardenia on the lapel of Howard's dark blue suit. Like all of Howard's models, she loved him. A well-heeled employee of the funeral home noticed her hesitation, and the uneasy task fell upon him.

The day before, Jocelyn had been pacing the funeral home floor when Howard's body arrived in the main parlor. Not much time had passed before one of the most bizarre postmortem tributes unfolded. Mrs. Babe Ruth, the wife of the baseball legend, came bursting through the parlor's double doors, drunk. Jocelyn recounted the incident to me.

Mrs. Ruth was about to make her way to the far end, where Howard's coffin lay, when Jocelyn summoned her to sign the guest book. Her breath reeking of liquor, Mrs. Ruth explained to Jocelyn that she had to be someplace else on the day of the funeral. However, she wanted to say farewell to the dear man who had given her the first modeling job she had. Certainly, this was not all Howard had done for her. He had been responsible for setting in motion the unlikely chain of events that led Mrs. Ruth to meet—and eventually marry—the baseball legend himself.

I wonder sometimes. If it had not been for Howard's introducing Mrs. Ruth to composer Sigmund Romberg, who then introduced her to a Broadway producer, who then gave her a small role in a show that opened at the National Theater in Washington, DC, the same city where the Yankees were then playing a game, and had it not been for the star of that particular show liking her enough to then introduce her to his good friend, the mighty Babe, then perhaps she and the Sultan of Swing would never have met. And if that were the case, then just perhaps Mrs. Ruth would still be just plain Claire Merritt Hodgson, a former model, and just maybe she would have actually arrived at the funeral home stone-cold sober, on the right day, and on time.

Wearing a long, ebony wool coat that partially obscured the pure white collar of her black dress, Mrs. Ruth staggered up to the half-opened coffin, leaned over the edge, and lovingly peered down at the artist who once found within her an alluring beauty so great that she became his muse . . . if only for a short while. Then, suddenly and rather unexpectedly, she descended to her knees with a thud. At first, it looked like she was going to fall on top of the spray of yellow mimosa covering the lower half of the shiny coffin, taking the whole thing with her on the way down. But then, it became clear that she intended to kneel before it, rather penitently. As she bowed her head in prayer, the short curls that veiled the sides of her face gently moved forward, covering her cheeks in a dark brown silkiness.

After a moment, Mrs. Ruth arose. Her mission complete, she made an unsteady beeline down the central aisle to the back. The long, flowing coat she wore, appearing much like a dramatic opera cape, whooshed past the carefully arranged rows of drab olive folding chairs that lined the long narrow path. When she met the grand double doors once again, she shoved them open with both hands. Stumbling onto the burgundy floral carpet of the adjoining anteroom, she turned and was gone.

Mrs. Ruth had departed as quickly as she had arrived—a day ahead of schedule.

⊡

It was a solemn yet inspirational occasion when people began to file in the funeral home for the Thursday afternoon service.

Many guests were distinguished in their own right. Some had achieved reputations of legendary proportions. A few were wealthy and famous. Others were just wealthy but not necessarily famous, and some were famous but of entirely modest means. And still others belonged in neither category. One such person was my handsome, blue-eyed blond Honnie.

His name was actually Harmon, but everyone just called him Honnie, pronounced as if it had a "w" in it, like the word "tawny."

Despite his youthful appearance, his eyes had witnessed a lot in such a short span of time. Eighteen years earlier, on a cold December night, his parents, Dr. and Mrs. Harmon Smith, died unexpectedly, and his entire world came crashing down around him. I became his guardian and witnessed his battle. The loss penetrated his heart deeply; it took everything within him, every ounce of strength and faith, to pick himself up and overcome it all. Eventually, he did, but it would take years, and much occurred in between, including a devastating war.

Just two months shy of thirty-three years of age, Honnie leaned against the wall of the funeral home in silence. Despite his uncommon good looks and outgoing personality, he would never rise to the lofty heights he could have easily attained. Fate had changed all that. But he shared something in common with everyone who attended the funeral that day. Young and old, well known and wealthy, tradesman or mere pedestrian, everybody who was present to pay tribute to this self-proclaimed common man's uncommon life had themselves led remarkable lives. Each had an important and fascinating story to tell. And, no doubt, they would tell you about it, if only you asked. I certainly did.

So on that sunny afternoon, many people arrived, wanting to honor Howard.

From Ohio came Senator John W. Bricker and Senator Robert A. Taft, the son of the former president and one of the most powerful senators this century had ever seen. There were former governor George White, Governor Frank Lausche, Congressman Robert Secrest, and Judge Harry Vodrey. The honorable judge so loved Howard's portrait of him that it was said he would not give his beloved Christy portrait away for even $5 million.

Roger Ferger was at the funeral too. His life was absolutely fascinating. As a young boy, Roger stopped outside the main office of *The Cincinnati Enquirer* during the wintertime and caught a brief glimpse through the window of the newspaper's editor in chief, smoking an unlit cigar, while a green visor shaded his eyes from the bright light bulb dangling above. Newspapers and typeset script surrounded this man's desk. To the young, destitute Roger, these were the badges of success. That was all it took to instill within him an unstoppable determination to achieve the same post in his own life. Years later, he also became not only the editor of *The Cincinnati Enquirer*, but the publisher and owner. Roger eventually related this story of self-determination to Dr. Norman Vincent Peale, who disclosed it to the world in one of his sermons and then later in his book *Positive Imaging*. Naturally, Dr. Peale was at the funeral too, along with his wife, Ruth.

From South Carolina came Governor James F. Byrnes, and from North Carolina, there was Thomas Yawkey, an orphan who inherited a lumber and iron empire from his uncle and then purchased the Boston Red Sox, owning it longer than anyone in history. Congressman Edward Eugene Cox of Georgia showed up. And so did Vice President John Nance Garner from Texas. Howard's painting of the former vice president hangs in the US Senate.

Thomas Gilcrease, the Oklahoma oil tycoon, philanthropist, and art collector, struggled to find an available seat in the front row. So did his friend Robert Lee Humber, a distinguished lawyer, state legislator, and the driving force behind the North Carolina Museum of Art. Three years earlier, Robert described to Howard the magnificent art foundation that Thomas Gilcrease had established in Tulsa and Gilcrease's vision of preserving the art of the American West. Convinced, Howard donated to the Gilcrease Institute his painting of humorist Will Rogers and Chief Bacon Rind, once the wealthiest Indian chief in the entire world. Howard told Robert that he could not think of any better place for these works to permanently reside. What Howard didn't know was that Thomas's grand dream far exceeded his means to support it. Thomas was nearly bankrupt.

Other notables who made the pilgrimage included publisher William Randolph Hearst Jr. (the son of the legendary newspaper magnate); writer and news broadcaster Lowell Thomas; movie actor Bert Lytell; master violinist Fritz Kreisler; reporter Bascom Timmons, who once advised various United States presidents, from Coolidge to Roosevelt; and Democratic politician and former postmaster general James A. Farley—all from New York.

Business tycoons were well in attendance, especially IBM's founder, Thomas J. Watson, who topped the list. Watson's company had become so powerful that just weeks earlier the US government filed an antitrust suit against it, alleging that it controlled more than 90 percent of all of the tabulating business in the country. On Howard's last and final birthday, Thomas sent to him a telegram that read: "I am looking forward to sitting for my portrait when you start painting again but in the meantime you must take good care of yourself and get well soon." The portrait was simply not meant to be.

New York energy executive Paul Clapp arrived, along with his wife, Rosalind. And so did W. Alton Jones, the president of Cities Service Company, a holding company that controlled oil, gas, and power subsidiaries, including thousands of miles of pipelines stretching from Texas to the East Coast. Albert V. Moore sauntered in. He was an extraordinary man who had the unerring ability to turn next to nothing into a business success. Decades earlier, Albert managed to pool five thousand dollars together and, with the assistance of a jib-nosed ex-tugboat captain named Emmet McCormack, turned a small-time cargo outfit into a colossal shipping fleet. Poor Albert—he died in January of the following year.

Hobart Ramsey, the vice president of Worthington Corporation—everyone called him "Hobe"—arrived with his much younger bride, Collette, in tow. Collette was one of Howard's favorite models; their friendship dated to the mid-1930s. She was so vivacious and talkative that anybody who would have just met her would never guess that she was going deaf. At the time of the funeral, she had lost nearly all of her hearing, but that didn't deter her.

Like everyone else there, Collette was running the race of life, but for her, the competition was much more difficult, the terrain much more steep, and the stakes much greater. Her race was the equivalent of sprinting an Olympic marathon. She possessed hope and was guided by faith—the same wellspring that fueled

Howard. Collette's hearing was eventually restored through a miraculous surgical procedure. Praising God, she founded the Deafness Research Foundation to change the lives of millions suffering from impaired hearing.

Howard's other models were also there. In their soft, graceful hands, they clutched handkerchiefs of white cotton or silk, trying to hold back the tears. One model who maintained her composure quite well was Elise Ford. She stood in a corner by herself.

ELISE WAS A MODERN-DAY VENUS. When she passed by on a busy city sidewalk, every man would stop and stare. When women gazed at her, as they often did, the opposite effect might occur; envy would instantly consume them as they longed for her youthful, feminine charm. They might covet her slender figure or her symmetrically exquisite face. They might desire her porcelain skin or delicate hands. Or maybe they were after that special look she exuded, that glow of virginal purity. It was this last attribute, an uncommon virtue, that seemed to bathe her in an angelic aura wherever she went, whatever she did, and, of course, whatever she wore (or didn't, as the case may be).

Elise became Howard's favorite model, a perfect specimen that he thought most closely approximated his ideal girl of the future. Elise was certainly all that and much more; the future was well within her hands. She only had to seize it, but that is altogether yet another story.

On the day of Howard's funeral, Elise's appearance was dazzling. If her eyes were tearing that day, I didn't notice. A delicate, black fishnet veil descended from her small hat and fell just above her lips. With her eyes partially obscured, only the curls of her soft chestnut brown hair and the glistening red hue of her "Cherries in the Snow" lipstick were immediately apparent. Somberly, Elise just stood there, motionless, like a statue.

I wondered what images must have been firing through her mind that afternoon. Howard's sudden death must have awakened within her a newfound understanding of the passage of time. Perhaps she recognized her own mortality and finally felt the heavy weight of Age upon her shoulders. Or maybe she was thinking of something completely different, such as the long hours she spent posing for Howard or the sunny days she enjoyed painting alongside him.

Having been acquainted with Elise since she was a teenager, I knew that she was approaching forty years of age. However, she didn't physically appear like any woman I had ever encountered. Elise possessed a certain recalcitrance to the natural forces of time. Her slender, curvaceous figure still exhibited all the wonder and enchantment that, only two decades earlier, had attracted Howard to her.

Elise never disclosed to anyone her actual age, and it was said that when she was asked to list her age on an application, she wrote the number twenty-seven and perhaps a plus sign afterward. Nothing more. No dates, no years, just this magic number. Elise would regularly tear the dates off letters she received and cut them from the magazines pages in which she appeared. No one knew why she would resort to this drastic measure. Perhaps she just wanted to ignore time altogether in the hope that Age, that wise lady, would somehow completely pass her by unnoticed.

I'm sure she thought the talons of Age would never sink into her tender flesh. Oh no, not her, especially after all the paintings she had modeled for, and the posters, and the murals. Glamorous photos of her had been seen all over the United States in newspaper articles and magazines. Certainly, Youth would never abandon a creature this lovely. If this was truly Elise's belief, and I suspect it was, then one would think she fell into Youth's illusory trap, another victim lured by the myth and swept away in its fantasy. In this case, however, the truth of the matter was vastly different from what one would expect. Elise was a paradox.

Age can be relentless in its quest to consume people—to leave them withered and gray. Yet this wise lady of time is not always successful in her insatiable endeavors and was not so when it came to possessing Elise's spirit. To be sure, Elise's physical attributes were not entirely impervious to the forces of nature, but at the same time, she was seemingly immune to their most ravishing powers. It was clear to me, more so in hindsight than at the time, that Age had never achieved victory over Elise because Youth had actually never left her side. Years earlier, when Elise attained the talismanic age of twenty-seven, Age had attempted to lay claim upon her. It was a mixed blessing that both enriched her life and doomed it altogether. But Youth's spell was too strong. She simply refused to surrender.

◙

That afternoon, Elise's twelve-year-old daughter, Holly, roamed the crowded room. She resembled her mother, having the same soft brown eyes, over shadowed with heavy, dark eyebrows.

I caught sight of Holly's long, dark brown hair as she moved in and out of the undulating crowd. She looked lost, uneasy, and overwhelmed with a group this large. She was wearing her boarding-school uniform: a navy blue blazer, gray skirt, white blouse, white bobby socks, and saddle shoes. She must have been going to Grand Central Terminal later. After the funeral, a bus would probably deposit her there, where she would board the Boston Express. Other than the train porter, no one would be there to assist her. Her father was dead; her mother had other things on her mind. She would return to Daycroft, a school in Stamford, Connecticut, that had been her home since she was six years of age.

People continued to push into the already overburdened room. Helen Coxhead, who lived in Apartment 715, finally arrived; so did her next-door neighbors, Walter Thornton and his wife, Judy. Walter was the head of a model agency, and Judy had been voted the best-dressed woman in the city for three years in a row. Louis DiPalma, who owned the grocery store and meat market on Columbus Avenue, came with his wife. I hardly recognized Mr. DiPalma without the white apron he always wore when he stood behind the meat counter, politely taking customer orders.

The room was beginning to fill to the brim, but tall and lanky Will Hays somehow managed to push through the burgeoning mass in search of a seat. A lawyer by trade, Will was the former chairman of the Republican National Committee and had served as the campaign manager for President Harding. Appointed as the US Postmaster General, he resigned a short time later to assume the presidency of what would become the Motion Picture Association of America. As head, he cleaned up the immorality in Hollywood by instituting the Production Code, a set of censorship regulations governing the production of movies. As usual, Will looked like a man on a mission in that room. He soon found a seat.

▣

SOME OF THE GREATEST MEN IN AMERICA finally arrived to pay their respects. Through the grand double doors they silently passed with no fanfare whatsoever, but everyone knew their names. These men were giants. Living legends. They were the nation's war heroes.

From New York came Captain Eddie Rickenbacker, the World War I flying ace, or, as the press had dubbed him, "America's Ace of Aces." Howard had painted Eddie Rickenbacker's portrait twice, first depicting him as a young, swashbuckling lieutenant dressed in his army air corps uniform and perched high above a blustery summit in the midst of an airplane dogfight. The second portrait was in 1943, when Eddie was president of Eastern Airlines.

Captain John D. Bulkeley of the United States Navy was also there. He called Howard "Pop" ever since he sat for his portrait in the summer of 1942, requiring him to take a two-day leave to do so. Known as the "Sea Wolf" for his bravery in combat in the European and the Pacific Theaters during World War II, John had emerged from that war as one of the navy's most decorated officers. It has been said that General MacArthur would have never uttered his prophetic remark—"I shall return"—had it not been for this brave captain. For it was John who, in March 1942, spirited the great general, his family, and staff out of the Japanese-infested waters of Corregidor and to safety in Mindanao. John's miraculous feat earned him a Congressional Medal of Honor.

General Raymond S. McLain of Oklahoma passed by without seeing me and continued on down the aisle. He commanded the 45th Infantry Division in Sicily during World War II and was instrumental in the Normandy invasion. From the corner of my eye, I spotted General Baird Markham, also of Oklahoma, who directed the militia during the 1921 race riots in Tulsa. It was a tragedy I shall never forget. Howard and I were there, in the midst of it, as we witnessed many people tragically die.

Lieutenant General James Doolittle didn't miss the funeral. Jimmy, as he was called, successfully led a daring air raid over Japan years earlier and was awarded the Congressional Medal of Honor.

Now, General Douglas MacArthur was extremely proud to be an honorary pallbearer that afternoon and definitively said so when he first received word that his presence was needed. "I have known Howard Chandler Christy for many years," the great general announced to the public, days earlier, "and have admired his work for even longer than I have known him. He was an outstanding artist and an outstanding citizen. He employed his brush and canvas to depict the real America. This nation will miss his genius and his patriotism. He was an inspiration to millions. He certainly was an inspiration to me."

In one form or another, Howard's spirit and loyalty to country motivated each of these living legends. In turn, they viewed him as a true American patriot.

BY THE TIME THE HEROES ARRIVED, the room was near capacity, but there were still many more people who would come: Howard's artist friends. They made a strong showing.

Ivan Olinsky, the Russian portraitist who lived down the block, came, and so did Arturo Noci, an Italian-born artist who loved painting scenes of New York City until he died the following year. Sculptor Wheeler Williams showed up; he had sculpted the west pediment for the Interstate Commerce Commission building in Washington, DC, and later the Robert A. Taft memorial on Capitol Hill.

These artists were good and well respected, but they were not the true, bright stars that afternoon. The special artists—those clever magicians who delighted the masses and achieved great fame and fortune doing so—arrived much later, yet just in time. To these men, time was everything, leisure a scarcity. In many cases, glamorous models were at their beck and call. And for all of them, valuable commissions were well in abundance. Each second was precious, as their work was in great demand.

Every few minutes or so, just before the service began, one of these special artists would make a grand entrance. When he did, the crowd certainly took notice. Bodies shifted, heads turned, and piercing stares could be felt. People couldn't keep their eyes off these distinguished gentlemen because they weren't just artists; they were national celebrities. These were the great illustrators.

And so the great illustrators arrived one after the other.

First, Mr. and Mrs. Rube Goldberg walked in arm in arm. A Pulitzer-Prize-winning cartoonist, Rube was best known for his clever drawings of absurdly complex machines performing relatively simple tasks. His name has become synonymous with confusing, overly engineered systems, the type for which the government is regularly criticized. Rube also wrote the screenplay for *Soup to Nuts*, the first movie to feature the uproarious Three Stooges. Interestingly enough, Rube is perhaps the only illustrator to have his name defined in the dictionary as a word—an adjective, in fact. On the day of Howard's funeral, he looked just like his photo from all of the cigarette and scotch ads for which he posed. That jovial face, the colorful bowtie, those moon-slivered eyes, and the perpetual grin that stretched from cheek to cheek made him who he was: friendly, funny, and cheerful.

Dean Cornwell made a special appearance. As he strolled in, one surely could not ignore his strong receding hairline or the elongated ears that twisted forward like that of an elephant. Distinctive round-frame glasses outlined his mustachioed face. Aside from his magazine illustrations, Dean was a noted muralist and a master of painting large canvases. In fact, in 1933, he completed the largest set of murals ever to then be painted on canvas. The commission, granted to him in 1927, was for the Los Angeles Public Library. According to Dean, the only studio that would accommodate canvases this large was in London, so he traveled there. And, of course, he needed artistic inspiration. So he ventured to Italy to see the Renaissance masters and to study the Byzantine mosaics. When he sought to paint a bishop for his work, he set up shop in the Little Church around the Corner in New York City, because no church would ever allow vestments to remain in an artist's studio. He used models constantly and, on rare occasion, the camera. Sometimes, he employed a shortcut, such as projecting a photostat onto the canvas, but generally, he simply used red pencil or sanguine chalk to sketch out his figures. Many preparatory drawings were made before he applied paint to canvas. In everything he did, the work was carefully researched and expertly executed. For more than five years, Dean labored on for this epic work and was paid only fifty thousand dollars. After it was finished, he declared that he received no profit from it; the price merely covered his cost and transportation. The labor on these works, he said, "had to be written off to personal satisfaction and love of art."

In the funeral parlor, an unsettling stillness permeated the air. Time was running out and the service was about to begin. Could Howard's other artist friends have forgotten him? I was beginning to wonder.

Then, something startling and unforgettable occurred.

A mass of windswept gray hair passed though the doorway and down the center aisle. It looked like Mephistopheles, but this devil was wearing a double-breasted suit. The jut of his jaw and the wide arch of his nose defined his distinctive profile. But it was his bushy, black, villainous eyebrows that disclosed his true identity: the incomparable James Montgomery Flagg. Everyone called him either Jim or plain ol' Monty.

NEW YORK BORN AND BRED, Monty had painted some of the most beautiful women in the United States, but his most notable creation

James Montgomery Flagg, as he looked in 1917, in front of his famous Uncle Sam poster, commanding "I WANT YOU" (Arnold Genthe Collection, Library of Congress, Washington, DC)

was actually a painting of himself. He used his own face to create the likeness of Uncle Sam for a World War I army recruiting poster—Uncle Sam, pointing his finger at us and commanding, "I WANT YOU." The image adequately portrayed Monty's visage and manner. Naturally, it became an instant hit. Four million copies of that poster were printed, prompting hundreds of thousands of young men to enlist in the US Army.

Truly a man of the age, Monty was a modern-day Leonardo Da Vinci, who sucked the marrow out of life but was never completely sated. Aside from being one of the most brilliant illustrators ever to have his work grace the pages of an American magazine, he had a mind like a roulette wheel and a sardonic wit to match.

Monty started his career at the age of two and sold his first illustration at the age of twelve. By the age of fifteen, he was on the staffs of both *Life* and *Judge* magazines. You name it, and he could draw it, paint it, or sketch it, and that he did, churning out over 250 works a year, with three months saved for vacation. Unlike Howard, Monty stuck purely with illustration. He never ventured into portrait painting, except for the occasional dalliance, but only if he and his sitter had a particular affinity for one another. Some of his critics might pan his illustration in favor of fine art, but Monty would adamantly disagree. "The difference between the artist and illustrator is that the latter knows how to draw, eats three square meals a day, and can pay for them," he would say.

In his heyday, Monty's work was highly sought out by newspapers and magazines. By the time of Howard's funeral, nearly every major magazine in the United States had featured Monty's work in one form or another.

Monty loved art but only beautiful art. He accepted nothing less and despised so-called modern art, considering it a fraud on the public. According to him, an artist could only achieve greatness if the artist was endowed with natural talent. Application and practice were also necessary. Monty always provided his gifted fans—the future artists—with a written response. His instruction to them was a simple message: "Draw continually from life—people, objects, anything," he advised. "Carry a sketchbook with you—and draw, draw, draw. Don't let 'modern' art fool you—it is phoney—this includes Gaugin, Van Gogh, Matisse, etc. Observe—don't merely look—study line—shadow, form, color with your mind, before you waste paper—then you won't waste it."

Monty didn't limit himself to just painting or drawing. He wrote scores of newspapers and magazine articles, authored several books, and acted in over a dozen movies, many of which he produced and directed. Wherever he was and whatever he was doing, one could be certain that his strong personality was the driving force behind his ambitions.

Rarely in doubt, Monty was never at a loss for words. Self-assured, he prided himself on his outspokenness and would tell everyone what he thought. His friends loved him for it, and those who didn't like what he had to say, he didn't want to be around.

Monty would often make charcoal sketches of his special acquaintances: stars of Hollywood and Broadway, US presidents, politicians, statesmen, military brass, authors, artists, humorists, and other celebrities. He referred to these impromptu drawings as his fifteen-minute sketches. His sitters loved them. So did the country's newspapers and the magazines, several of which printed them. Of course, he could often be found sketching what seemed to be one of his favorite subjects—himself.

Wherever Monty Flagg went, he was just as famous as the people he sketched, and he knew it.

MONTY STRUTTED DOWN THE AISLE of the funeral home, looking like he was worth a million bucks. No doubt, he was worth that princely sum . . . at one point . . . had he not spent it over decades of hedonistic living and cavorting with the likes of John Barrymore and other actors. As usual, he had arrived with the same flamboyant flair that made him one of the most famous and instantly recognizable figures in the history of American illustration.

It was getting down to the wire now. Every seat was filled; people stood on both sides of the aisle, and some leaned against the walls.

Arthur William Brown entered, but he had no place to go, other than to stand in the back with his wife, Grace. With his illustrations of pretty girls and clean-cut men, Brownie made a cool Wall Street million early on but lost it all in the stock market crash of 1929. It is said that he arrived from Paris a few hours too late to sell.

William Oberhardt, who was widely and affectionately known as "Obie," was the last in the door, I think. If not, he certainly was the last person to sign the guest book. Obie had spent the better part of his life delineating the human head on paper. With pencil and charcoal, he drew some of the most famous people in America. It was Obie's strong adherence to technique and capturing the sensitivity of individuals that caused him to be selected to draw a head of Speaker of the House Joseph Cannon for the first front cover of *Time* magazine.

WHEN THE PROMENADE OF CELEBRITIES WAS OVER, the casket lid was closed, and the service began. Hymns were sung, Bible verses were read, and more tears were shed.

After the service ended, I walked down the aisle and saw Elise once more, still standing in the corner. Our eyes met just briefly, only to acknowledge each other's presence.

The funeral entourage departed and proceeded some twenty odd miles north to Hartsdale, Westchester County, New York, where Howard was to be laid to rest in the center of two graves in St. Luke's section of Ferncliff Cemetery. He would have liked his final resting place, as it is serene and pastoral—the perfect setting for an artist who loved nature.

The air was cool that afternoon, a little blustery even. Snow covered parts of the cold, wet cemetery. In a few weeks, the surrounding land would be full of flowering trees and budding flowers. Howard was right. Spring was almost there, only he did not live to see it.

◉

IN THE DAYS FOLLOWING HOWARD'S BURIAL, many sentiments were published in America about his life and his work. But there was one tribute that seemed to speak to Howard's passion in life—beauty. A minister of a small church in Zanesville, Ohio, situated not far from where Howard once lived, gave a short eulogy on the Sunday after Howard's death. Having never met Howard, he said this:

Again and again we read in our newspapers glowing accounts of hometown boys made good in the metropolitan areas of our country. By sheer persistency of effort and a strong and unbreakable faith in their purpose and goals, they won the acclaim of many in high places.

So there went forth from Muskingum County a young man by the name of Howard Chandler Christy who, as a boy, walked the same streets you and I walk each day of our lives. A log cabin not too far from here and a beautiful oil painting in the halls of Congress—this is the story in but a few words, of the creative genius of a small town boy whose name was Christy. Can any good thing come out of Muskingum? The skeptics still ask. To honor the memory of such a boy, plans are already underway to exhibit the paintings and water colors of Ohio's distinguished artist.

And so I quote the immortal words of Abe Lincoln. 'It is altogether fitting and proper that we should do this.' As long as appreciation of beauty and art abides in human hearts, so long will the name of Howard Chandler Christy live on—the name of a small town boy who lived near Zanesville.

The American delegation signs the United Nations Charter on June 26, 1945, in San Francisco, California. Dean Virginia C. Gildersleeve of Barnard College is shown seated. (Special Collections, Lafayette College, Easton, PA)

Christy's 1947 painting titled The Signing of the United Nations Charter *sparks a controversy as it is unveiled in 1954, a day before the ninth anniversary of the actual event. (Special Collections, Lafayette College, Easton, PA)*

CHAPTER THREE

Moments of Pleasure

*M*Y FRIEND RUTH JOHNSTON finally returned from Chicago. I was upstairs alone when she knocked on my apartment door, and Callie greeted her. Footsteps—the sound of heels clicking on the hardwood floor—followed. Then, complete silence.

Standing at the edge of the balcony, I could see Ruth was fixated upon an immense, unframed oil painting that sat in front of the fireplace. All I could see of her was the back of her short champagne hair and colorful dress. Howard's Goliath of a painting completely dwarfed her.

As I stood there, looking down, I couldn't help but think she and this painting were dear, old friends to me. In the summer of 1946, when she moved in next door, she and I became the best of friends. During this same span of time, Howard's painting— nine feet tall and fifteen feet wide—had been languishing by the fireplace for nearly six years.

It was certainly too long a period for any painting to sit in one place without a permanent home, I recall thinking. It had to go. However, the commission was not yet paid for in full. Through the decades, I had become accustomed to seeing the studio filled with many works in various states of completion for weeks, if not months, on end. Howard's portraits were generally finished within the span of a few days and then, after a brief curing period, transported unvarnished to the sitter. Mural-sized paintings such as this were a completely different matter. Several months of labor were needed to complete the job. When finished, the canvas would be carried off—generally by several strong, burly men—only to be unveiled days later in some lavish ceremony replete with dignitaries, long speeches, and a swarm of spectators.

This sizable painting was not exactly one of those prized trophies. Yet it was certainly no ordinary commission. To Howard, this *was* America. It was what he so loved about this country: united effort, teamwork, freedom, and, most of all, peace for the entire world. This painting also captured something else that was dear to his heart—leadership and stewardship. He felt that these two virtues, which America reflected from the time of its founding, made it greater than any country on earth. He wanted to portray these attributes on canvas for posterity. In doing so, he had captured history in the making. He called it *The Signing of the United Nations Charter*.

COMPLETED IN 1947, *THE SIGNING OF THE UNITED NATIONS CHARTER* was the last of Howard's mammoth-scale historical paintings, and, from a global perspective, it was arguably his greatest. Two devastating world wars, each occurring within the span of a few decades of each other, precipitated the need for a powerful world organization—a global watchdog—dedicated to achieving peace and resolving disputes among countries. The result was the United Nations.

Howard's painting depicts the morning of Tuesday, June 26, 1945, when the charter—bound like a book and printed in five different languages—was signed in the Herbst Theater of the Veterans War Memorial Building in San Francisco. He wanted to portray the momentous occasion when the United States delegates signed the document establishing the illustrious international association, arguably the most important in the history of mankind.

On the auditorium's brightly lit stage, there were eight United States delegates, encircling an enormous round table covered in blue frieze cloth. To the far left of the table was President Harry

Truman; Secretary of State Edward R. Stettinius Jr., who was shown seated and signing his name to the document; Commander Harold Stassen; Barnard College Dean Virginia Gildersleeve; and Representatives Charles Easton of New Jersey and Sol Bloom of New York. To the far right were Senator Arthur Vandenberg from Michigan and former congressman and senator Tom Connally from Texas. In the distance was a smoky blue semicircular wall, in front of which were fifty United Nations flags, each hoisted on a tall flagpole and illuminated by floodlights.

Democratic congressman Sol Bloom, who had been Howard's good friend and advocate in Congress for many years, assisted with marshaling the various delegates to pose for the painting. He also negotiated the $10,000 commission, and later wrote Howard, stating, "I know it is going to be a beautiful painting, for it will be very historic as it is being painted from life."

On an early February morning in 1947, Howard had traveled to the White House and sketched President Truman, and he had painted many of the delegates, such as Dean Virginia Gildersleeve, in our studio.

Knowing how the wheels of government turn, Sol cautioned, "Certainly you would not want to send this painting out to San Francisco before it is accepted by the United Nations in New York and also the Congress."

Howard listened. After placing the finishing touches on the painting, he did not move it one inch. And so, this is where it remained in the weeks following his death, as it waited for final approval.

"OH, RU-U-TH," I EXCLAIMED, seeking her condolences as I approached her.

She turned to meet me but didn't hug me as I had hoped she would. Her blue-gray eyes didn't seem to confer any compassion on my plight. But that was understandable. Ruth had many melodramatic events in her own life. Her first husband, Milton, a World War I veteran, deserted her in 1930, leaving her to raise their two young daughters on her own.

"You have had enough sympathy, Nancy," Ruth politely said to me. "Now it's time to get to work."

She was right. Howard's financial affairs were not entirely in order. Numerous debts remained to be paid. Like many people, Howard bought on credit. He owed money for artist supplies, art packaging and moving, frames, stationery, flowers, books, tailoring, laundry, and dry cleaning. Louis DiPalma, the butcher, was owed over $140 for meat, and the $1,000 funeral bill remained unpaid. Most important, taxes were coming due. There was much to be done.

After we talked briefly, Ruth returned to her apartment. It was then that I started the difficult process that consumed much of my life for the following months. I rummaged through drawers and shelves, closets and cabinets. I reviewed and sorted letters, notes, memos, and receipts. And I organized bills and invoices, statements and bank books. Through the years, I had kept track of all of Howard's comings and goings, becoming his social secretary, public relations manager, and shrewd advisor. And, in the end, I had it all—every last shred of paper relating to his life from the time I first met him—the good, the bad, the humorous, the tragic, the embarrassing, and even the mildly incriminating.

As I combed through the stacks of correspondence, I discovered many fascinating letters. Some were from US presidents and their wives. Others came from politicians, movie stars, rich industrialists, congressmen, senators, socialites, and, of course, a few scant ones were sent to him from his models—those lovely women of timeless beauty whom everyone called the Christy Girls.

I too was once a Christy Girl. Yet in the end, it was I who would become Howard's wife. Everyone thought of me as *the* Christy Girl, the model who truly began Howard's career as the foremost illustrator of his time. But that was so many years ago.

Among the bundles of correspondence, there was just one letter that stood out among the rest. It was carefully placed in an envelope postmarked May 17, 1932. As I tugged at it ever so slightly, the crisp folded leaves of periwinkle blue paper slowly emerged. With avid interest, I unfolded the pages and quickly began to read the paragraphs, all written in white ink.

I recognized the script as being from the hand of Dorothy Dianne—one of Howard's winsome brunette models—a starlet who preceded Elise Ford but who never quite rivaled her. Dorothy, however, did have some talent. She later starred in a play at the Ambassador Theater called *Young Sinners*. Given her character, the play's title was indeed fitting.

There was no mistaking Dorothy's penmanship, and the content was exactly as I would have expected it to be—a paean of unquenchable adoration for the gifted artist who immortalized her.

Howard's sketch of model Dorothy Dianne, 1933 (Courtesy of The Illustrated Gallery, Fort Washington, PA)

She called Howard "Dearest" and said that his voice was like a breath of pure inspiration, and his power was ever increasing. She feared life without it and needed his guidance. She wondered who he was painting and whether it was fun. Then, she announced her own plans:

A little girl might live in a quiet hotel, up high where the wind is cool, and where she can see the world below. On very special days she might visit the famous Howard Chandler Christy and have lunch in his lovely dining room. And on even more wonderful occasions, the great artist might desire to paint her and then show the world his great love for this strange girl. Is she strange? Is she loved, this creature? She is warm, and adoring at your unique shrine always, dear Sir. Does it not make your heart pulsate and your pride glow? Do you like the plan or object. I await the King's pleasure in the matter. And Oh King! If you would answer soon. The girl is lonesome and her eyes are almost dewed with tears of unconsoledment.

She had scratched through the "ed" in the last word, claiming that she had changed her mind, and she signed it, "Obediently yours, Love—Dorothy."

The letter read like a riddle, an enigmatic fantasy.

Was this yet another illusion in all of Howard's exquisite creations? My wondering mind longed to think so, but my heart knew otherwise.

Next, I discovered a small Christmas card with two black Scottish terriers on the front. Each was cartoonishly drawn, with big plaid bows encircling the napes of their necks and miniature stamped envelopes protruding from their mouths. "Merry Christmas" read one. "Happy New Year" read the other. Written on the inside were the unmistakable double Ds of Dorothy's initials. "Not one wish, but two billion is my greeting for you," it said. "A Christmas of Cheer, And a Happy New Year!" Then came her personal message: "My love forever and ever is yours,

D. D." Dorothy had inserted the word "billion," along with her love, of course.

No, this was no deceptive trick, just one of Howard's adoring models who threw herself at him at every chance. And there were others—many of them.

In the days that followed, I continued to gather the papers I would need to bring to the estate attorney. But one afternoon, as I was passing by the bottom of the stairs leading to the second floor, something extraordinary happened. The hairs on the back of my arms and neck began to rise. I felt like I was standing in the middle of the Arctic, but this was late spring. I moved away and the air became warm again. Then, as I moved closer in again, chills ran up my spine.

It was a cold spot.

Frightened, I ran out the door and down the hall. I pounded on Ruth's door. As soon as she opened it, I ran hysterically to her. After calming me down, she said she would investigate my apartment. Minutes after leaving, Ruth returned and shut the door. She said that she could feel the normal warmth at the entryway of my apartment, but as she moved past it and toward the stairs, the air became strangely frigid in one particular spot. She walked through this area and found that the temperature around it was normal, but as she turned to leave, she walked through the spot again. It was icy cold.

Ruth's daughter, Jocelyn, told me years later that the same experience happened to her when she was asked to look after the apartment of her neighbors, Elmer and Kate Greene, following Kate's sudden death. While Elmer transported his wife's body for burial in Massachusetts, Jocelyn and her friend stayed at his apartment. As they entered the bedroom where Kate had passed away, each of them noticed a distinctive icy cold spot in the middle of the room. Finding no explanation, they believed it to be Kate's spirit, returning once again.

As for my apartment on that afternoon, Ruth did not have any explanation for the unusual temperature change. But I did. It was

Howard's spirit, returning to let me know he was still there. He was telling me good-bye.

◳

UNRAVELING THE ESTATE of the most famous artist in America was certainly not an easy feat. Naturally, I hired the best attorneys in the city.

To this day, I can still recall sitting in the backseat of a yellow taxi cab, being hurriedly shuttled through midtown Manhattan and then down the long succession of streets forming the shadowy canyons of Wall Street. It was there that I arrived at my destination: 14 Wall Street, a gray stone skyscraper resembling the legendary Mausoleum of Halicarnassus, perched atop the slender Campanile of St. Marks. It was in this formidable tower—once occupied by the great banker J. P. Morgan—where the esteemed assemblage of lawyers, known simply as White & Case, practiced their profession.

Despite the imposing exterior, the firm's interior was quite spartan, as if to convey the distinct impression that these attorneys meant business. Within the firm's expansive hallways, a cloistral hush prevailed. Elderly men, wearing gray office jackets and grasping files and well-sharpened pencils, shuffled from office to office. They were the firm's messengers, culled from the ranks of retired stock-exchange runners. Lawyers in charcoal gray suits strode through the unadorned passages, chatting in the faintest of whispers. All of the employees of this firm were men, even the stenographers and receptionist.

Edmund Beecroft, a middle-aged lawyer who concentrated in trusts and estates, was sitting in his office when I arrived at his door. He rose as I entered, and his male assistant made the customary introduction. Naturally, I took over.

Mr. Beecroft, I see that there are no women in your office.

Women are not employed here, Mrs. Christy. They would simply be a distraction.

Well, Mr. Beecroft, my late husband would certainly not have approved, but we aren't here to discuss that, are we?

Howard believed that, in any trade or profession, women were just as able and hardworking as men. He even felt that women had a comparative advantage in many respects because of their beauty and charm. His artwork regularly conveyed his thoughts of this gender superiority. Thus, Howard would never have accepted the banishment of females from any workplace, especially one that is as respected as the legal profession.

A faint smile broadened across Mr. Beecroft's face as he nodded at my insinuation.

No, we are not, Mrs. Christy. Please, have a seat. By my count, your husband left a probate estate of slightly over $57,000. A sizable sum, to be sure, but it will not keep you comfortably living for more than ten years. Of course, there is the cooperative apartment at the Hotel des Artistes that you and he owned. According to recent sales of similar apartments in that building, it looks like that would have a fair-market value of $8,188.50. Your husband had no real property but had numerous bank accounts and some Treasury bonds. Then, we have his daughter, Natalie, to contend with. Oh, that may be interesting. . . . You see, under his will, she gets next to nothing. And, Mrs. Christy, she may contest it too, for all we know.

Howard's only child—his daughter, Natalie, from his first wife, Maebelle—lived in a small apartment atop the fifth floor of a brownstone building on West 64th Street, just three blocks south of where we lived. Despite the close proximity, she rarely visited her father in his later years. There was always a slight tension between them. In fact, there was a tension between her and most people. She had been estranged from her husband, Ira, since the late 1930s. No one knew exactly why. She said nothing and kept to herself. Natalie was secretive that way, almost paranoid. She lived with her mother, Maebelle, and her daughter, Carolyn, Howard's only grandchild—just three lonely women, living together in close quarters.

Yes, Mr. Beecroft, I do see your point. What can we do?

That afternoon, the two of us hatched a plan. Howard had left a duly executed will, but it was dated April 1927, and much had changed since that time. His will gave Natalie his real property in Ohio and the sum of only $10,000; his former servant Lavinia Lemon was to receive the sum of $1,000. I was to receive the rest of his estate. The problem was this: all of Howard's real property in Ohio was sold years ago. Miss Lemon was nowhere to be found.

Mr. Beecroft and I decided to proceed as if no will were in existence. Thus, his will was never probated; I kept it. No further mention was ever made of it. Under New York law, I would receive one-third of his estate and his only child, Natalie, would receive the rest. The apartment would transfer to my name, and there would be no fight between his only daughter and me.

Weeks after that meeting, I discovered that Howard had more bonds and several thousand dollars in cash stuffed away in a safe deposit box at a Fifth Avenue bank. In all, his estate was valued at over $77,000. His paintings, those that were left in the apartment, including *The Signing of the United Nations Charter*, were valued at only one hundred dollars. His furnishings: $250. Yes, there were other holdings—bank accounts that held substantial sums of money, accounts that never appeared on any estate inventory or tax return. We all have our secrets, and why Howard maintained those accounts was *his* secret.

Howard's estate eventually was settled and, aside from our co-operative apartment, I was left with only the small sum of $21,000.

As for the enormous painting that sat in my living room for those many years, the United Nations finally paid the bill. One day, a group of burly moving men entered the apartment, disassembled it, rolled it up, and hauled it out the studio entrance. It disappeared down the stairwell to the side of the front door.

For a time, the painting was placed in storage, only to be unveiled at a ceremony in New York City commemorating the ninth anniversary of the charter's signing. The whole affair proved to be somewhat embarrassing for the United Nations, as no other painting was executed depicting any delegation other than the United States. That was not surprising. Congressman Sol Bloom, an entertainment impresario, had simply engineered the whole feat to make the United States appear great. Sol was known for that, especially since he orchestrated part of the 1893 Columbia Exposition in Chicago. In the 1930s, Howard had painted Sol's portrait for the United States Capitol. But that was then . . . .

▣

AFTER HOWARD'S DEATH, my life moved on without change or incident for nearly five years. The one exception was Bobby Conneen, my "Prince of Hearts."

We met one night while I was quietly sipping a drink at the Café des Artistes. The place was dimly lit, illuminated only with the faint glow of light cast upon Howard's nude murals and the flickering candles sitting upon the restaurant's white-linen-covered tables. From the corner of my eye, I saw a tall, handsome man enter the doorway, wearing tall dark brown riding boots, khaki jodhpur pants, and an old tweed riding jacket. He held a riding crop in his right hand and was like no other man I had ever seen before. His physique was slender; his facial features were strong and well defined. His closely shorn curly brown hair slightly receded from the two corners of his forehead. His youthful appearance conveyed an aristocratic air, like that of an English duke. Within seconds, our eyes met. He came over, and that was that. We spent the rest of that evening chatting about his life and mine.

He said he was a former show-horse jumper—a gentleman jockey—who had competed in some of the biggest steeplechase events on the East Coast and in the Midwest. During the mid-1920s, he rode one of Al Capone's prized horses to victory, after which Mr. Capone threw a grand party for the horse and him. But the life of riding champion steeds broke Bobby physically in two. While training a young horse in Michigan, he was thrown and nearly died. Bobby spent weeks in the hospital with a fractured skull and a broken neck. His professional riding career was over, and when his wife saw him lying helplessly in his hospital bed, unable to move, their marriage was over too.

Robert F. "Bobby" Conneen, as he appeared in his fox-hunting suit in 1961, by Robert Oliver Skemp (1910–1984) (Courtesy of Joseph Conneen, Jr.)

After that fateful night at the Café des Artistes, Bobby and I spent many more romantic evenings together. To me, it seemed that the days and nights would never end, until one fateful day when he simply vanished.

Eventually, I received a letter from him. He apologized and said he was working at a thoroughbred farm in upstate New York and did not know when he would return. It was July 1957, a hot summer month, and he said that he was working physically harder than he had ever done before in his life. He was doing this just for us, he said, and wanted me to know that he loved me more than anything in the world and would wait for me forever. I believed him.

That particular year seemed longer than any other. I was again alone and secluded myself in the studio apartment. There, I found great comfort . . . surrounding myself with the past.

It was in that same year that Howard's friend Penrhyn Stanlaws died. I recall picking up *The New York Times* and seeing his obituary. Like Howard, Penrhyn was an illustrator of beauty and a glorifier of the young American woman. He created the "Stanlaws

Girl," who, for many years, had appeared on the cover of magazine after magazine. And like Howard, Penrhyn eventually turned from painting beautiful women to portraiture. But it was the manner of his death that intrigued me the most. Just days earlier, Penrhyn lit a cigarette in his Los Angeles studio, sat down in an overstuffed chair, and quietly fell asleep. The cigarette fell from his hand, igniting the chair's upholstery and everything else. A fire quickly swept through his studio, and he burned to death at the age of eighty years, the same age as Howard when he died.

Monty Flagg was right. "Artists don't die," he once said. "They blow up!" A few other friends of Howard did as well.

It seemed that the great illustrators of beauty had the most tragic and profound deaths. First of all, there was Howard's friend Harrison Fisher, the creator of the "Fisher Girl." He lived across the hall from us, drawing and painting his women with long tresses, flowing ribbons, and billowing feathers. Howard proclaimed him to be "the king of magazine-cover illustrators" because he had painted more covers for *Cosmopolitan* magazine than any other. Harrison suddenly and unexpectedly died in 1934. He went to the hospital for a routine appendectomy but died the next day from other causes, including cirrhosis of the liver.[2] He was only fifty-six years of age.

Next was N. C. Wyeth. Wyeth spent his days illustrating magazines and books, creating romantic images for such works as *Treasure Island*, *Robinson Crusoe*, and *The Last of the Mohicans*. On an October morning in 1945, he and his four-year-old grandson were returning from a visit to the post office when their station wagon stalled at a railroad crossing near the artist's home in Chadds Ford, Pennsylvania. A southbound train from Philadelphia broadsided the vehicle and sent it hurling through midair. Both the artist and his grandson were instantly killed.

Then, there was Haskell Coffin. He too painted beautiful women for magazines and then turned to portraiture. Moving to St. Petersburg, Florida, in 1940, he ran out of money and was evicted from his hotel. Suffering from depression, he became a charity patient in a mental hospital, ending his life by leaping from the third-floor window of his hospital room. Two orderlies found his lifeless body on the lawn.

Nationally known illustrator and portrait painter McClelland Barclay was certainly saddened by Haskell's death. Years earlier, Haskell sent one of his girls to McClelland, who needed a model. He hired her and eventually married her too. McClelland had an untimely end. His death is somewhat of a mystery. Stationed in the South Pacific during World War II, he was serving in the US Navy when his boat was torpedoed. His body was never found.

After seeing Penrhyn Stanlaws's obituary and thinking about all of the illustrators of beauty and their untimely demise, I realized something. Compared to that of his friends and contemporaries, Howard's death was actually quite beautiful, if not ideal. At the end, he discovered what he had searched for his entire life—true beauty.

So in those lonely, dreary months, I remained alone in the studio apartment like a cloistered nun. All I had left were memories . . . those splendid, indelible thoughts of Howard; the people we met; the places we visited; and the lives we changed.

How I missed those halcyon years when true talent reigned and beauty was revered. How I longed for those days when I was Howard's only model. I so yearned for the magic of Youth that I lost myself in those golden memories of long ago.

In the corner of the studio sat my scrapbooks, sixteen in all. Over the years, I had filled them with my remembrances. One night, in the despair of my self-imposed dungeon, I sat down and opened one.

The binding creaked. The page edges were frayed. Photos that were once well affixed fell into my lap. Newspaper clippings, once crisp and bright, had turned brown and crumbled in my fingers. All of what I had saved many years ago was old . . . as was I.

Page after page I turned, until I came to one bearing a photograph of a stately mansion. It was Howard's former home in Ohio, a big barracks of a place. In fact, that is what he called it: the Barracks. The home sat high atop a steep, craggy cliff overlooking the east bank of the Muskingum River, just at the point where the river narrows into a large bend. A sequestered structure, the columned mansion rambled to the ridge's very edge. Acres of farmland, comprising a system of steep ridges and lush lowlands, surrounded it. And together, this homestead and its verdant acreage became one the most enchanting places on this earth. For this is where I first discovered true beauty and where my heart longed to be on that somber evening.

The Barracks, as Howard's home looked from the southeast in or around 1913, a year after Nancy first arrived there. Many years later, she saw this same photo in her scrapbook, reminding her of her early days as a model for Howard, who was then the second most popular illustrator in America. (Special Collections, Lafayette College, Easton, PA)

Upon the instant I saw that faded image, it was as though someone had turned off the television, and the clamor of the city streets that had been ringing in my ears, day after day for years on end, had suddenly been silenced. I closed my eyes for a moment and then opened them again. The once dark and lonely studio had become full of bright light, brimming with the trees, flowers, and birds that I had seen years ago. And that momentary silence was gradually replaced with the long-forgotten sweet sounds of nature.

In my heart, I felt an unimaginable peace.

Even now, I can still remember that magical place, and I remembered it quite well then, on that particular night, as I looked through my old, crumbling scrapbooks.

Although it was decades ago that I first ventured there, it seemed as though it were only yesterday.

Howard stands to the far right of the imposing south portico of the Barracks, his Ohio mansion that sits high atop the crest of a 200-foot bluff, overlooking the Muskingum River (left). His dogs—Sargent, a Great Dane, and Bill, a brindle Bull Terrier—are in front of his daughter, Natalie. The other people in this circa 1912 photo are unidentified. (Special Collections, Lafayette College, Easton, PA)

CHAPTER FOUR
A Lovely Place to Be

*I*T DID SEEM AS THOUGH IT WERE ONLY YESTERDAY when I first travelled to the Barracks.

It was a cloudless day in May; the sweet scent of an unusually early summer was in the air, and a half-mile winding drive was all that it took to reach a place that I so closely believed to be heaven. That day, too, I had arrived there, not knowing my fate, just as I had three weeks earlier when I first met Howard.

It was the spring of 1912, and I was sixteen years of age, a poor, flaxen blonde from Poughkeepsie, my home for many years.[3] There was nothing left for me in that gloomy town, save for my widowed mother, who often complained of heart problems. My sister, Gladys, and I cared for her, along with my brothers, Milton and Frederick. My father was deceased. And my mother looked after all of us as best she could in a small, narrow house along Bellevue Avenue.

For me, the only means of a decent livelihood was from the scant wages I received, working with many other young women, sitting among rows of tables stacked high with tobacco leaves on the upper floor of a large, dusty cigar factory on Main Street. I had learned a good trade, but it would never give me what I so wanted in life. It was time to leave.

Full of ambition, I was intent on becoming an artist's model, like those beautiful girls I saw on the front covers of the newsstand magazines. I could do that too, I thought. I was slender and relatively tall. Without heels, I stood at five foot seven and a half inches. The only thing I lacked was experience, but that would come in time, I knew. First, I had to travel to the place where all the great illustrators of beauty lived and reigned: New York City.

One day, I quit my job, packed my bags, kissed my family farewell, and headed for the train station, where I boarded an express that would take me to where I longed to be. In my purse, I carried a letter of introduction from a family friend, addressed

A sample of Gibson Girls is seen in this 1900 pen-and-ink drawing by the artist, titled Picturesque America: Anywhere in the Mountains. *In the spring of 1912, Gibson was considered to be the most famous illustrator in America. (Library of Congress, Washington, DC)*

Charles Dana Gibson in his Carnegie Hall studio in May 1913 (Bain New Service; George Grantham Bain Collection, Library of Congress, Washington, DC)

to the illustrious Charles Dana Gibson, who, at that point in time, was the most popular illustrator in America and the creator of the most famous woman in the world—a refined and elegant lady who never truly existed . . . except on paper. She was called the "Gibson Girl."

KNOWN SIMPLY AS DANA TO HIS FRIENDS AND FAMILY, Charles Dana Gibson rose from humble beginnings to become the most celebrated illustrator in America during the late nineteenth century.

Born in Roxbury, Massachusetts, in 1867, he started his artistic career when his father gave him a pair of scissors. He then went to work cutting paper silhouettes of dogs and elephants to be hung in his family's parlor. The local milkman was suitably impressed and bought two for three cents.

At the age of fifteen, he became a messenger on Wall Street but changed back to art when he won a one-dollar prize at the Stock Exchange for a sketch of the recently assassinated President Garfield. This one dollar meant more to him than his monthly salary of fifteen dollars. Sensing the desire to draw, he left high school and enrolled in the Arts Students League, where he continued his education for two years. Gibson's first published drawing was of a dog barking at the moon, which *Life* magazine purchased for four dollars and published in March 1886. After his newfound success, he marched into the same office the following morning with a bundle of more drawings. The editor refused them but extended an encouraging, "Come in again."

This setback did not dissuade Dana. He traveled to every publishing house and lithographer in Manhattan but was met with the same disappointing response. Eventually, he learned to use the back entrances of the big publishing houses to avoid being seen leaving from the grand front entrances with an armful of rejected work. True to his Yankee upbringing, Dana never gave up but refined his artistic style, relying on talent, hard work, and pen and ink, which he claimed was an "unconscious throwback of New England heritage" because "pen and ink are as unyielding as rocky soil."

By the late 1880s, his drawings could be regularly seen in all of the top American magazines. His income rose exponentially, as did his public stature. But it was his greatest creation, the Gibson Girl, who debuted in 1890 in *Life* magazine, that made him a star. Tall, confident, and statuesque, the Gibson Girl looked liked a marble goddess, yet exuded a style and sophistication of the Gilded Age. Her head was crowned with rich, lustrous hair, piled high in an elegant chignon. Her dainty nose was slightly upturned, while her gaze seemed distant and aloof yet sexually alluring. The long, flowing dresses she wore were the latest fashion and served to highlight her attractive hourglass figure, swan-like neck, and ample but delicately rounded bosom. Young women regularly imitated the Gibson Girl's look, even to the point of adjusting the tilt of their hats, the length of their skirts, the style of their hair, and the size of their sleeves.

According to the artist, the Gibson Girl was never a single woman but a composite of many. "I have hundreds of girls pose for me, and I have no favorites," he once declared. "I look for beauty whenever I can find it, and I don't think it can be discovered concentrated in a single individual."

Dana did have hundreds of the prettiest women in America posing for him. Many were paid; others simply volunteered. Society girls would regularly travel to his studio, along with their chaperons, for the chance to appear incognito in his magazine illustrations. Naturally, once published, the magazine would be left conspicuously open in the family parlor for the model's suitors to discover her likeness by surprise.

Young men would also regularly show up at Dana's studio doorstep. From drawing board to printing press and then to the public, a new figure was born—the "Gibson Man," an imaginary hero who eventually changed how American men looked and dressed. The Gibson Man was clean-shaven and had a chiseled jaw, broad shoulders, and a slim waist. The male population quickly took notice. Facial hair all but disappeared among the younger generation, while padded shoulders began appearing in American suits. Men trimmed down, choosing to favor a svelte waistline rather than an extended stomach, considered then to be a mark of wealth.

Dana drew what he saw and, along the way, redefined the concept of romance for Americans. Old World tales of medieval princes and princesses inspired contemporary stories of love and chivalry, with men in white tie and tails and women in dazzling gowns. From the comfort of their armchairs, Dana's loyal stable of readers could experience the grand pageantry of the belle époque, where high society, money, and the quest for European titles of nobility appeared to be all that mattered, amid a backdrop of opulent mansions and horse-drawn carriages, fanciful opera boxes, and lavish drawing rooms.

Using satire and pathos, Dana lampooned society, only to find himself a welcome figure in its upper ranks. Yet years earlier, as a mere messenger boy, he was chastised when he knocked at the door of railroad baron Cornelius Vanderbilt. But as a famous artist, he became an eagerly sought guest. Indeed, Dana was regally feted with ceremonial dinners, where often he would serve as the toastmaster.

Undoubtedly, it was the Gibson Girl's unprecedented popularity that made its creator a household name, for her name and likeness spawned a vast commercial enterprise that included clothing, goods, and furniture. Her image could be found on matchboxes, calendars, umbrella stands, postcards, and even silverware and dinner services. The art of pyrography—in which an image was burned into wood—led to Gibson Girl chairs, plaques, and wood panels. People danced to Gibson Girl waltzes, polkas, and even entire musicals.

Although she was merely a lovely figment of one man's imagination—an illusion of beauty—the Gibson Girl captured the affection of millions of people, including my own.

I WILL BE THE NEXT GIBSON GIRL, I thought, as I sat, half asleep, on a train speeding southward. When I would arrive at the studio of Charles Dana Gibson, I knew that he would surely welcome me.

Ah, Miss Palmer. I have been awaiting your arrival. Please come in and try on this beautiful dress. I want you to be my next Gibson Girl of 1912.

The ebony evening gown was of the latest fashion. My heart pounded as he politely gestured toward an Oriental screen at the studio's far corner. I took the dress and excused myself to assemble everything without disturbing my hair, piled high with appropriate formality, just like the girls in his illustrations.

As I presented myself, the silky fabric puddled at my feet, and ascended my body with a narrow fullness, tapering at my waist where it was pulled tight. In that one short instant, I became the pinnacle of elegance even though no one but him ever saw me.

His eyes stared at me for what seemed like an eternity. Then, he looked down with great intensity, working quickly with his nibbed pen over an old wooden drawing board. From time to time, he glanced up but was otherwise lost in his work, magically turning ink into flesh.

It is finished. What do you think of it?

Just then, the train in which I had been traveling for over two hours came to a sudden stop, jolting me awake. My daydream was over, but my adventure was only just beginning.

Outside of Grand Central Terminal, a bright future awaited.

IN THOSE DAYS, MANHATTAN WAS A BUDDING, SEPIA-TONED CITY, intent on becoming the most modern metropolis in the world. Its spacious streets and tree-lined avenues were filled with trolleys, canopied motor coaches, push-carts, horse-drawn wagons, and the occasional lavish carriage guided by a pair of shiny black geldings. The city's crowded sidewalks also surged with a mass of humanity—gentlemen clad in dark suits and long wool coats, with stiff felt derbies or tweed caps; ladies wore ankle-length skirts, tight-waisted coats, and flowing hats. Everyone seemed busy; they all wanted to get somewhere, including me.

That afternoon, I made my way through the bustling streets to the studio of Charles Dana Gibson, located high above Carnegie Hall in a sixteen-story tower, where painters, musicians, photographers, and dancers worked each day and often slept. I avoided the elevator, a device I did not quite trust then, and climbed the tower's many steps until I arrived at the ninth floor and found his studio, number 90–1, and knocked at his door.

Mr. Gibson, please forgive my intrusion. My name is Nancy Palmer. I am from Poughkeepsie. We have a mutual friend. Here—I hope you have the time to read this letter she wrote to you. It tells of my interest in becoming an artist's model.

I see.

I handed the letter to him, and he quickly read it. He wore the apparel of a prosperous man of affairs: a tailored black business suit, high wing collar, and a black silk necktie that swelled from the top of his vest. His cheekbones were distinct, and his forehead rippled as it approached his balding head, which, with the starched collar, made him appear much like a boiled egg sitting on top of an ivory cup. Yet he was one of the handsomest men I had ever met.

All right, Miss Palmer. I will call you within the week. I trust you will be residing in the city.

I will, Mr. Gibson.

Very well, then.

Saying nothing more, he closed the door. A few days later, I received a call requesting that I come to his studio. This time, when I arrived, his secretary greeted me, and what I witnessed was nothing less than magnificent splendor.

The studio of Charles Dana Gibson was a cavernous place with double-high windows shrouded in heavy, dark Victorian curtains and large woven tapestries draped from ceiling to floor. Plush Oriental divans lined the interior walls. The artist, looking rather lonely, sat before an old drawing board in the center of the room. By his side sat a small table, on top of which was a collection of half-filled bottles of ink and thinner and several white handkerchiefs.

Are you ready to pose for me today?

I nodded my head like a young schoolgirl.

Please stand over there in the light, where I can see you better.
Splendid.

As I stood there motionless, he continued to talk.

"Now, as curious as it may seem, I never consciously sat to work to create a special type of American girl," he confided to me. "Indeed, my efforts have, I hope, been broader than that. As an anecdote, in my particular case, I have for years made it a rule to have no model more than twice consecutively, however admirable the person may be as a model or however successful the character may be portrayed."

My heart sank as he said those words. He sensed this, I felt, and then asked me to shift more toward him.

You know, there are some modern academic philosophers who say that women are losing their femininity . . . that they are rapidly approaching the masculine in their actions and appearance. Indeed, the president of the National Academy of Design and the director for gymnastics at Harvard have recently agreed on this issue. But I think it is a bunch of rubbish, Miss Palmer. What do you think?

I completely agree with you, Mr. Gibson. Women may be getting stronger and more independent in their ideas and actions, but they are still quintessentially feminine. Over the years, that singular constant has not waivered, despite changing fashions. Women are still and will always be women.

He paused and then turned back toward me. "When the sun becomes an icy ball," he said, "women may no longer be women but not before that. Men love women as ardently as ever," he added. "The feminine charm has not diminished, the call of sex to sex is as strong as ever, and the average woman can arouse the man as much as when Anthony and Cleopatra went boating."

After a short period, he stopped drawing and looked up. *I know of one particular illustrator who idealizes women in his work. He has lifted the so-called weaker sex to new heights until she has, in fact, become the stronger of the two. With his paintbrush, a person of average feature becomes more beautiful if you can only imagine that. I am speaking, of course, of Howard Chandler Christy. Perhaps you have heard of him and his Christy Girl?*

Oh, I have!

Splendid! Well, he is presently in town for a short while . . . and in need of a model. You show great promise, Miss Palmer. Would you care to meet him?

I most certainly would, Mr. Gibson!

Very well, then, I shall telephone Christy today and make the introduction.

Although I felt overcome with joy, I was filled with some trepidation.

The Old Waldorf-Astoria, as it appeared at the intersection of 5th Avenue and 34th Street around the time of April 1912, when Nancy Palmer first met Howard Chandler Christy. The Astoria's covered carriage driveway is immediately facing. (Detroit Publishing Company; Library of Congress, Washington, DC)

"You're a beautiful girl and a very promising model, so you needn't be nervous," he assured me. "I think Christy will want you, and I think I had better warn you too. If Christy chooses you to go back to Ohio with him, you'll come back to New York as Mrs. Howard Chandler Christy."

Arrangements were made. At 12:30 the following day, I was to meet Mr. Christy in Peacock Alley at the old Waldorf-Astoria, an imposing palace of a hotel that had hosted some of the most famous people in the world.

The old Waldorf-Astoria was actually two separate buildings joined together. Large, ornate lobbies on either end swelled with the hotel's clientele, who were funneled through an opulent corridor called Peacock Alley, so named because women would often preen for the members of the opposite sex and the envy of their own as they strutted in the most fashionable of clothes.

That day was no different.

Underneath its high coffered ceilings and etched-glass chandeliers, the pageantry of the noonday business unfolded in glamorous splendor. Broad-brimmed hats with plumes of ostrich feathers bobbed by. Expensive furs fluttered in the air, and glistening strands of jewels and pearls dripped down from the necks of fair ladies.

I affirmatively decided that I still needed to find that singular spot on the hotel's first floor that was even more visible than all the rest. So I found an unoccupied chair, settled in it, and nervously glanced at my watch, reassuring myself that Howard Chandler Christy would eventually find me. The minutes slowly moved by, but at last, when he did see me, it seemed as if time had stopped.

Miss Palmer, I presume.

I looked up, and my eyes immediately met his. My pulse raced.

"I know you must be the girl Gibson spoke of," he said in a reassuring tone. "There is no one else here like you."

I just stared at him, absolutely speechless . . . primarily because there was no one else in that entire hotel like this man—or in the whole state of New York, for that matter. He exuded a youthful air, like a

Howard, as he looked around 1912, when he and Nancy first met (Special Collections, Lafayette College, Easton, PA)

modern-day Adonis. Although he was thirty-nine years of age then,[4] he looked to be about twenty-five. And he was precisely as Charles Dana Gibson had described: handsome, with piercing blue eyes and reddish dark-blond hair.

He wore a dove-gray suit, with a vest of similar color but piped in black. His heavy silk cravat held a stickpin bearing a single glistening diamond. These are the indelible memories I have of that first meeting—my first impressions.

"I am Howard Christy," he continued, "and I am very glad to meet you."

And I am Nancy Palmer. Pleased to make your acquaintance, Mr. Christy.

I rose and extended my quivering hand. He grasped it firmly but in a warm manner, and quickly it became still.

And I yours, Miss Palmer. Have you been here before?

I have not.

Well, then, you must first call me Howard, and then I will tell you everything I know.

I shall. And please call me Nancy. Everyone in my hometown does.

Well, Nancy, many years ago, when I was but a young man, Colonel John Jacob Astor—the very same man who recently perished on the RMS Titanic—*decided to build this impressive structure in which we are now standing to adjoin the Waldorf Hotel, built by his cousin, William Waldorf Astor; the new addition was called the Astoria. The opening gala of this combined hotel caused as much sensation in New York society as the opening night of the Waldorf Hotel four years before. The event occurred on a cool November evening, and I was there to witness it all for* Leslie's Weekly.

How were you so fortunate to be here at this hotel and at that very moment in history?

The magazine's editors commissioned me to create an illustration for their upcoming issue. I'm an illustrator. I paint what I see.

What did you see?

That particular night was stormy. A crowd stood outside the hotel, drenched in the rain and hungry for a glimpse of glamour among the awaiting carriages that lined the covered driveway. Policemen kept spectators at bay as New York's aristocracy entered the Astor gallery for the first time. It was like being in a European castle. Orchestral music echoed throughout the spacious rooms as the wealthiest of the wealthy and the most socially notable families in all of the world stood in groups on the open floor, mingling and observing. It was an event to see and at which to have been seen. There were a great many youthful people, both men and women, who, by traditional standards, would be considered handsome or beautiful. The person who intrigued me the most, however, was actually none of them but an older woman.

As Howard stared down the long, busy gallery of the Astoria, he recalled this woman's appearance, just as if her ghostly apparition was floating right there before him.

"Her hair was white, lightly flecked with black," he said. "She wore a gray gown of some soft material, with touches of black in its makeup. Her gown and face were in absolute harmony, with perfect contrasts and balanced with ideal effectiveness. There were scores of far younger women there, but this one stood out plainly defined, observed by all."

His vivid description impressed me because I could not envision anyone who saw beauty as he did. He could see things that others simply could not. I longed to know more.

So, if I may ask of your observances, I assume there is more to true beauty than just youth.

Oh, yes. Age is of no consequence in the realm of true beauty. Someday, you will learn the secret. Come; let us go. Shall we?

As our arms linked, his face exuded a soft smile. This is how Howard and I first met, and this is how I will always remember him: young, handsome, smiling, and with a secret.

We strolled down the long gallery to the Palm Restaurant, a lavish and exclusive establishment, where many of the most prominent people in the city dined each night.

I have several business acquaintances I would like for you to meet. I think you will find them quite cordial.

By the far wall of the restaurant, two quiet, serious-looking gentlemen were huddled around a table, deeply engaged in conversation. As soon as they saw Howard, they immediately rose and moved in our direction.

Miss Palmer, I'd like to introduce you to Clarence Vernon of Street & Smith Publications, and Mr. Hines, who is one of the publication's editors.

The two men greeted us, and then we all sat down at a round table set with a large bouquet of white and purple flowers in the center and encircled with numerous sets of crystal glasses. On the tablecloth, silver forks, knives, and spoons of varying sizes were aligned in precise fashion, like the instruments of a surgeon.

Howard informed me of the importance of these particular gentlemen:

Street & Smith specializes in fiction: adventure stories, mystery dramas, and rags-to-riches novels. You know, the sort of thing one might pick up in a five-and-dime store. The editors develop the characters and plot, their stable of writers write about them, and then we, the illustrators, bring the whole thing to life, and it is published in magazines and books. All of it is seamless magic.

Seamless magic?

Yes, pure magic . . . and all of it is quite seamless. He smiled, then whispered in my ear, with his left hand shielding his thoughts from the others. *To them, it's all about the money.*

He then turned to these gentlemen to discuss the deep business at hand—scenes he would illustrate in the coming weeks. Myriad details, editorial comments, deadlines, and storylines filled the air. I, of course, remained completely silent during each of the luncheon's various courses.

After a couple of hours passed, Howard's guests departed. He and I were alone once more.

Overwhelmed and nervous, I was entirely unsure of myself or of my standing with this great artist. I felt quite certain that I did not impress him and that he would surely not want me to be his model. This feeling grew even stronger until, as we approached the lobby, his calm, genteel manner assured me otherwise. Somehow, he intuitively felt my precise thoughts.

"I think I know what question you want answered," he said as he turned to me with a grin. "And I do have an answer for you. I am certain that you are the model I want."

His words gave me great comfort.

Art imitates life in this Christy illustration, published in September 1912 for Gouverneur Morris's The Penalty, *a popular serial illustrated for* Cosmopolitan *magazine and later adapted into a 1920 movie of the same name, starring Lon Chaney. Howard used Nancy as the female model for this work, perhaps inspired by their first meeting at the old Waldorf-Astoria Hotel. The male model is Noel Talbot (David Noel Maitland Talbot: 1880–1954), Howard's British caretaker for his Ohio home, The Barracks.*

Howard asked me if I wished to dine with him and perhaps see a light musical that night. There was nothing in the world I wanted more, and so I readily accepted his invitation.

That evening at dinner, Howard sketched out in words his remarkable life, and I began to fall under his spell.

To this day, I can still see it all in my mind, everything that he told me. First, he spoke of his childhood and then of his early years in New York, studying to be a painter. He mentioned seeing and painting the tragedy of the Spanish-American War, which led him to his current work. But of everything he mentioned, the most intriguing to me was the beauty he saw at his home, sitting high atop the Muskingum River in Ohio. He talked of groups of well-dressed passengers traveling on large steamboats and of a pastoral setting so inspiring and pure that the vision of it, in my mind, was just as heavenly as it smelled.

"You would like this place," he said. "It is said to be the most beautiful view in the state of Ohio."

And so, there it was . . . just a short description of what I would later encounter, yet from his assurances, this tranquil spot where he lived sounded to be so wonderful, so enchanting that it brought me closer to him and unknowingly pulled me into his magical world. Could what he said be true? Did such a land truly exist, or was it all simply a fantasy? I longed to know.

I want you to see the place for yourself, Nancy. I want you to be my model. I know that you feel that you are inexperienced as an artist's assistant, but from what Gibson told me and from what I see, you show great promise. There's no need to be nervous. You possess the right requirements, and I prefer to train my models anyway.

His words were reassuring. But in my mind, I still felt that Gibson's earlier prediction—that Howard would eventually ask to marry me—was a complete fabrication of its own. How could he want to wed me? For here was a man whose sole purpose in life was to find beauty and to paint it, not to fall in love—and certainly not with me. There was nothing beautiful about me or my background. I am just an ordinary working girl. This was something I kept turning over in my mind as we were together that evening; something I could not forget.

After the musical finished, we made our way from the bustle of the theater lobby to the crowded sidewalk, where a taxi cab awaited in the din of the after-theater traffic. Howard opened the door, and I slid into the backseat. He stood by the side of the taxi and closed the door, firmly gripping the sill of the open window, as if he did not want to leave until I gave him an answer.

Yes, Howard, I want to be your model, and there is nothing I would love more than to see the beauty you have described.

So it is settled. I will send for you in the coming week. And, as I mentioned, once you are in Ohio, be sure to change trains at Trinway. From there, you'll want to take the train to Zanesville and then the one downriver. It follows the river's west bank and stops directly across from my home.

We said our good-byes, although neither of us wanted to part. As the taxi pulled away, Howard's calm voice resounded in my mind, along with brief images of the paradise he described. Soon, I would learn the truth.

Within a week, a letter from Howard arrived at my doorstep, along with a train ticket. Promptly, I left New York City, stopping briefly in my hometown of Poughkeepsie to pick up some additional dresses and hats, and then took an early afternoon express, the destination of which was Ohio. My journey to this strange new world was just beginning, and my head was swirling with dreams waiting to come true.

◉

AS DAWN BROKE, I awoke in the front seat of a passenger train car barreling at full speed across the countryside of Ohio.

Adjusting my hat, I pressed it against the window to peer out. The landscape was vastly different from anything I had ever seen. Everything was so lush and green. There were crested hills, flowing streams, and plentiful cornfields that seemed to stretch for mile upon mile. I saw quaint old farmhouses and barns, both old and new, and well-traveled dirt roads. But what I remember most was the bright sunshine that illuminated the unspoiled land on that perfect day.

Within a short time, the train pulled into Trinway Station, a charming Victorian depot with sloping curved gables and leaded-glass windows. Steam rose from the station platform as I stepped down from the car. An attendant greeted me. The young porter graciously assisted with my luggage and hat boxes, lining them up in two neat rows. Once done, he tipped his hat and walked right past me, as if I were a mere apparition, and continued to the far end of the platform toward the front of the train, where there was a man standing alone in the smoky haze. The man dropped some coins in the porter's hand and then slowly emerged into the daylight until his face and body clearly appeared within view. He was just as I had remembered from days before.

"Thought I would meet you here so that you would make the right connection. Did you have a pleasant journey?" he called to me, softly following with "Good morning."

Upon seeing him once again and hearing his gentle voice, my heart skipped a beat.

Oh, yes, I did. The countryside is invigorating. There's so much to take in. Good morning.

I'm so pleased. Here—let me help you with your cases. The train to Zanesville will be departing shortly.

In that brief moment, a sense of tranquility and great thanks came over me. With Howard, everything would turn out all right.

We boarded another train, and the hour-and-a-half train ride to Zanesville quickly passed. From there, we took the downriver train, which, as Howard had described, brought us just a little over ten miles south of Zanesville, until it came to a complete stop in a grassy field at a point below a bend in the river, where the two banks narrowed.

After we climbed down the train steps with my luggage, the locomotive chugged up again and continued its journey downriver, eventually disappearing into the horizon. Moments later, all that could be seen of it was the faint trail of smoke that floated above the treetops.

I paused to collect my bags as Howard pointed upward to a great sandstone cliff across the wide river.

There it is! My home! It sits on a bluff called Christy's Knob.

I was entirely oblivious to what he had said until I looked up. On the ledge of the sandstone cliff, an immense white mansion was shining brilliantly in the sun. Four tall chimneys pierced the sky. And slightly beyond it was an enormous white staff with the American flag gently flapping in the wind.

Although this place was more than a quarter of a mile away, it seemed so grand in my eyes. In fact, everything on that particular day seemed beyond the realm of imagination.

Howard's mansion, The Barracks, as it looked from the Muskingum River around 1912. At the base of the bluff is South River Road. The home's driveway, which winds from the road to the top, is at the far right and not shown. To the left, rising diagonally, is a pathway that traverses up the side to the tennis court at the top right. (Courtesy of Jaye and Melodie Hayes)

I turned to Howard, struggling to find a way to express my thoughts, but I simply could not. He said the first words.

Well? What do you think?

Oh, my! What a place to live in!

I had it built just a few years ago, according to my own plans. I call it the Barracks.

A brief smirk came from my lips.

Whatever for? The name makes it sound like a military encampment. But this is far from it. It's absolutely beautiful, like a castle in the clouds.

Its name comes from my fondness for the US Army when I painted during the Santiago Campaign in Cuba. Sometime, I will tell you about that. But this is where I grew up. My family lives in a house next to the place I built. Come; I will show you.

Together, we gathered up the luggage and boxes and walked down a wide path leading to the river's edge to where a launch was docked, waiting to carry us across the moving current. We boarded as he told me more about those who had journeyed to his home.

I receive all sorts of guests here, mostly writers, publishers, and close friends. Artists too.

Really? I would love to know more.

You will, and you'll certainly meet many people too. Some are quite famous. At one point, even Evelyn Nesbit, Gibson's young model, stayed at my home. You may recall that her millionaire husband, Harry Thaw, murdered architect Stanford White in the summer of '06 over an affair. Shot him point-blank during a musical revue on the rooftop of Madison Square Garden.

But why did she stay here?

Hearst's newspapers had a field day. Best press since the Spanish-American War, they said—gorgeous model, wealthy husband, famous architect, and, of course, cold-blooded murder in a crowded restaurant filled with society. Perfect ingredients for a good story . . . don't you think? Everyone called it the trial of the century. Evelyn had to hide out from the newspapermen, and here, on Christy's Knob, no one would ever find her. I assured her of that. You know, Nancy, sometimes I have unexpected visitors too. I don't even know they are going to arrive or even why. I hope you don't mind.

Unexpected visitors? Whom do you mean?

One might say my home has become a bit of a tourist attraction, or perhaps I am. Just four years ago in the summer, a group of young canoeists left Zanesville on a Saturday afternoon. By nightfall, they had landed in Philo, the town directly across the river from my home. Their campfire could be clearly seen, and it attracted a neighboring man who knew all about my place. He could see my lantern hanging on the flag staff. I raise it each night as a beacon for the boats that ply the river.

And they saw the light and decided to visit?

Yes. That, and the clever man told them that I set off dynamite and rockets . . . for good fun . . . in the evenings.

Dynamite! Undoubtedly curiosity must have got the best of them.

So much so that they rowed their canoes right over here to the edge of the landing and, thinking the lantern looked more like a shining star, climbed the side of the hill to see it better. They came up the side by the tennis court, breathless and sweating. My family and I, on the other hand, were comfortably seated in lawn chairs by the side of the croquet court. As it was summer, we entertained them for a while, and they entertained us. They returned the next morning, and I gave them a tour of the place.

So do you actually set off dynamite?

His eyebrows arched as he smiled.

Well, on occasion I do use a bit of explosives to disgorge the old tree stumps on the hillside. People can hear it for miles around. Keeps the villagers on their toes.

Although I did not know it then, I would later discover that not only was Howard the talk of the neighboring towns and villages but also of the entire country.

The boat launch arrived at a sandstone ledge on the river's east bank, just below Howard's home. A horse pulling a hay wagon slowly descended from the winding gravel drive until it came within view. Sitting atop was a dashing, clean-shaven young man with raven-black hair. He tipped his hat.

Good afternoon. I trust on this fine day you had a pleasant journey.

Nancy, I would like to introduce you to Noel Talbot. He's my summer caretaker here at the Barracks.

'Tis a pleasure to make your acquaintance, Miss . . .

Palmer. This is Miss Nancy Palmer from New York. She has traveled here to model for me.

Ah, yes, the new Christy Girl. Fine choice, Howard. Most certainly the public will adore her as much as they have of all your creations. If you are ever in need of any assistance, Miss Palmer, I am most certainly at your disposal.

Noel climbed down from atop the driver's seat and came to the edge of the road to where a set of steps led down to the landing. He was exceedingly handsome and muscular, with finely chiseled features and a sophisticated British accent that gave him an air of mystery and worldliness. It made me wonder all the more if this wonderland was indeed a fantasy, and I was merely the unsuspecting girl who had fallen down the rabbit hole.

It's a pleasure to meet you too, Mr. Talbot. For some reason, you seem so very familiar to me. Have we met before?

I don't believe we have, Miss Palmer, as I am certain that I would have remembered such a beautiful face.

That's it! Howard's illustrations . . . I've seen you in them.

Oh, yes, well, ol' Howard employs me from time to time to model for his pictures. You may have seen me on the front page of some Sunday insert or monthly magazine section of the newspaper. Howard loves doing those. They can be found all over the United States, you know. Then there is Cosmopolitan *magazine, where I have been a regular for years. Although it seems like an eternity at times. Whenever Howard needs a man for his illustrations, I seem to be his man—caretaker and model. He's quite resourceful, you know. He even uses his own father and mother for modeling work, as well as some of the children up the way in Duncan Falls. Saves on expenses.*

I just knew this man looked familiar. But it took a few second to make the connection.

Yes, I have seen you before . . . many times! You . . . you are the Christy Man! And I have seen you in Howard's books as well . . . with his Christy Girl.

Oh, quite! I am practically in every book he has done for the past four years.

Noel seemed embarrassed, but I could tell he really wasn't. He wanted to tell me everything.

Remember Alfred, Lord Tennyson's The Princess? *For that, Howard conscripted me to dress in a full suit of armor to become the proverbial knight in shining armor. And just when I had placed my helmet on, his huge dog, a Great Dane, bolted across the room and came bounding up to me. With his big hairy paws, he pounced on my chest, knocking me flat on my back. Bloody near killed me. It took three grown men to lift me to my feet. Well, that was the end of that; the big brute of a dog was forever banished from the studio.*

Noel smiled brightly.

Now, Miss Palmer, I am no longer required to dress up as the knight. Howard has me wearing the latest men's fashions—stiff Arrow collars, Kuppenheimer suits, pen-point toe shoes, or, in the summer, white buckskins. Much prefer that.

Mr. Talbot climbed down from the wagon driver's seat and then walked to the steps leading down to the landing.

Good models are hard to find, Miss Palmer, especially those who can hold a pose long enough to suit Mr. Christy. Based upon first impressions, I know you have what it takes, as they say.

Thank you, Mr. Talbot, for your words of encouragement. I hope to do my best.

Mr. Talbot leaned down and grabbed my bags.

That's all you can do, Miss Palmer. Act like the greatest model in the world, and the world will think you are. It's all about the illusion or, as Howard would say, seamless magic.

Noel Talbot, Howard's caretaker, modeled for Howard's 1911 illustration titled "The Valiant Knight and his Dutiful Squire." The knight is imagining his wife and newborn child as he prepares for battle. This illustration appears with many others in Alfred, Lord Tennyson's The Princess. *(Private collection)*

One by one, Mr. Talbot took each of my suitcases and hatboxes and carefully placed them in the back of the hay wagon and then climbed back up to the driver's seat. Howard and I were at the back of the wagon when, in a moment of youthful exuberance, Howard surprised me.

Here—let me help you up.

His strong arms grabbed me by the waist. As he pulled me close, our eyes briefly met, and I could see a faint smile on his lips and a twinkle of mischief in his eyes. For an instant, I thought he was going to kiss me, but instead, he grabbed my waist and hoisted me up to the rear of the wagon.

Howard! Is this how you treat your guests?

He laughed, and Mr. Talbot did too, as I quickly brushed away the hay clinging to my dress.

You'll make a country girl out of her yet, Howard!

Oh, I would be satisfied with just a simple city girl who loves natural beauty . . . the beauty of freshly cut straw and an old hay wagon . . . and maybe a long ride to Duncan Falls.

Just then, from the corner of my eye, I could see a shiny burgundy motor car with white tires descending the sloping curves of the tree-lined driveway. The calming sound of its rumbling became more distinct until, through the trees, I could see its polished brass grill and headlights gleaming in the afternoon sun. Howard saw it too and looked at me.

Now, that's how I treat my very important guests. All the others have to ride in the back of that hay wagon. But you're different. I wanted you to get the best of both worlds.

He laughed again as he helped me down. This time, I laughed as well. But Noel reflected a more demure manner.

Mr. Christy is showing you his humorous side, but I assure you that he's quite serious. He doesn't break out the motor car for just anyone. You must have what it takes.

When the car came to a complete stop at the edge of the road, Howard's chauffeur—suitably dressed for the part in tall black boots, long tan duster coat, and gray tweed cap—got out and opened the passenger-side door for me. Then he opened the door for Howard to take the driver's seat.

Thank you. I'll drive this train now! Noel, you can pick up the caboose.

Without missing a beat, the chauffeur quietly hopped in the back of the hay wagon. His boots dangled at the edge like that of a rag doll.

Howard engaged the motorcar as he turned to me and said, *Now, here comes the fun part.*

He pushed forward the hand break and, with a small jolt, we began to lurch up the steep gravel incline, moving forward ever so quickly.

Hold on tight!

And off we went, scaling the heights above the lovely blue Muskingum River.

The higher we ascended, the faster we moved. Flickering beams of sunlight danced on the car's hood and brightened the shady patches of the road ahead. The breeze, faint with the scent of honeysuckle, whipped my hair back until my long curls simply unfurled and fluttered in the wind. My handsome driver couldn't seem to keep his eyes off me.

The way your hair floats . . . in the changing light—love it! I think I will borrow it for one of my magazine covers someday.

Howard turned forward to watch the road, but his eyes continued to glance back at me.

Maybe I'll add in a long, flowing scarf too. Now that would be something!

The car rolled on, and I felt so alive.

For once in my life, I was truly living. I was finally free . . . without any cares.

As we approached the top of the ridge, on either side of the drive billows of pink and white lilac blooms ushered us to the right and then begged us to continue on. These flowers were not like anything I had ever seen. Howard slowed the car so that I could admire the view, and I told him what I observed.

"Why He Missed the Aeroplane," an illustration of a motoring couple, was one of the first works Howard painted of Nancy Palmer as his model. To the left is the original work; to the right is how it was reproduced for periodicals. (Private Collection)

They smell so heavenly! And they're absolutely gorgeous. Aren't they?

Over the din of the car's motor, he replied, *Yes, they are. They only last for a few weeks and are gone, but they'll be back again next year.* He revved the engine and exuberantly shouted, *Spring is here!*

And again we were off, flying over the winding drive and kicking up a cloud of dust and gravel behind us.

To the left, nestled in the green hillside, was a quaint cottage with a steep wooden-shingle roof and a stone chimney. And to the immediate left of that was a huge five-story barn, painted a buttery yellow. Behind everything was a sloping pasture, where cows meandered and rested. When the car moved to a point near the top, it slowed, and Howard pointed with his left hand to the humble cottage.

Howard's rising popularity precipitated the sale of picture postcards depicting his Ohio home, along with various rooms within it. This postcard shows his sprawling estate, including his parents' house to the right. An eighty-foot flag pole sits amid a long grape arbor (center). (Collection of author)

Howard, with his Great Dane, Sargent, stands on the bridge in front of his studio barn. The cow pasture is behind. In the left foreground, Bill, Howard's brindle Bull Terrier, quietly observes in front of an old stone lamppost. The springhouse is to the far left, and the tack room (not pictured) would be to the immediate right. (Special Collections, Lafayette College, Easton, PA)

That's the springhouse there. It's where we keep the milk and cream. In the summer, on really hot days, we go swimming in the cold pool that's inside. And over there is the studio barn I built three years ago. The second floor, below the walkway bridge, is where the horses are stabled, and the cows are milked. The floors above are used for my painting. And to the left of the barn is the tack room, where the saddles, reins, and other equipment are stored.

He accelerated the car toward the top of the ridge, and as we passed over it, an old, weathered, gray stone post came into view. Perhaps an immense scrolling iron gate was once hinged to it, but none was there then. It simply marked the beginning of his well-manicured domain.

In the middle of the lawn, a croquet court awaited, and the same tall flagpole I had seen across the river had a mammoth American flag flying atop. There were many chimneys—more than I had seen earlier. On top of the mansion's roof was a glass-paned belvedere—a sequestered spot to see the river. Below, three stately white columns lined the front veranda.

Directly across from his home to the east was a sprawling Victorian farmhouse with a long front porch. The rustic retreat was connected with a pebbled walkway and flanked by a long wooden arbor with Concord grapevines entangling it.

Who lives over there?

My parents. When I was a young boy, I lived there too. And you know what, just behind it is an apple orchard. I'll show that to you too.

We drove on . . . . On the hillside overlooking the river, there were no trees, save for a few sparse old specimens, mostly buckeye, beech, and ancient oak. Those that surrounded his home were in their youth, except for a single, huge laurel in front of the old farmhouse. I distinctly recall the flowers. Iris lined the walkways. Heliotrope bloomed in great profusion. Dogwood and rosebud trees exploded with the color of fireworks. And there was even a cultivated rose garden containing row upon row of the most exquisite-smelling varieties in the world.

Howard enjoys the summer air with his daughter, Natalie, on the stone stairs leading to the bluff overlooking the Muskingum River, circa 1912. To their backs is the vine-covered pergola, decorated with Chinese lanterns and supporting a railed walkway. (Special Collections, Lafayette College, Easton, PA)

Howard pulled the car around to the south side of his house near two sturdy white columns perched on stone plinths. A peacock crossed in front of the car but stopped short just long enough to display all of the iridescent eyes on its splendid feathered tail.

Is that a—

Peacock! We have several of them roaming the grounds. They are beautiful creatures, and they know it. To them, it's all about their appearances. Such vanity!

Howard opened his door and was nearing me to open mine when suddenly, the exotic bird darted across the green and mysteriously disappeared.

Tall sliding glass doors on the south portico glided aside, and out came bounding a grayish beast resembling a small horse. As this creature came closer, I could see that he was not a horse at all but a massive dog, the largest I had ever seen. Yet when his paws hit the ground, it was as though I was in the front row of the Kentucky Derby. Bounding and jumping, this dog looked like he was going to collide headlong with Howard until, at the last moment, he put his brakes on and jumped high in the air. When he descended, both of his front paws miraculously landed on Howard's shoulders, and a red, beefy tongue slathered up the side of his master's cheek.

Hello, old boy. Hello. Good to see you. . . . Missed you.

Howard petted him until the large beast calmed down and eventually landed back on the gravel walkway.

Nancy, this is Sargent, my Great Dane. I named him after my favorite painter, John Singer Sargent. He rules the roost.

Well, hello, Sargent. Up close, you don't seem to be so brutish at all. In fact, you look to be a gentle giant.

Noel pulled the hay wagon to the side and jumped down, keeping his distance. *Umm, quite. Well, perhaps he just has a natural affinity for men who prefer to dress up as tin cans.*

Nipping at Howard's heels was a brindle Boston Terrier, a stout black-and-white dog with pointy ears and an upturned nose. He was about a tenth of the size of Sargent and much less rambunctious.

And this here is Bill. On most mornings, you can see him chase the blue jays and cardinals over the front lawn and into the cow pasture. And in the afternoons, when he is completely exhausted, he just sits . . . and watches the world go by. Nice life, eh, Bill?

The patient dog rendered a satisfied bark and then just sat and observed the commotion of my arrival.

From the front veranda, an older couple descended the steps, along with two young ladies, one in a long black skirt and white blouse, and the other in a long gray dress, banded at the waist by a dusty rose ribbon. They strolled down the walkway and approached us.

Nancy, I would like for you to meet my father and mother, Francis and Mary Christy. And these are my two younger sisters, Rose and Hope.

Howard's father was tall, lean, and gaunt, with short snow-white hair and a Van Dyke beard. He looked like the quintessential Kentucky colonel. Elegantly dressed in a three-button, black suit and ivory tie, he possessed the same genteel demeanor as his son, along with identical piercing blue eyes.

Howard's mother stood quietly by, exuding a serious air. The others followed suit, greeting me in turn—first his father, then his mother, and then his sisters.

Welcome to the Barracks. It's so good to have you here.

I am very pleased to make your acquaintance, Miss Palmer. If there is anything you need, please let me know. As Howard's mother, I treat all of his female models who come here as though they were my own daughters.

So delighted and so excited, Nancy. This place needs more of a feminine touch. Hope and I have tried to do our best, but now that you are here, you can help us. We also want to hear all about New York City and how you and our brother came to meet.

In the background, Noel worked quickly, shuttling my cases and hatboxes to the front of the mansion and then up the stairs. He returned and went back several times as Howard's sisters and I chatted. But on his final trip, Noel approached me.

I think you'll like it here, Miss Palmer, very much so. You never know who will pop in for a visit.

I'm sure I will, Noel. Thank you again, especially for your kind words of encouragement.

In the distance, I could hear the elder Mr. Christy muttering under his breath to his wife, "I think she's thinner than she ought to be, don't you, Mother?"

Mrs. Christy said nothing but only looked at her son, who was entirely preoccupied with his sisters' conversation with me. "Yes, sir," Mr. Christy said to his wife. "We're going to have to fatten her up."

From the south portico, a colored woman came walking down the steps.

Sorry, Mr. Christy, so sorry. Sargent was a-sittin' in the dining room by the glass doors all day, just a-waitin' for ya. When ya came drivin' up, I just hadda let 'im out.

It's all right, Virginia. He's part of the family, as are you. Please meet Miss Nancy Palmer. She will be staying with us for what I hope will be a long time.

Pleasure to meet you, miss. Are you Mr. Christy's new model?

Yes, I am.

Ohhh! You sho' is pretty. Where's you from?

Poughkeepsie, New York, ma'am.

Neva been there, but I'm sho' it's a fine place. I hopes you like to eat, Miss Palmer, because I sho' do plan on servin' a hearty dinner tonight. Hopes you like apple pie too!

Yes, I do. After living in the East for all of my life, I can't wait to have some Midwest cooking.

Howard's mother interjected. *Here—please allow me to show you to your room.*

Inside Howard's home, the tasteful and well-decorated rooms were spacious and inviting. The walls and furniture proclaimed his vision of beauty, but I could tell that they needed a feminine touch here and there. The scent of warm fresh bread and cinnamon filled the air. Howard's mother and I climbed the steps to the second floor and turned down the long hallway.

Sensing that someone else was there, I peered back, and a pair of girlish brown eyes peeked out from the crack of a doorway. Below, a white-stockinged leg and the frills of a white skirt were partially hidden.

Mrs. Christy, who is the young girl in the room down the hall?

That's the room of Howard's daughter, Natalie.

He never mentioned he had a daughter. How old is she?

She'll be thirteen in July. She used to live with her mother and Howard in New York City, but now she lives here.

Her words left more questions in my mind. What happened to her mother, and why was she not with her? There were so many things that I needed to learn . . . and in time, I would.

In time, the truth would be revealed.

I hope this room suits you.

The bedroom had two high picture windows overlooking the cliff and river below. I felt like it was a bedchamber in the high turret of a medieval castle, and I was the young princess.

Yes! Oh yes, this is simply splendid, Mrs. Christy.

I am glad you like it, dear. If you need anything, I will be downstairs. Please let me know. Dinner is at 6:30, and breakfast is at 8:00 a.m. sharp.

The room was indeed splendid, as was that cloudless day. Outside, the blue river sparkled. The green foliage shimmered, and the birds were singing high above the treetops without any cares in the world.

LATER THAT EVENING, A SIZABLE FEAST WAS SERVED, just as Virginia had promised.

As coffee was poured, I asked Howard's father to speak of his younger days.

Mr. Christy, Howard said that you served in the Civil War.

Eh? What about the War?

Noticing that his father had difficulty hearing, Howard interjected, *Father can't hear very well, Nancy. In his regiment, he was in charge of lighting the match that would fire the cannons; the sound impaired his hearing. Please speak a little louder.*

Mr. Christy, I said that Howard said you had served in the Civil War!

Ah, yes, I did. Served for two years, nine months, and three days—62ⁿᵈ Ohio Infantry, Company B, 116ᵗʰ Regiment. Saw thirteen battles in my time, and that doesn't include skirmishes. Never had a major injury.

You must have been rather young when you joined.

The Union only wanted men eighteen years of age or older. Friends of mine, boys scarcely seventeen years of age, were mustering in and fighting at the front. I was sixteen years of age on September first of '62, about to turn seventeen, so I couldn't lawfully join . . . but I did. Fibbed about my age! Told 'em I was eighteen.

Why?

Patriotism, my dear! I also wanted to be with my friends in Dixie to fight for the Union. And I did. First went to Columbus, Ohio, to get a uniform. Was given two months pay and a twenty-five-dollar bounty. Then I traveled to Suffolk, Virginia. By November, I saw fire while on a raid at the Blackwater River, a dividing line between Union-occupied territory and the Confederacy.

Natalie's brown eyes were completely fixated on her grandfather as he told of his heroic past.

Grandfather, please tell Nancy about the time you were nearly shipwrecked.

All right, little one. Around New Year's Day 1863, my regiment was ordered to report to General Foster at New Bern, North Carolina. So from Norfolk, Virginia, we boarded the steamer Catawba. *Once at New Bern, we stayed until February '63; then we took a steamer called the* Convoy *south to Beaufort, South Carolina. A heavy storm came up on us, knocking everything loose on deck overboard. The wind was so heavy and the waves so high that we were nearly shipwrecked off Cape Hatteras. And if that were not enough, once we arrived at Hilton Head, we were left at sea for sixteen days without water, due to a misunderstanding between Generals Hunter and Foster as to where to disembark. The exposure to the cold and wet weather gave me rheumatism at age seventeen. Still have it.*

Natalie was excited at her grandfather's fearlessness and patriotism and wanted him to tell more stories of the War between the States. So she prompted him even further.

Nancy, that's not all. Just before the announcement of the Confederates surrendering, a few of them kept popping up. Grandfather saw it. So did General George Armstrong Custer.

JAMES PHILIP HEAD (103

"[A]nd pretty soon Custer came out at the head of his [troops] on a big, black stallion," Mr. Christy exclaimed, "and splashed these men all to the devil!"

Excited at the thoughts of his earlier days, Mr. Christy added a few more words.

And I also saw Lincoln in a stovepipe hat with his son, Tad, reviewing the Army of the Potomac. I can remember it like it was just yesterday.

Howard rolled his eyes and excused himself, just when his father began to recount another story. After a few minutes, I became curious.

Mrs. Christy, where did Howard venture to?

He's probably outside on the steps of the pergola, dear, looking at the river. He likes to do that after dinner. Why don't you join him. Noel will play the piano. Noel, please play a nice song for us.

Certainly, madam.

To the north of the house, just off the living room, was a long pergola that spanned the bank of the cliff and supported a walkway. A row of columns set atop a gray stone wall lifted the giant arbor, framing the river and valley below in a series of picture windows. Hanging in each was a Chinese lantern that cast a romantic alabaster glow.

As I walked through the living room's threshold, I could see across the lawn a single lantern dangling from the flagpole, along with the many dimly lit windows in the home of Howard's parents. To my left, down the side of the bluff, there were the remains of huge tree stumps, appearing like the extracted molar teeth of some colossal giant. And at the far end of the pergola, I saw the ashy-red glow of a lit cigar and faint wisps of smoke rising and encircling one of the descending orange globes.

Lovely evening, isn't it?

He took the cigar away from his lips and turned to me. *It's even more lovely now. I hope you are settling in all right.*

I am. Your family is so kind to me. I really feel like I'm at home.

I'm so pleased. If there is anything at all you need, please let me know. Anything. I want you to be as comfortable as possible.

Across the river, flickering lights from distant windows speckled along the valley as the moon's silvery glimmer illuminated
the ebbing water. I longed to know more.

My, what a gorgeous scene. Where does this river lead?

*As I child, I would sit here on this same cliff and ponder just
that. I dreamed of being a passenger on one of the many steamboats
that would journey up and down the river. I just wanted to travel
to big places, where I could "paint big pictures of big things." I
knew I would do just that . . . someday.*

*But does this river really lead to big places, just as you had
imagined?*

*The Muskingum forms at the confluence of two rivers in
Coshocton and then runs 111 miles south to Marietta, where it
joins with the Ohio River. So it is long and vast and can take people
to where they want to go. But floating on one of those powerful
sternwheelers as it plies this river, a boy can get to any place in
the world . . . any place he wants to . . . not only in his dreams,
but also in reality.*

And did it get you to where you want to be?

Most certainly. It brought me to you.

When he said that, my face lit up almost as much as the shining
moon. I politely changed the subject.

*Noel and you both mentioned Duncan Falls earlier. Is that
far from here?*

*About a mile north. It's a small town. I go there from time to
time to pick up my mail and drop off paintings to be shipped out.
We will go there at the end of the week.*

Is there really a falls in Duncan Falls?

*Well, that's a matter of some debate. Oftentimes, as they say,
there are two sides of a story. There is the truth and, of course,
then there is the figment of someone's imagination.*

Illusion?

*Precisely! And the two are sometimes hard to separate. That's
where the artist comes in. A painter of beauty strives to portray the
truth, but invariably he appears to create an illusion—something*

too good to be true that no one would ever believe it. Yet it's the truth, and it's what the painter sees. The same is true about how Duncan Falls got its name. Over time, four different stories emerged.

But what is the truth?

Well, I'll let you decide that for yourself. One story is that there was indeed a falls or rapids, and a certain Major Duncan was trading there when his servant was attacked by Indians. Another story is that Mr. Duncan came from Pittsburgh and hoped to end the hostilities between the Indians and settlers but was fired upon. Then there is the story of the Irish explorer named Duncan, who nearly drowned when his canoe sank. Finally, there is the most outlandish tale of them all.

As he began to tell this last story, his eyes lit up, and he puffed on his cigar.

Years before, the Shawnee Nation built an "Old Town" on the site of present day Duncan Falls. Around 1774, a trapper named Duncan came from Virginia. The Shawnee chief assisted him, and for several years, all was well, and he was greatly respected. But as time went on, some of the Indians became greedy and stole from his traps on the west side of the river. Incensed, Duncan staked out his trapping grounds and shot at every Indian who came near them to poach. He killed a few too. The Indians didn't like that one bit, and they decided to hunt Duncan down like a dog. But he was sly and more skilled at maneuvering through countryside than even they were. He evaded their attempts. As he didn't have a boat to travel across the water, the Indian scouts were astonished to see him on both banks of the river. How did he do that, they wondered?

Magic?

Yes, but the illusion was eventually uncovered. In the river there was a row of stones that led to the main channel. At night, Duncan would hop from one stone to the next until he reached the main channel. There, he would place a sturdy log across and carefully walk to the other side. The Indians were completely perplexed.

So they decided to lie in wait on both sides of the river and keep watch. When Duncan crossed one evening, they ambushed him. Arrows came flying and buzzing around him. Eventually, he was hit, and just as he fell, one of the Indians cried, "Duncan falls!" Later, his body was found a half mile downstream in a place called Dead Man's Ripple. So, Miss Palmer, which of these four stories is true?

I think the first is, Mr. Christy.

No. It's the last.

He looked at me with a silent grin and then turned toward the flowing river bathed in the vibrant moonlight.

You see, that story is so fantastic, so incredible, that no one would ever believe it, including you, but that's the truth. And with the truth, there is no need for artifice or illusion. The same is true with beauty.

I wondered what he was thinking just then as he stared out into the quiet darkness. I did not want to be bold, so I gave him a compliment instead.

Howard, you have such a charmed life. Look at yourself. You have it all.

It hasn't always been that way. While my childhood was idyllic, there were times in my life that were not so.

What do you mean?

To appreciate the glorious vistas on the mountain's summit, one must first trek through the deep valley below.

He turned away and said nothing more; he didn't have to. I understood what he meant, yet I wondered what his earlier life had been like. A moment passed; only once did he look at me, and then it was only for an instant.

Tomorrow will be a long day, I know. I should probably retire.

Then good night, Nancy.

Good night, Howard.

I returned to my bedroom but did not turn on the light. I wanted one last look of that moonlit river from my open window. Down below, I could see Howard on the steps and the glowing embers of his still-lit cigar. His eyes were fixated upon the starry heavens, and his mind was deep in thought. Perhaps he was thinking of the Indians who once inhabited this great land, centuries ago, or maybe he was contemplating the beauty from the truth he sees.

I turned away, for somewhere, far in the distance, a dog was barking. When I glanced back to where he was standing, he was gone.

Howard stands on the stone steps of the pergola of his home, looking west over the Muskingum River. (Special Collections, Lafayette College, Easton, PA)

Howard paints an illustration for Gouverneur Morris's The Penalty, *a popular serial that ran in* Cosmopolitan *from August 1912 to April 1913. Nancy Palmer became the model for the story's protagonist, Barbara Ferris. The painting in this photograph appeared in the March 1913 edition of* Cosmopolitan. *(Harper's Bazaar, August 1915)*

CHAPTER FIVE

Of Youth and the Magnificent River

*A*T SEVEN O'CLOCK THE NEXT MORNING, I opened my eyes. Outside my bedroom, floorboards creaked under busy feet as the soft murmur of voices broke the silence. Soon, the home's occupants were quietly stirring below. I pulled back the covers, stretched, and began preparing for the morning. Before long, I became distracted by the sunlight, opened the sash, and peered out.

The rippling water serenely moved along the tree-lined river-banks. Midway up, the head of a young man bobbed up and down as he swam closer to shore. He swiftly approached the foot of the bluff and pulled himself up onto sandstone ledge. Completely naked, his chiseled young body shimmered in the early light as water dripped from his loins and onto the rocks. With my heart beating fast, I pulled my head back inside and just stared at my yellow spring dress cascading down the bed. I didn't want to look again, but eventually, I couldn't help myself. It was Howard.

He dried off; then vanished.

A half hour later, the sound of a bugle playing reveille pierced the morning air. I hurried downstairs, only to hear Howard's voice.

Nancy, Nancy.

It seemed to be coming from the dining room. When I peered in, no one was there. Just then, the front door opened. As I rounded the stairs, Howard slowly turned around.

Why, good morning!

"You do that every morning, or was that especially for me?" I asked.

That's a part of everyday life here at the Barracks. Morning begins with reveille and the flag.

Through the window, he pointed at the American flag gently rolling atop the staff in the center yard.

Men and women have fought and died for that flag. I experienced death and am grateful to be alive. Howard's mood suddenly changed. *Come—let's take a brief walk. There are a few things that I would like to show you.*

Before we go, I have one question. Was that you calling my name minutes earlier?

I was outside, sounding reveille.

I am certain I heard your voice.

Together, Howard and I went into the dining room. A full minute passed as we stood in complete silence, except for the faint sound of pans clanging in the kitchen. Howard stared straight at me.

See, there's nothing here.

Then, from the corner of the room, we both heard a voice, just like Howard's.

Nancy, Nancy.

Ventriloquism? Or more of your seamless magic, Mr. Christy?

Howard's eyes twinkled. He chuckled as he walked to where the voice was coming from. *No, that's just Polly.*

Howard swiftly whipped off the white sheet covering a brass bird cage. The pugnacious green parrot underneath let out a few short, pert whistles and started jabbering. His tiny claws danced on the wooden swing until it swayed.

Hello, hello. Nancy, Nancy. Howard, Howard.

I laughed with such utter delight . . . and complete relief.

The excited bird continued. *Lovebirds, lovebirds.*

I bet he can be a bit of a troublemaker at times.

He sure is. Polly, quit that! You must not frighten or offend Miss Palmer. She thought you were a ghost or, worse yet, me!

With innocent eyes, the parrot squawked and uttered another remark. *Sorry! Sorry!*

While I was working in my studio last month, I distinctly heard what I thought was my sister Hope calling from the house,

"Howard, telephone." So I quickly ran there only to discover that Polly was indeed the culprit.

Now that's a smart bird!

We both bade Polly good-bye as Howard slid open the dining room's large plate-glass doors. As we crossed the threshold, Polly uttered, *Good-bye, good-bye. Lovebirds!*

Would you believe he's thirty years old? Once, he escaped from his cage and flew to a limb over the bluff. I called to him, but he wouldn't come. So I climbed the tree. When I got him, he bit me. On the way down, all he said was "All right, all right."

Howard and I both found amusement in these anecdotes and at each other as we laughed and strolled along the gravel walkway by the bridge leading to a secluded tennis court.

My sisters like playing a match here every day. I do as well but only when there's time.

From there, we continued up the lawn and over a short bridge spanning the front of the great studio barn.

During the warm seasons, I work here. In the winter, I prefer the warm hearth of the main house.

Inside the great barn sat his tall easel, upon which lay a blank artist board and before that a modeling stand.

That's where you will be posing for me later.

Howard gazed around the barn's immense interior with a glow of wonderment.

It took eight carpenters an entire year to build this. No blueprints. I sketched it out in my mind. When the carpenters took the final measurements, they discovered that my calculations were spot on.

We climbed the narrow wooden steps leading to the fourth floor and peered out the large north window, as it provided the best view of his estate—a lush landscape resembling a Thomas Cole painting of the Hudson River Valley.

You see the pergola over there? Just outside your bedroom window, there's a railed walkway. We can get a better view of the river there. I'm thinking of enclosing it this fall so that it becomes one long gallery. What do you think?

That's a splendid idea.

It would be a nice spot to see the sunset in the winter.

A short time later, we returned to the main house but not before Howard became distracted by an old burnished cannon that sat by the edge of the bluff. With immense precision, he began to describe how it fired. I became lost as his voice drifted off. Over the horizon, there were small skiffs and other boats moving northward up the river . . . and I began to wonder then what it was like to live here when Howard was a boy.

And so, once the charge is punctured through this hole, a fuse is inserted and then lit.

Howard then stood up as if he had just remembered something important.

My father's job during the Civil War was to ignite the fuse of the Swamp Angel—a cannon. While it was pounding Charleston Harbor, its breach burst on the thirty-sixth round. Never was replaced. You know, Nancy, nothing in this world lasts forever.

Howard's face suddenly turned sullen, but I piped up, *So what's that all for?*

At first, he did not answer me. He shied away, as if he had some secret that he wanted to keep. *You'll see. I know you want some coffee.*

I do!

Well, you will have that and much more. Let's go get some breakfast.

Breakfast at the Barracks was an event to be remembered. Howard's parents; his sisters, Rose and Hope; and his daughter, Natalie, were seated around a long table in the dining room. His dog Sargent was lying quietly on the floor. Bill, his other dog, was conspicuously absent.

Howard, where's Bill?

He's been banished. He likes chasing skunks.

After we sat down, grace was said. Virginia brought out sizable platters of eggs and bacon, pork tenderloin, and fried mush. Enough to feed a platoon. As the conversation flowed consistently, Sargent just buried his head between his paws and whimpered. Whenever one person stopped talking, another picked up. And when it came time for Howard to speak, everyone listened intently.

Each week, I receive some mail. Just a few days ago, I got a letter from a gold miner from the Klondike who apparently read Rex Beach's novel The Ne'er Do Well. *He saw my illustrations, including the one on the front cover showing you, Noel, carrying*

Marie St. Germain in your arms from boat to shore.

Noel interjected to reveal the illusion behind Howard's magic.

Ah, yes, you did that the year before. But if truth be told, we were never posed that way. In fact, we were never in the water. Howard had us lounging on a wooden bench. It was quite cozy, I dare say.

Howard continued with what he had read in this letter. *The gold miner said in his letter, "He never could have held her like that. That Rex Man may have been a ring-tailed, stem-winder, bull-necked Swede, but he couldn't carry a skirt that way—he'd drop her sure as hell."*

Noel's face looked a bit puzzled. *Marie bit me during that interlude.*

The front cover for Rex Beach's 1911 best-selling novel, The Ne'er Do Well, depicting Howard's illustration of models Noel Talbot and Marie St. Germain

Yes, she didn't like you at all. Can't understand why.

Perhaps it was my smooth and creamy English charm, Howard. Or maybe it was the fact that I kept dropping her. She didn't quite possess the narrow-waist as you had portrayed her.

Laughter filled the room as Bena, one of Howard's colored housekeepers, overheard the conversation and added a few more words. *Mr. Christy's pit-chers fill all of da best-sellers, Miss Palmer! It's his pit-chers which make them sell so well. They's the best I'se ever seen.*

With each word spoken, I began to see Howard's world unfold. The illusion dissipated.

Noel's eyes turned to mine.

Bena is right. Howard has a new story for Cosmopolitan *magazine. It's called "The Penalty"—it's sure to be another pot-boiler. Or is this one a bodice ripper?*

Howard interjected, *It's a grand story! Noel is Wilmot Allen, and you, Nancy, will be Barbara Ferris, a beautiful twenty-two-year-old woman who's the daughter of a famous physician and has more suitors than she can count on both hands. Barbara's an artist and is in the midst of sculpting a clay bust of Satan when she happens upon a legless street beggar named Blizzard. As it turns out, Blizzard's not really a street beggar but a wicked and dangerous man. He runs a hat factory full of pretty young women. He has also lent a considerable sum to Wilmot, Barbara's friend, who is trying to woo her. Barbara is warned of Blizzard, but she pays no attention and solicits Blizzard to become her model. There are more twists and turns in the story. You see, Barbara's father is the doctor who mistakenly amputated Blizzard's legs when he was a child, changing him into a bitter man bent on vengeance and motivated by a life of crime.*

I laughed. *Ah, such drama! I can't wait!*

When Howard and I once again returned to the studio barn to begin the day's work, an oak spindle-back chair greeted us near the doorway. Draped across it was a long gingham apron. It was as if unseen hands had placed all of it there while we were having breakfast. I spoke about this mystery to Howard.

That wasn't here earlier.

I had Noel bring it down from the hayloft.

How is that possible? We left the barn and went directly to the main house where we saw Noel standing at the front door.

He works quickly.

Howard's demeanor was mysterious, but I sensed that he liked to keep certain secrets to himself.

You may keep on the navy blue skirt you are wearing, but I would prefer that you change the blouse. I have one upstairs that you will find hanging on the wardrobe rack. Please try it on, and then put on the apron.

I went upstairs to the hayloft and followed Howard's directions. With my blouse buttoned and apron tied around me, I promptly returned.

Wonderful. Please sit in the chair, lean forward, throw the apron to your right side, and place your hand on your chin. No, make that your thumb and forefinger. Roll up your sleeves, and then assume the same pose. I want it to look like you have just been working on that clay bust all day long, and you now wish to reflect upon it.

I did exactly as he instructed and held perfectly still, trying not to move one muscle . . . except for my lips, upon which were many questions.

I always imagined illustrators using a white canvas, long sable brushes, and a palette smudged with oil paint.

That's a misconception. White canvas could work, but oil paints take weeks to dry. These panels have to be ready to ship to the publisher within days of their completion. I prefer an artist board. It's lighter, less expensive, easier to ship to New York City, and, most important, a perfect match for the medium—watercolor. A lot of what I do for publication will be reproduced in black and white, so the use of color is unnecessary. A gray palette is what I use and this white paint called gouache to provide highlights, soften lines, and correct mistakes.

You make mistakes?

We all do . . . especially me.

I couldn't believe what he said. How would Howard Chandler Christy, the second most popular illustrator in America, ever make a mistake? I refrained from saying anything, and he continued.

At the end of the following week, I am going to Duncan Falls to ship out the next batch of paintings. You are welcome to accompany me.

I would like that very much.

Wonderful. Don't move. You have captured this scene for me. Please don't spoil it. He smiled and gave a wink.

Am I making a good impression?

Wait until the next painting, when Noel will join you. If you don't bite him, my impression will be far greater.

While Howard painted, I told him several stories from my youth. His eyes danced as his left hand moved from side to side. Then, he paused to dip his brush in the watercolor tin. And every so often, he would stop and stare straight at me, squinting and nodding his head. I couldn't tell if he loved me or absolutely hated me.

Howard's birthplace, a two-story log cabin located along Meigs Creek, McConnelsville, Ohio (Special Collections, Lafayette College, Easton, PA)

I'm curious, Howard. What's your first childhood memory?

The summer of 1876. My family lived in a two-story log cabin down on Meigs Creek, about twelve miles south of here. I was born there. One sunny day, when I was three, my father scooped me up in his arms and placed me under a shady tree while he plowed the fields. Down the way, a man with a handlebar mustache rode on a bay horse. As he neared the fence, he yelled out that the Indians had massacred General Custer at Little Bighorn. That was my first memory.

You were moved by what he said, weren't you?

I wanted to know more about this Custer and why Indians had killed him. What was that battle scene like? I wondered. And I could almost picture it in my mind, as a young boy would, inspiring a great love of history in me.

It seems that this one singular memory helped make you into the man you are today.

When I was boy, the excitement of warfare—anything that pitted man against man—thrilled me. These visions bred romantic thoughts of courage, duty, and honor.

But was it really romantic?

No. Eventually I learned that there was nothing romantic about conflict—nothing beautiful at all, only ugliness and tragedy. But to discover that, I had to see the horror firsthand.

In Cuba, during the Spanish-American War?

Yes. This changed me completely.

A sharp whistle pierced the air. My ears perked up. *What was that?*

Sounds like a whistle to me.

The sound occurred again.

Yes, it does. Where is it coming from?

Outside.

I shook my head with a humorous look of disapproval.

Well, that I do know. Please enlighten me a little more, Mr. Christy, because I do think the country air may be getting to me.

Well, Miss Palmer, I would say it came from the springhouse.

Go and take a look. I assure you there are no Indians in these parts—haven't been in over a hundred years.

Can't you go and see what it is, Howard? You know this area better than I do. Please?

Not now. I need time to envision the next illustration. But if there are Indians, I will certainly stand at the ready to defend you.

Another piercing whistle sounded and then, moments later, another, until I felt completely uncomfortable sitting in that spindle-back chair.

All right. I can't bear it any longer. I shall investigate it myself. With a look of distain, I rose, threw down my apron, and marched right out the door.

And report back too! I need you here no later than three o'clock to finish the job.

INSIDE THE SPRINGHOUSE, a large cement pool was dug into the ground and filled with water. By the side of the door was Howard's father, humming a Civil War tune.

I had hoped you had heard my call. Has Howard been talking to you about his boyhood days? I suspected he was.

Good afternoon, Mr. Christy. Yes, he only mentioned his first memory—a man with a handlebar mustache riding up to your farm to announce that General Custer had been killed.

Ah, yes, I saw General Custer during the last days of the war. He came from nowhere, through the trees and smoke, and slaughtered those last few rebels shooting at him.

Every last one of them?

Yes. Every last one. I suppose Natalie told you the story.

You did last night.

Oh my ... well, my memory is fading, dear. I can't recall what I did the day before, but I can still recall what happened many years ago like it was only yesterday. In any event, I want to tell you something. Just between you and me, I think you will prove to be Howard's best model yet.

To the left of the studio barn is Howard's springhouse, which contained an indoor swimming pool. On unseasonably hot days, Howard and his guests would take a refreshing dip here. (Special Collections, Lafayette College, Easton, PA)

Howard's father, Frank, with "Polly," Howard's talking parrot, circa 1912 (Courtesy of Maxine Christy Peters)

Mr. Christy looked at me as he said this and then nodded with approval. *He's had many models, but I can tell you that you will help him as much as he will help you. For that, I want to give you this.*

A glass of cream?

To be a true illustrator's model, you need some flesh on your bones, and this will help.

I didn't know what to say. I was flattered but reluctant to add more weight to my frame.

Well, Mr. Christy, these are only illustrations, not photographs.

Makes no difference at all, dear. A painting portrays only what the painter sees, and a painter needs a great model to give him inspiration. Real men want real women—women with curves. Bean poles don't sell magazines or books. Never have, never will.

He lifted the glass to me, and I took it.

All right Mr. Christy. I accept your offer, but let me ask you this. Does your son really like me? Will I become a great model?

Howard does like you. I have never seen him happier in all of my life. And as for your second question, I don't have a perfect answer. Never been able to predict the future. So I will tell you a story instead.

Please do.

When Howard was a boy, a man named Russ Bethel was running for sheriff here in Muskingum County. He was tall and thin and had long, slicked-back raven hair, coal-black eyes, and a well-trimmed mustache. He came to see me one day to ask for my vote. When he dismounted from his black steed, his coat blew open to reveal two shiny medals pinned to his vest. Howard asked me what those were, and I told him that Sergeant Bethel was awarded them for bravery. Unlike other Civil War veterans, Bethel never talked about his wartime battles, but that afternoon, my son insisted that he do. Bethel told him that he was the color bearer during the Battle of Atlanta. Carrying the flag and keeping it safe was the most important job any soldier could have because it inspires men to fight. But it was also the most dangerous job a soldier could have. Well, during that battle, several men were killed as they grasped the flag in their hands. The first color bearer was shot on a road near the front line. The next soldier held the flag until he was shot in both thighs and collapsed. A sergeant grabbed the standard and hoisted it high, but it soon fell to the earth along with him. He was dead. A rebel then lunged forward to snatch it up at the same moment the sword of a Union army captain came down on his neck, severing head from body. Bethel then picked up the flag and carried it during the rest of the battle. He was wounded himself, but he never told Howard this.

What did Sergeant Bethel do with the flag?

After hearing about how the men carrying the flag had died, Howard was so filled with excitement that his eyes were as wide as blueberry pies. Bethel told him that bullets were raining down, and men were falling all around him as the Union troops were falling back. In the distance, Bethel saw a single apple tree standing defiantly in the haze, and he started running to it for safety. He ran as hard and fast as he could. Yards behind him, his men saw the flag advancing. So they turned around and quickly followed. When he got to the tree, he looked back and saw that his men were right behind him. Bethel couldn't just stop there, so he continued on and, of course, the Union won the battle.

What was the second medal for?

Howard asked exactly the same question. Bethel said it was given to him for being the first to plant the flag at Petersburg and left it at that. Howard was deeply inspired. He had heard dozens of other stories about soldiers single-handedly killing and capturing the enemy, to the point where he could almost smell the blood and gunpowder. Yet none of those men ever received a medal. Sergeant Bethel's story was different; it moved Howard. You see, the former sergeant never mentioned that he fired a gun, brandished a sword, or ever injured anyone. It was daring fearlessness that made him a hero. Fearlessness—Howard always considered that his favorite virtue.

I think you answered my question, Mr. Christy. Thank you for the story and, of course, the beverage. Both were quite refreshing.

I'm glad you liked them, dear. Just remember . . . in life, keep going forward, choose your path wisely, and, most important, be fearless. Never give up. Greatness will surely follow.

I'll be certain to remember that. Thank you.

Oh, and one more thing. Return here each day upon the call of my whistle. I'll supply you with another glass of cream and a few more stories.

I returned to Howard, who was sitting and reading a stack of pages.

So did the Indians capture you?

I rubbed my left wrist with my other hand. *Yes, they did. I barely managed to escape.*

Good, 'cause I need you. Once we get this serial done, I have several more. And a few will involve Indians. Always good to have a model with personal experience on the subject matter. Oh, you have a little white stuff on your upper lip. Is that cream?

With the tip of my tongue, I discreetly brushed off the last traces.

◻

BY MIDAFTERNOON, HOWARD was nearly finished with his first painting of me.

Howard, how does the whole illustration process work? I recall seeing several books for which you illustrated the magazine pictures, and some of these books only had one of your illustrations. Just one!

Almost finished; one more minute.

The artist board faced me, and I could see that Howard had signed his famous signature at the bottom. He placed his watercolor tin on the table, dried his brush on a white cloth, and crossed his legs as he turned to me.

"Now I'll try to answer your questions — the *Cosmopolitan* engages me to illustrate the story," he said. "The writer probably does not know who is to illustrate the story. Then the book publication is still another matter."

Why is that?

"They—the book publisher—would have to buy the illustrations from the *Cosmopolitan*, and it would be a very expensive performance, and they could not buy one unless they purchased the entire number. So you see they get someone to make a frontispiece and publish the book at much less cost."

I suppose to the publishers, it's all about making money.

It's always about the coin. Human nature. Artists try to see beyond that. So how do you like the painting?

I simply adore it, but I don't look that beautiful.

You're mistaken. You actually are that beautiful . . . only you just don't see it. Sometimes things are not always what they seem. You might think with absolute certainty that what you see is so very beautiful, but, in actuality, it may be quite different. And what may appear to be common may actually be exquisitely beautiful.

I do feel that what I see is indeed there. Isn't it?

Sight is often clouded by feelings, emotions . . . bias. And there are some who fail to notice the small details that provide the greater truth.

Truth?

Outward appearances are merely a façade—a ploy to entice others. But eventually, if one looks closely enough, beyond the illusion, and sees the inner soul, one finds the truth, and therein lies true beauty.

Can you really see my inner soul, Howard?

Oh, I have . . . and what I see is quite remarkable.

But do I really look that beautiful?

For some reason, women always seem to think that their outer appearances matter most. They long to be faultlessly perfect in feature, and so they constantly fret about their hair, complexion, lips, eyes, figure, and so on. Vanity of vanities; all is vanity.

Every woman feels that way.

A woman's looks are not so important to the artist painting her or to the man who truly loves her.

Doesn't any man want a gorgeous woman on his arm? Doesn't any artist want a perfect female specimen sitting in front of his easel?

"Perfection of feature is not enough," he said. "Beauty must be more than skin deep."

And I replied—but in a somewhat outspoken manner, *Every man loves a beautiful face and figure. Women want this too, so they can at least dream about such beauty if they aren't so fortunate to possess it.*

There are many who are lovely to look at, but after one gets to know them, one may find that they are quite ugly in character and temperament—bitter, sad, jealous, vain, or just plain filled with contempt for others, especially for those who are happy.

I see your point.

Now, those lovely women eventually age. And no matter how beautiful they appear on the outside, with time, they eventually reflect their own inner truth. The same goes for men. It's not what is on the outside that truly matters but that which is within. That's true beauty . . . and true beauty lasts forever.

Forever?

Yes! With true beauty there's life everlasting . . . immortality. True beauty comes from the heart. What is on the outside is simply all an illusion.

Immortality . . . . Howard, I would love to be immortalized.

You have, right here. And once this is published, you will be immortalized in the Cosmopolitan. *And it shall span the ages. It's as fixed as the stars, and no person can ever change that.*

As a child, I wanted to live forever.

Well, you're not the first one. Your image certainly will, but as far as you personally . . . that's another question.

His response startled me. I hesitated for a moment and then decided to change the subject altogether.

So getting back to our earlier discussion, what do you feel is most important when it comes to the qualities of a woman?

"Beauty—but with character to back it up. For without character,

there is no true beauty of face."
And what do you feel is most important when it comes to the qualities of a man?
"That he be a reliable friend."
It's fascinating how men perceive a good bond with a chum, yet it's completely different when it comes to a bond with a woman. Isn't it?

A good friend is hard to find. And I detest insincerity. I think you'll agree that it's rather unimportant if a man is beautiful or handsome on the exterior. Inwardly? That's an entirely different matter; the same is for women—integrity, loyalty, and truthfulness. It's so important to be truthful. From my childhood, I learned about this virtue through an important if not embarrassing lesson.

I would love to hear it.

When I was a young boy, an old peddler stopped by my uncle Finley's farm with a horse-drawn cart of his wares. Uncle Fin saw two sets of suspenders, and he just knew that my brother, Bern, and I would love to have them. So he set about thinking of a plan by which we could earn them. Uncle Fin's farm had a rat problem, and he was determined that Bern and I would solve it. Forty dead rats would earn a pair. Naturally, Bern and I set to work setting up traps and catching them. A few days later, I saw Bern catching more rats than I was and became envious. At least twice a day, Bern would catch a rat, show it to Uncle Fin, and throw it over the hill. I saw exactly where he was tossing them. Soon, I was just as successful as he was. Finally, when Bern scored forty dead rats, I did too, and we approached Uncle Fin. He was pleased with my brother. But when it came to me, he questioned whether I had caught all of the rats I had brought to him. I told him, 'No, I didn't.' I had no idea how he knew. He paused and then said that Bern had caught a rat by the left hind foot, and then within minutes, so had I. After that, he said that he would give me a pair of suspenders too but not because I earned them. I asked him why.

Howard looked down briefly and then looked at me squarely in the eye in such a way that I sensed he felt uncomfortable yet proud.

He said that I had told "the truth."

That's what you are after, Howard, isn't it?

The truth is everything, especially when it comes to painting. You see, there is no trickery, no artifice when one paints what one truly sees. The truth is always there, waiting to be discovered. One only has to look closely.

I so wish to hear the truth . . . and see it too. Tell me more about your youth. I want to feel it wash over me, like I was there . . . with you.

Ever so briefly his eyelids shut, and then when they reopened, he began to tell me what I longed to hear.

"I can close my eyes and hear it," he said, "and then I can see that old river too. There is nothing that I've ever seen that I can't recall as if it was yesterday. That's the way my memory works—in pictures, always in pictures."

Sitting back in his chair, he looked up at the barn's beamed ceiling as if he were thinking about some great painting he was about to begin, prompting him to recount those glorious days of long ago.

[Howard's Voice]

I HAD AN IDEAL CHILDHOOD, growing up on this farm, overlooking this majestic river. I felt so absolutely invincible then, as if I could do just about anything . . . and I pretty much did.

I rose at the crack of dawn, brought the horses in from the field and got them outfitted for plowing. I milked the cows and fed the chickens. All this occurred before breakfast. Yet somehow, I always found time to have a little fun along the way. Those times will never be forgotten.

My brother, Bern, and I liked to fish on the river, and he knew when the fish would bite—early morning and twilight. On many of those mornings, it would just be us—a couple of young, tanned whippersnappers, one slightly taller than the other, wearing knee-high trousers, straw hats, checkered shirts, and no shoes—walking along with bamboo poles and my brother's dog, Turk. Bern was always a couple steps ahead of me. I lingered behind only because I was busy imagining.

On many mornings, a veil of ghostly fog would shroud the river valley. I imagined a smoky battlefield where the scattered trees were soldiers, and the distant sound of a hunter's gun was the beginning of a deadly encounter.

Smiley, stop your dawdlin'. We are going to be late, and the fish'll be all gone.

Back then, everyone called me Smiley, especially the steamboat captains, on account of I smiled a lot.

Hey, Bern?

What?

Hey, Bern?

What? What do you want, Smiley?

Did you bring the angleworms?

Yeah, I did. Got 'em right here.

He held up a tin can filled with the slimy creatures as he walked ahead of me with his dog.

Just want to make sure. When you are going into battle, you've got to be prepared. An unprepared soldier gets wounded or killed. Then, he's no good to anyone.

You've been reading too many stories, Smiley. There are no Rebels here. Never have been. Stop your talk!

I remained quiet, but it wasn't too long before Bern wanted to complain about something else I was doing.

Quit it! Quit swinging your shoes at me, Smiley!

I'm not doin' nothin', Bern. Just playin' with Turk. He's going to help me scout for Rebels. There's a bloody skirmish 'bout to occur. We have to be at the ready!

Aw, you're just daydreamin' again. That's all you do, Smiley. No use in that.

Howard draws upon his own childhood with his older brother, Bern, to portray two young brothers in James Whitcomb Riley's 1904 best-selling book, Out to Old Aunt Mary's.

Through the fields we plucked our way, climbed over the old wooden fence, waded in the Salt Creek, and hurdled over bushes and briars. Somewhere near the edge of the river, the two of us would argue, as brothers often do, and get into a rough-and-tumble that would last only a minute or two until we would come to our senses, dust ourselves off, and continue on our way.

What about here, Bern? It's shady, and the fish'll be bitin' just fine.

Naw, I want to get closer to the lock. We can find a lot more fish there until the steamboat comes.

The river had a series of locks and dams at various points. As the riverboats made their way from Zanesville to Pittsburgh and back again, the locks would be used to raise or lower them at places where the land was not level.

Bern wanted to fish near Lock No. 9, a short distance north of home. Sitting by the ledge, we baited the hooks and cast our lines as Turk gleefully galloped up and down the riverbank.

I could hear Bern softly repeat some poem he had memorized.

"Backward, turn backward, O Time, in thy flight; Make me a child again, just for to-night," he said. "Mother, come back from the echoless shore; Take me again to your heart as of yore; kiss from my forehead the furrows of care, smooth the few silver threads out of my hair."

Is that something you learned in school, Bern?

Naw, just practicing my elocution. It's called "Rock Me to Sleep."

Sounds real pretty. One of my favorites is Longfellow's "Evangeline." I often dream about the scenes in it. One day, I want to bring them to life. Maybe I will.

In his youth, Howard's relationship with his older brother, Bern, was close and brotherly, yet marked with moments of contention and envy. These scenes from Out to Old Aunt Mary's *reflect those early days of wonderment and languor when Howard and Bern delighted in each other's company while surrounded by the natural beauty of the Muskingum River Valley.*

Keep on dreamin', Smiley. You've got a long road to travel.
Well, I have a favorite verse too.
What's that?
"'Tis a lesson you should heed; If at first you don't succeed,
Try, try again; Then your courage should appear, For, if you will
persevere, You will conquer, never fear, Try, try again."
Who wrote that?
It's from my McGuffey Reader.
Bern shook his head in complete disgust. *Awww, that's no
poetry. That's just a grade-school primer.*
*Well, I heard that McGuffey has sold almost as many books as
the Bible. It should be poetry!*
The early morning mist lifted as the minutes passed, and the
sun rose higher. About the time that our wicker basket was half
filled with catfish, the faint whisper of a whistle would break the
air. Instantly, I recognized this hypnotic sound.
*Bern, the early steamboat's a-comin', and she's gonna lock
through. I've got to go!*
*All right, but you had better be home soon. Mama will fry these
up. You don't want to miss that. Go!*
And I did. I dropped my fishing pole right where I stood and
sprinted back to our family farm, where Turk and I climbed to
the highest spot on the bluff.
Excitement swelled within me as I wondered which riverboat I would see. Would it be the *Carrie Brooks*, *Lizzie Cassel*,
Bessie Siler, or *Valley Gem*? Or maybe the *Lorena* that had the
most beautiful calliope whistles of any of the riverboats. Who
would be the captain and the pilot? To this day, I can still see
the heavyset Captain Davis proudly standing over the hurricane
deck, and Captain Martin telling jokes to the elegantly dressed
ladies with parasols, and Captain Beckwith calling out orders to
the deckhands below. I wanted to see it all play out like actors
performing upon a stage. But this was much better. There was no
magic or illusion on that river. Everything was real.
One short, shrill whistle, followed by a louder, deeper one,
would rise to the heavens. Together, the whistles blended into a
single perfect harmonious chord, only to abruptly cease, leaving

a lingering echo that would resound back and forth among the hills. An instant later, another blast would pierce the air, the same as the first, alerting the awaiting lock tender.

Along the still-foggy horizon, I could barely see her, yet I could hear the brief whistles, the lively music, and the boisterous laughter. And as she drew closer, I could see a band playing on her main deck and crowds gathering at her rails. Eventually, she would arrive and ease in the lock as the lockmaster cranked a long iron arm until the gates closed.

The musicians with their silver horns would play a lively tune as the passengers enjoyed themselves. Minutes later, the gates would open, and she would majestically glide out into the channel with a surge so powerful that all of the other boats and skiffs nearby would bob up and down and smack the river's edge. Yet that magnificent steamer remained untouched—invincible.

On the side deck, a cabin boy, dressed in white, might near the rails to shake a tablecloth over the side. Oh, how I envied him. He was going someplace, while I was only working on a farm. At that time, there was no place I would rather have been than on that riverboat with those society people.

Just as the mighty ship neared the crest of the bluff, the captain and pilot would wave. In return, I would send back a hearty greeting. But as my arm lowered, my broad grin would quickly fall. I longed to be there with them, traveling far away to big places.

Later, when the noonday steamer headed north, I was back at the same spot, eagerly awaiting the encouraging waves of captain and pilot. They always did that, you know. They never forgot me. Turk and I would wait there patiently as that Pittsburgh riverboat wound her way up the river, passed the bend, and simply disappeared. The echo of her distant whistles became a lingering reminder that she would be back, and so would I.

Nighttime was no different. When everyone was fast asleep, out the window I went, dashing across the yard to that special place at the bluff's edge, where Turk would find me. At first, I could see nothing and only heard the sound of the distant bell and echoing whistles drawing near. But soon, out of the darkness, a big northbound steamer from Pittsburgh would suddenly appear, like a far-off star, gleaming with light and energy.

Now, two steamers were in sight, one trailing the other. The ships' captains engaged in a cat-and-mouse game of racing one another for the lock. Onboard, the firemen would throw more coal in the boilers. Smoke would pour out of the funnels, and a round of whistles would shatter the peaceful night air. The riverboats would move faster into the inner channel, crossing their own swell, as each vied to be the first to arrive.

They're coming, Turk. Two of them!

Fire would leap from the steamer's tall stacks as they went roaring and hissing by. Inside each of the brightly lit wheelhouses, I could see the captains and pilots look up and wave at me, while Turk let out an accepting bark. He and I waited patiently, until the last chime whistles were barely audible, and only a faint haze ascended in the moonlight, like an Indian campfire from long ago.

"Do you see that smoke away down the river?" I said to Turk. "Well, I'm going farther away than that someday, and I'm going to learn to paint and draw. I'm going to learn how to become an artist, how to paint big pictures of big things like that! Never anything little, do you understand?"

That dog just sat there wagging his tail. He understood.

[Nancy's Voice]

HOWARD ROSE FROM HIS CHAIR and walked toward the open barn doors and over the short bridge, where Sargent and Bill were patiently waiting.

It's almost four o'clock. He said this as he scanned the horizon, much like a weary sea captain looking for his lover amid the windswept breakers. It was as if Howard had some unfinished business.

Is something the matter?

Not at all.

Howard, you did travel much farther than those riverboats ever did. And you are painting big pictures of big things.

Not exactly. . . . I'm more than well paid for my work. I can't complain.

But you will . . . you will paint big pictures of big things someday.

They forgive everything but greatness.

Howard, you are great. And I just know you will achieve your dream. Never give up. That was the advice your father gave me today.

Life is much like a book. Each has a beginning and an end. As for my life—my book—I am just halfway finished, I feel. The characters have been introduced; the themes have been established; the story is just now taking root. And now, with you, I begin a new chapter, a good chapter. So yes, someday I will paint big pictures of big things.

Indeed, you will.

We will, Nancy. We will do all those things together.

But you are the artist. I can only cook, sew, and do needlepoint.

There you are wrong. You are my muse and model, something every artist needs.

All right. We'll do all those things, then, together. Now, I want to hear more about your story. Did you ever travel aboard one of those steamboats as a boy?

Howard stepped away from the door and returned to his chair. He began to talk of those early years once more.

[Howard's Voice]

I COULD NEVER BE CONTENT just sitting on top of that bluff, watching those riverboats pass by. I had to be there, with them.

First, I would swim alongside. At least I tried, but when I learned I could not win the race with those mighty giants, I would simply fall behind in their frothy wake and admit defeat, believing that the next time would be different.

Upon occasion, I stole more than a few rides, which was easy. Just below the cliff to my home was a landing, where the riverboats often stopped and where I hopped on. From the gangplank, I would run straight up the stairs to the hurricane deck, where I could always find the captain with one foot on the bow rail, looking down at the point where passengers, freight, and livestock came aboard like a modern-day Noah's ark.

Well, hello, Smiley!

I put one foot up on the rail and leaned forward, just as he did.

Hello, Captain! Where are we going today?

Heading to Duncan Falls and then Zanesville.

Ah, sounds like a fine plan.

We also have some guests I would like you to meet—men from back East. They want to build a railroad along the side of the river.

A railroad! Now that'd be something!

Indeed, it would. I just might need to change professions.

Nah. No train could ever beat this steamer. Never.

Smiley, a train moves faster and can carry more cargo and passengers than this ship ever could. Times are changin'. Nothin' is forever.

Sensing a bit of trouble on the gangplank, the captain might shout out some orders to the deckhands below.

Careful with those crates, boys! I don't want the owners comin' after us. Dawson and Peters, once those hogheads are rolled in, be ready to pull in the lines.

Minutes later, the captain would reach for the rope dangling from a large bell that hung directly between the twin smokestacks. Tugging at it, the bell would loudly ring. We were off.

Steady as she goes, Captain!

Good day, Smiley.

I'll see you again real soon, Captain.

Next stop for me was one deck up and farther back: the wheelhouse. A shiny teak door with a huge pane of glass would swing open. Eagerly, I would make my way inside, only to find standing there a chubby pilot with a face like Santa Claus. He was keeping vigil before an enormous varnished steering wheel that gleamed in the sunlight as it rocked. To keep it steady, the pilot rested his booted foot on a single spoke.

Well, well, if it isn't the Barefoot Boy from the Blue Muskingum. How are you, Smiley?

Doin' fine, sir. Grand day, and you?

Can't complain. Looks like we have some company today. They come from the East.

Toward the back of the pilothouse, a group of distinguished gentlemen in silk top hats, high collars, and long, double-breasted frock coats were busy discussing business. When the captain arrived, he introduced me. I shook their hands, and each of them made me feel honored.

I always tried to make conversation whenever I was in the pilothouse, especially when guests were there.

"Well," I said daringly to the captain, "who are you going to vote for?"

"Why?" responded the captain.

"I want to see Russ Bethel elected," I replied, believing that Bethel, a Republican, was the best candidate for the job of sheriff.

"Well," the captain responded, "we are all Democrats." He turned to the pilot and said, "What do you think about it?"

The pilot just nodded in agreement. Somehow, he knew that I had done a little investigation of my own.

"Well, if he's good enough to have you electioneering for him," said the captain, "we'll vote for him for sheriff."

That was my first successful sales effort. Russ Bethel was elected county sheriff that year.

Following that initial conversation in the wheelhouse, it wouldn't be too long before my assistance was requested. Upon the pilot's call, I put all of my weight on a shiny brass pedal. As it gave way, I bounced up and down like a leap frog. Overhead, the whoosh of steam filled the tall brass whistles and the pilothouse rattled and shook like an earthquake was occurring. Just two long whistle blasts, and my job was complete.

Over the front of the wheelhouse was a long slanting roof that, on the underside, had the image of a steamboat with smoke trailing from her tall stacks. When the captain began talking again, my ears perked up.

Gentlemen, I see you are admiring that steamboat picture. This young fellow here drew it. Smiley's going to be a great artist when he grows up.

The distinguished men simply nodded and smiled.

The following day, my father called me into the house and handed to me a copy of the Zanesville newspaper.

"Never, as long as you live, go near the river again or get on one of those boats," he said, "unless you wear your shoes and stockings and are dressed properly! Look at the article in this paper! Do you want to disgrace your family?"

Nervously, I read the story, which mentioned the gentlemen I had met the previous day. After mentioning their big plans for transforming the river valley, they were quite taken by a drawing of a steamboat which, to their surprise, was done by a barefoot urchin in a straw hat who lived on a farm at the boat landing. This was my first brush with fame, all of which proved to be more of a lesson in the end.

I never forgot those riverboats. Every now and then, in my mind, I still ride them and am transported back to that joyous time in my life. The clear water still races along the steamer's sides. In the distance, state boats ease barges through the current. And by the river's edge, there are overhanging trees with full branches just barely touching the lapping water. Workers on the bank saw timber to buttress the canal. And I can still see cut logs stacked on mill boats and can smell the sawdust floating downstream. On the deck of that riverboat, the band still plays on while the chugging engine and beating paddlewheel add rhythm. My spirit is lifted . . . . Such glorious memories never to be forgotten. Yes, those times are never to be forgotten.

[Nancy's Voice]

HOWARD UNCROSSED HIS LEGS and looked down. The room grew silent.

I sensed he was thinking about his once-bare feet and raggedy boyhood clothes. But on that day, he wore a starched white shirt and khaki riding pants. His feet were clad in new, dark brown knee-high field boots.

With a slight smile, he looked up at me. *Now, if you will excuse me. There's something I must do.*

He left the studio barn and traversed the immense lawn with hastening speed. I followed and saw what Howard had magically sensed just moments before. Down the river, a white, three-story paddlewheel riverboat was furiously racing toward the Barracks. I have no idea how he ever knew it was coming; he just did.

As it moved closer toward the narrows, I could see smoke billowing from two tall stacks and a red paddlewheel glistening in the sun as it whipped the water into a creamy foam.

Quickly, Howard continued across the lawn—his stride matching the rise and fall of the beating paddlewheel blades—until he arrived in front of the flagpole bearing a gigantic American flag. Curiously, he lowered the flag to half mast and then walked over to the large cannon sitting on the bluff. Within a few minutes, the cannon produced a ferocious boom that resounded back and forth from the surrounding cliffs and hills.

Howard turned to me and began to gesture with his hands, as if to tell me something. But at that precise moment, a long, distinct whistle answered back from the boat pushing forward downriver, and the crewman dipped the boat's flag in salute. As the throaty sound echoed throughout the river valley, the smile on Howard's face grew wider. The steamboat captains never forgot ol' Smiley—the Barefoot Boy from the Blue Muskingum—and he never forgot them.

And so it was, on that very afternoon, that I began to learn of Howard's extraordinary life and his curious customs. Days later, he would tell me more of his early years, but wherever he was and whatever he was doing, he would always stop to acknowledge with great fanfare the approaching steamboats on that beautiful blue Muskingum River.

The Valley Gem, *one of many steamboats that Howard saw plying the Muskingum River, passes by the high-crested bluff of Howard's home as it heads toward Pittsburgh in this circa 1913 photo. (Special Collections, Lafayette College, Easton, PA)*

Nancy as Saxon, in Jack London's "Valley of the Moon," a serial that appeared in Cosmopolitan *magazine from April 1913 to December 1913. This illustration appeared in the October 1913 edition.*

CHAPTER SIX
A Glimpse of Heaven

*O*N THE STUDIO BARN, Howard stood over a large wooden crate. Natalie watched her father with great interest as he carefully tapped the nails into the smooth planks.

Summer had come early in Ohio. The uncommon morning heat had made everyone a bit uncomfortable, including the dogs. Even in the shade, Sargent and Bill panted restlessly. But after a while, they fell into a deep, quiet slumber on the sun-speckled floor as their master busily worked.

I just need one more nail.

In the morning light, Howard appeared cool in his white duck trousers, cream buckskin shoes, and snowy white shirt, sleeves rolled up to the shoulders and collar points upturned to his chin. When he finished the crate, he turned to me.

It's done. Now, we're ready for the paintings.

One by one, I handed to him the artist's boards, each bearing my image as Barbara Ferris, the heroine of the story, and he gingerly placed them in the wooden box. First, there was one of a devastated Barbara Ferris in an exquisite silken dress and almost in tears, kneeling on the floor before a chair; then, one of a discouraged Barbara, finding comfort in a white wicker chair; next, a painting of Wilmot and Barbara, viewing the finished sculpture of Satan; and one of Barbara standing in an elaborate embroidered dress, where she appeared "wonderfully young and beautiful." When Howard had finished this piece, he confirmed to me that I was just like this . . . and this is how the painting was captioned for publication.

In each of these, Howard had portrayed me in the latest fashions from New York and Paris. Ever since I was a young schoolgirl, I had known that there was something intrinsically alluring about a glamorous, well-dressed woman, as she alone can compel members of both sexes to convey admiration, if not envy. Howard explained to me that chic clothes capture female readers, while a beautiful face and curvaceous figure always attracts the males. Similar rules applied to illustrating men, except that handsome, well-cut clothes always seemed to interest men, while a lean, muscular physique and confident, square jaw invariably caused women to swoon. In the realm of illustrating beauty, these ideals became the pole stars for a budding illustrator's eventual success.

As the completed artist boards were placed in the crate—two months' worth of illustrations for *Cosmopolitan*—they were separated only by large squares of muslin cloth. Howard lingered over them and pulled out one painting he wanted to save.

This is the very first painting that I did of you, Nancy—the one where you are sitting pensively with an apron cascading down your lap. I think I will keep it for later.

Why?

He hesitated at first, but then gave me a candid answer. *I rather like it.*

Do you really?

Of course, and it's not due to be published until January of next year. So it can wait. These others will be published in the August and September editions of the Cosmopolitan. *They must be shipped now.*

I can't even begin to tell you how absolutely thrilled I am, Howard. I simply cannot wait to see the final issues.

By late June, the paintings for the August edition will go from editor to publisher, artist proofs will be made and reviewed, and from publisher they will go straight to the printing press. By mid-July, the final edition will be on the newsstands and the Cosmopolitan's *stable of subscribers will receive them in the mail. And by Christmas, you'll be a star.*

A star? Like a famous actress or singer?

Even better, because you don't have to perform for anyone . . . except me. Everyone will want to know who this new beautiful young creature is. Who is she? That's what they'll say. And I will tell them that she is my new model, Miss Nancy Palmer of Poughkeepsie.

My, oh my! I'm so flattered . . . and so grateful. How can I ever thank you?

Better not tempt me, as most assuredly, I just might think of a way.

Howard winked as he placed the wooden cover on top of the box and pounded in the final nail. When he was done, he took a short paintbrush, dipped it in his watercolor tin, and addressed the outside of the box in jet black. The return address was simply "Howard Chandler Christy, The Barracks, Duncan Falls, Ohio."

It's done. Now, I'm going to go into Duncan Falls to deliver this crate to the post office. From there, it will go to the editors in New York. Would you care to join me?

There's nothing that I would prefer more.

He rolled down his sleeves and adjusted his collar.

Well, then, we'll leave in ten minutes.

And we did. At precisely ten minutes after ten o'clock, the two of us rolled down the long driveway in a black horse-drawn buggy, carrying in the back that single wooden crate, like it was a coffin. We were simply the undertakers charged with the grim duty of taking the glorious contents to their final resting place.

I hope you don't mind this buggy.

Not at all.

I think it's a bit too hot to travel in the motor car. Don't you?

Not really. I rather enjoyed it the first time you took me.

At times, the radiator can be a bit temperamental, especially in hot weather, and the motor car breaks down. The road to Duncan Falls is not one that one wants to be stuck on. It's narrow in places. During bad weather, it's quite impassable. Usually, the riverboat is a better alternative. Today, the road is as dry as a bone, so a buggy ride will do quite nicely.

And it's quieter than a motor car, giving us a chance to chat.

As we descended the end of the drive and turned right onto the dirt road, Howard was suddenly reminded of something from his early years.

For some reason, sitting here with you and turning onto this road made me think of when I was four years old. I begged my father to take me to the studio of Charlie Craig.

[Howard's Voice]

IT WAS THE WINTER OF 1877. I had heard of Charlie Craig, an especially gifted artist who painted landscapes and portraits of Indians. I pleaded with my father to take me to see him.

Eventually, my father relented. One cold winter morning, we traveled upriver on the riverboat *Carrie Brooks* to Zanesville, where my father hired a driver and carriage. When we reached the Clarendon Hotel, the big Negro driver climbed down and offered his hand. I had never seen a Negro man before and didn't know what to do or expect. So nervously, I looked up and shook his hand. As I pulled my hand away, I glanced at my palm, thinking that a black print would be there. But there wasn't, and I realized that this man was just like me, only bigger. The driver saw the look on my face and threw his head back, laughing. His white teeth sparkled in the sun. My father swiftly took me by the hand, and we walked away.

Craig's studio was atop a narrow flight of stairs. Inside is what heaven would be like, I thought. The place was bright and airy, with sketches tacked to the walls in various stages of completion and finished paintings propped up in far corners. A glowing fire kept the room toasty warm. Seated in a chair, Mr. Craig welcomed us as if we were old friends. He had a pinkish face, red mustache, and a balding head encircled with sprigs of ginger hair. His smile was jovial and lacked any worries, as if to say that the work before him was more a hobby than a profession. But I knew that this was not the case. He was a serious and well-known painter, which is what I longed to be, even then, at the age of four.

He was in the midst of painting a landscape and held a brush in one hand and in the other, a big palette glistening with dabs of paint that were wet and juicy, just like spoonfuls of jelly—raspberry, blackberry, blueberry, mint, marmalade, peach, and lemon—heaped on an oversized platter.

With one brush stroke, he slathered on the canvas a sizable helping of paint. At first, I thought he had ruined the work, but then I saw how skillfully he worked it in to create a tree hanging over water with a distant shore and sky. Throughout that morning and early afternoon, his magic continued.

When we left, he instructed my father not to give me any colors until I learned how to draw. My dreams were crushed. Yet I didn't give up. As we left, I insisted that Father purchase a set of watercolors for me. Father listened, and he purchased my first set of watercolors and a little brush. This made me the happiest boy on earth. I never forgot that day in Charlie Craig's studio, as that was my first glimpse of heaven.[5]

In the weeks that followed, all of my spare time was spent drawing and painting. First, I painted some ears of corn tied together with a cord. After that, I wanted a live model, so I caught a cottontail rabbit in a trap and placed him in the family parlor. I drew several pictures but was never quite able to capture the wiggling of his little pink nose. Once I finished, I set him loose on the lawn. He wanted to stay, but I stamped my foot, and off he jumped, looking back at me. In return, I said a silent prayer, asking that he would remain safe and that hunters would not shoot at him, or, if they did, they would miss.

During that winter and the following spring, I ignored everything other than painting. When I ran out of paper, and I quite often did, I scoured every drawer and cabinet in the house to find more. Soon, my sketches and paintings of farm animals, birds, dogs, and steamboats began to line the walls of our home. My parents indulged my passion and allowed me to have a room in the attic to use as a studio. There, I secluded myself each day.

As the drawings and paintings progressed, I became more adventuresome and selected larger and more varied models. When my parents were out visiting one day, I led a full-grown ram named Cassey into the house, up the stairs, and into my attic studio. Cassey patiently posed for me as I lay on the floor and drew him. Yet there was just not enough time to finish the job. My parents returned home earlier than I had anticipated. As they approached the house, I heard them and quickly pushed Cassey out the door and down the stairs. He didn't move very far, so I pulled him by the horns. He got halfway down and then refused to move any further. And this is where my parents found me, desperately tugging at that stubborn animal.

Master Howard Clifton Christy! What in heaven's name are you doing with that beast in this house? Have you taken leave of your senses?

Why, Father, I am only escorting my lovely model down the stairs and to the door . . . just like any well-bred artist would do.

[Nancy's Voice]

HOWARD'S STORY MADE ME GIGGLE. Yet I found almost the same if not more humor in his real middle name: Clifton.

Your middle name is Clifton and not Chandler? You were born as Howard Clifton Christy? Oh my, now that's quite funny!

He smiled and then placed his finger to lips like an overgrown boy.

Shhh! You'll spoil the illusion.

When did you change your middle name?

That's a story for another time. Not now. Later.

Well, that one I would like to hear. Please tell me someday.

I will, Miss Palmer. And perhaps you might tell me why Anna is actually your real first name and not Nancy. And is it really Miss Palmer? Or am I addressing Miss Coon?

Ah, touché, Mr. Christy. Well done.

Well? What say you?

Ah, that's a story for another time too. Later.

He nodded and dropped the subject.

Howard so intrigued me. How did he know my real first name or last name? Who is this man? I wondered. He has so many secrets, and I long to learn them all.

I began my inquiry, starting with his brother, Bernard.

What did your brother think about your newfound passion of painting?

[Howard's Voice]

BERN WASN'T FOND OF IT AT ALL. My brother was neither artistic nor romantic. He preferred to go fishing. I, on the other hand, lived in an imaginary world of my own, where everything and everyone was beautiful.

One day, when the boys and girls from school were admiring a drawing I had made of a man in checkered trousers, Bern took out a bow and arrow and shot it clean through the middle. Perhaps he resented my work, or maybe he just wanted to pester me, just as I had done to him. In any event, I was furious, and a fight ensued. Boys and girls stood around us in a circle, cheering and then yelling, "Birthday fight! Birthday fight!"

Like all of the other rough-and-tumbles we had, Bern and I eventually ended up right in front of our mother, embarrassed, with dirty faces and tattered clothes.

My only interest was in drawing and painting. I had no interest in school.

In my desk, I kept a drawing tablet. When the time was right and the teacher was not looking, the tablet would slowly emerge from the dark recess of my desk, and I would hastily draw anything that caught my interest. I sat near a window that overlooked the river. One day, I spotted a Jersey cow standing in the shallow water on the far side of the river. She was under a clump of willows, just swatting her tail at the flies. Now that would be a nice picture, I thought, and out came my tablet.

Master Christy! What, may I ask, are you doing?

Nothin'. Just drawin', Mr. Baughman.

I see. Well, when you are in school, you must pay attention to me, your teacher, and not to the animals outside.

I understand, sir.

Mr. Baughman did not, at first, seem to share in my interest, but the rest of the class did.

I became popular with all of the children, including the older boys, who, after obtaining permission to sit next me, would silently slip books under their desk to me. While the teacher was speaking, all eyes would be on me, drawing steamboats on the inside covers of geography and history textbooks. At one point, the teacher discovered the system I had devised, and his stern eyes were on me too.

Master Christy! Did I not tell you before? Were you not listening?

Sorry, Mr. Baughman.

The teacher abruptly snatched the book from my hands and was about to pound me on the head when its owner jumped up and quickly grabbed the teacher's arm.

The boy screamed, *Don't hit him! I won't let you do it!*

He held on tight until my teacher's grasp loosened. The book tumbled to the floor with a loud smack. In those days, some boys were not frightened by anyone. They would sometimes insult if not physically assault their teachers with impunity.

Mr. Baughman never hit me. Instead, he verbally affirmed in my mind what I had suspected for years.

Master Christy, I think you have a gift.

Why, thank you, Mr. Baughman. I think so too.

But please entertain that gift elsewhere. Now, listen to the lesson.

Days afterward, my teacher spoke to Father and told him what he had seen.

Your son has a gift, Mr. Christy. He draws pictures so readily and so lifelike. I would suggest that you encourage him in that regard and hone his artistic skills.

If I had the means, Mr. Baughman, I would surely do so. At this point in time, I do not. So I will leave it up to the good Lord to decide what's best.

Being strong Presbyterians, my parents possessed an unwavering faith that everything works for the greater good. They prayed for the best and, eventually, things seemed to go precisely that way.

At ten years of age, I began to make a name for myself. The town butcher was in need of a sign for his shop, and I painted one. Rising four feet, my painting of a bull could not be missed by those who passed by his shop in Duncan Falls.

"It was a beautiful job," I later declared.

Soon, everyone wanted to know who this artist was. Yet few could guess his tender age.

◻

ONE DAY, DURING A HISTORY LECTURE AT SCHOOL, Mr. Baughman mentioned President James Garfield.

The president had been assassinated only a few years earlier. Mr. Baughman said that he had seen the log cabin schoolhouse where the president once taught for a term in the spring of 1851, before he became a congressman. In describing it, he said that it looked remarkably like a nearby building, with which everyone in the class was familiar. So I sketched this building, and when Mr. Baughman was satisfied, a trip was arranged for me to see the actual one-room schoolhouse where Garfield taught, a few miles south of Duncan Falls, along a stream called Back Run. Once there, I sketched the Back Run schoolhouse, and Mr. Baughman sent the final drawing to Senator John Sherman—the same senator who would later enact the famous antitrust act that bears his name. The local newspapers reported my artistic efforts and soon the *Toledo Blade* offered me a job as staff artist. For my sketch, I received no money, but the prospect of being hired by a big Ohio newspaper thrilled me.

Barely thirteen years of age, I didn't know what to do. I didn't want that newspaper to know how young I was. Yet more than anything, I wanted to draw. So I sought advice from a trusted friend who was much older than I.

Well, Howard, you could always start wearing some shoes and fib about your age. I suspect that the shoes won't be too difficult for you but lying will. Why don't you just tell them the truth and not accept.

Thank you. That's precisely what I will do.

The following day, I sent a letter to the editor of the newspaper, declining the offer, and I never heard back.

[Nancy's Voice]

You really wanted that job, didn't you?

I did, but I knew in my heart that I could not have it. Sometimes, we have to sacrifice things we want for that which is right. Three years later, my life changed forever when I went to New York to study art.

I would love to hear about that.

You will. We're almost near Duncan Falls. I want to show you a few things when we get there.

The road to town was shorter than I thought. When we began, there were tall sandstone cliffs to the east, but as we neared the town, the cliffs trailed off, and only small houses on sizable green patches of land, level with the road, remained. The one constant along the way was that majestic river, gently flowing to the west. By the time we reached the center of town, it was nearly noon.

Well, here it is, the Duncan Falls post office, such as it is.

Howard took the crate and marched on in, placing it on the counter. Standing by, I could not help but ask more questions as we waited for the postman.

What happens with the original paintings once they are published in magazines?

They are returned to me. I make arrangements to have a few of them framed at E. P. Church & Company in Zanesville. Some are sent to New York, some go to Indianapolis, and others are given to people right here in this region. The rest I stack up in the studio barn.

Why?

Because they're worthless.

How can works of such beauty have no value?

Well, I am glad you think so.

In my opinion, they are priceless, Howard.

These paintings are considered commercial art, rather than fine art and, therefore, not worth much of anything, once the image on them is published.

What's the difference between the two?

Commercial art is art for hire. A publication commissions the artist to make a painting or drawing that will later be published in a magazine, book, or newspaper. Fine art is art for art's sake.

I still don't see the difference—why one is worth practically nothing and the other is worth so much. Wasn't Michelangelo commissioned to paint the Sistine Chapel?

He was.

And I have seen many copies of his work. So then, he was a commercial artist! Yet his work is priceless, isn't it?

It is.

Then, of course, there is Winslow Homer and Frederick Remington. Aren't they commercial artists?

Yes, they were for many years, but then they became fine artists.

I understand their work is considered valuable too.

Yes, especially now that neither is living.

Well, I am thoroughly confused, Howard. I just don't see the difference between the two categories of art. It shouldn't matter whether one form is made for publication and another isn't. What should matter is whether the art is beautiful or not.

Yes, Nancy. I agree.

The postman arrived, took the crate, and placed it behind the counter. He then handed to Howard a bundle tied together with twine.

What is that?

Magazines. I subscribe to about thirty of them, domestic and international.

He untied the bundle and fanned out the stack. There was a *National Geographic*, one from *International Studio*, periodicals from England, and some from France and Germany, the names of which I cannot pronounce.

How do you ever read so many magazines?

Quickly, usually at night, when everyone is asleep. I am especially partial to the pictures. He winked and then reassembled the periodicals into a single stack, which he secured with the twine. *Come on—let's go get some fresh fruit.*

We traveled to the local fruit market, where bins of ripe peaches, plums, apricots, pears, and bananas awaited Howard's choosing. With an order in hand, the grocer filled up several large wooden crates and placed them in the back of the buggy.

We'll take two watermelons. Oh, and please add a crate of oranges as well. Thank you.

Yes, Mr. Christy.

From a basket of strawberries, Howard took a single ripe specimen, and, with his eyes closing in on mine, he gently placed the fruit between my lips. As I bit into its soft flesh, I sensed a degree of sensuality—a heightened flirtatiousness—that I had not experienced from him before. It was as if he was testing me and enticing me, both at the same time.

Delicious, eh?

Yes, quite sweet.

I so adore them. They will even be better when July rolls around. I can't imagine anything more enjoyable than a bowl full of strawberries.

I can!

What?

Cherries.

Well, there will be plenty of those as well. And you haven't had cherries until you have tasted Ohio cherries, but you will just have to wait until next month.

I suppose.

And then there are blueberries too, but those come later, and then apples in the early fall. So you will have to stay for those as well.

I certainly will. I'll stay for as long as you want me to, Howard.

I hope so. I have another place that I would like to show you.

We traveled to a mercantile shop along Main Street, which, from the outside, also appeared to possess a variety of curiosities and amusements, along with the more traditional dry goods of a small-town store.

It's in here, Nancy.

He pointed to the door, and within moments we were inside, surrounded by canned goods, bolts of cloth, and porcelain dishes. To the side wall was a wooden bird cage filled with yellow canaries, chirping and flapping their wings.

I'll take the whole bird cage.

The proprietor looked at him as if he had lost his mind.

The whole cage, Mr. Christy? You mean the cage itself or all the birds in the cage?

The whole, entire cage with all of the birds—every last one of them.

He bargained with the proprietor, placed a few coins on the counter, and then we left. In the back of the buggy, the bird cage joined the crates of fruit, and the canaries, now blissfully happy, continued to chirp away.

So, what are you going to do with all those birds?

We'll take them home. Set them free. They will keep us company for a while in the studio, and then one day, something will startle them, and they will fly away.

What will become of them?

Like us, they will live out the rest of their lives.

Howard snapped the whip, the black horse began to trot, and the buggy moved forward. As we left the edge of town, we came to a crossroads, and Howard suddenly became excited.

Did you see that?

See what?

The young girl in a white dress. Did you see her? She just crossed the street.

No. I was admiring the river.

I must find out who she is.

We traveled farther down until we ventured upon a young boy walking by the side of the road. As it turned out, it was one of Howard's models, Raymond Crumbaker.[6]

Raymond?

Good afternoon, Mr. Christy.

I just saw a young girl crossing Main Street. She had the love-liest long brown hair tied with a bow and was wearing a white dress, white stockings, and black shoes. Do you know who she is?

That's Eleanor Foster.

I must find her. Where does she live?

Up north on Main Street with her parents, Mr. and Mrs. Foster. Her father is a blacksmith. James and Fannie Foster—that's their names—at 237 Main Street.

Raymond Crumbaker (1903–1980) and Eleanor Weaver (neé Foster) (1904–1987), two of Howard's young models, standing at his home, the Barracks, circa 1913 (Special Collections, Lafayette College, Easton, PA)

As soon as Raymond gave the address, Howard turned the buggy around, and we were heading back into town at full speed.

The rest of that afternoon was spent in the front parlor of the Foster home, where Howard made his plea to Eleanor's father. A bargain was struck, and Howard was more than pleased. He had secured a new young model in the span of three hours.

By the time we neared Howard's home, it was early evening. The sun was setting over the west bank of the rippling river, making it appear like an azure ribbon speckled with Grecian gold. The road before us, though rough in places, became a path of glowing, polished amber.

I wish it could be like this always, Howard.

You mean summer?

Yes, summer—when the air is always fragrant and sweet, the river always sparkling and blue, and the fruit always ripe and delicious.

Sometimes I feel that we are put on this earth so that we can experience just a small taste of God's beauty, if only to prepare ourselves for the unimaginable beauty yet to come.

I wish to think so too.

Nancy Palmer, as portrayed by Howard in Gouverneur Morris's "The Seven Darlings," a popular serial that ran in Cosmopolitan *magazine from September 1914 to March 1915. The story was later produced into a best-selling book of the same name.*

CHAPTER SEVEN
An Unexpected Visitor

*D*AY TURNED INTO NIGHT; night turned into day. Each splendid week unfolded into the next. Before long, we were knee-deep in June.

Nancy, please hold still.

I'm trying, but it's hotter than the hinges of Hades up here.

I assure you it's not any warmer here than it is in New York City.

Howard worked all morning upstairs in the barn's studio, a spacious room two stories tall, ascending from the top floor. A large window facing the north provided the perfect amount of light. Underneath the pine rafters, Howard worked on the last scenes of "The Penalty" and was about to begin work on Jack London's new serial, "The Valley of the Moon."

The yellow canaries Howard had purchased weeks earlier swooped down and encircled us until they found a place to roost. Others just sat, comfortably perched on Howard's easel.

I don't mean to complain. It's just that this long dress is made of heavy dark wool.

Everything must be authentic. I can't have you wearing summer clothes when it's supposed to be winter.

Shortly past noon, I began to fade from the heat and humidity, while Howard was contemplating his next great work. He seemed to be moved by it.

In a few more weeks, I am going to work on "The Seven Darlings."

Seven Darlings?

It's another romantic serial—a family with six daughters and one son with the surname of Darling. I'll need you to pose in a bathing suit, darling.

Ah, well, I'm sure it will be much cooler.

It certainly will, darling. And each of the six sisters will be you, but captured in different poses and in different lights.

I decided to return the favor of his flirtation. *Splendid, darling. I can almost envision it now. By the way, darling, what's that curious bug on the ceiling?* I pointed to where a black insect was roaming near a group of small mud pipes cemented to a beam.

That's a mud dauber—a wasp. Quite common in these parts.

Well, that creature makes the most perfect little home for itself. You see it? Looks like the pipes of a church organ.

Howard studied it for a moment and then turned back.

A pipe organ mud dauber—each pipe is of a different color, culled from mud gathered from a different place.

How do they do it?

One might say that the mud dauber was born to have a special talent.

Very much like you.

What do you mean?

You were born to paint, Howard, and paint well.

There you're too kind, but I must say, you are quite observant. Talent always comes from within, like that of a budding flower. Take, for instance, Queen Anne's lace. Have you ever looked closely at that flower? Queen Anne's lace is one of the most exquisite creations in all of nature. So perfectly it forms, like a globe of downy snowflakes. After seeing it, I don't see how anyone can ever doubt there is a God.

I feel the same way about roses . . . and you have such an exquisite garden filled with so many varieties—all sweet-smelling, and each created as if it were a special gift.

There's so much more that I would like to show you.

I would like that very much.

We shall begin today. Let's take a short journey together.

That is how I shall always remember that summer as we explored the paradise surrounding his enchanted home—Howard and I in our tall boots, riding horseback in search of the ancient Indian mounds he and his brother once excavated as boys; the late-afternoon tennis matches and rounds of lawn croquet that I always seemed to win; Howard finishing an afternoon landscape while I, with umbrella in hand, stood over him to protect his still-wet canvas from the soft, fragrant rain; the two of us in his covered motorboat, flying at full speed up the river and then, hours later, soaking in the last minutes of the sun's golden rays along some deserted beach at the river's edge across from his home.

It was there on that beach, as we reclined on the warm sand in our bathing suits, that I first raised the question of meeting Howard's notable friends.

Someday soon, I'd love to meet your guests—the ones Noel spoke of when I first arrived.

You will. You already have.

Not the locals. I mean the famous ones—the writers, publishers, actors, and authors, like Rex Beach and Charles Scribner. I mean, do you actually know Harrison Fisher and James Montgomery Flagg, the famous artists?

Just as I know Charles Dana Gibson, the most famous illustrator in America and the very man who introduced you to me. I count these men among my closest friends. We're all in the same brotherhood—the Illustrators of Beauty.

I would love to meet them!

Don't be such a social climber, Nancy.

Howard! I'm not. I'm just curious.

You'll meet them.

When?

Have patience.

I do, and I'm still waiting.

Well, to answer your question, I've just received word that Mary Roberts Rinehart, the best-selling mystery writer, will be staying with us shortly. Over six years ago, I illustrated her first book, The Man in Lower Ten. *I'm certain you will find her quite interesting. And I'm . . . I'm thinking of a having a July Fourth celebration for her.*

Mary Roberts Rinehart . . . and a July Fourth celebration. How simply divine!

Howard (far left), his dog Sargent, and several of his models wade in the Muskingum River in front of his motorboat around 1912. In 1908, Howard had the boat constructed after his friend Colonel Foster gave him the engine as a present. (Special Collections, Lafayette College, Easton, PA)

After swimming, Howard, his dog Sargent, and several of his models relax on the beach directly across the river in front of his home. Nancy is to the far left with a hat on her foot. (Special Collections, Lafayette College, Easton, PA)

Howard, playing a game of tennis. The tennis court, accessible by a rustic log bridge, was located directly over the bluff and to the south of his home. (Special Collections, Lafayette College, Easton, PA)

Howard (far left) and Nancy (by Howard's side) enjoy a summer afternoon with friends near the Barracks. (Special Collections, Lafayette College, Easton, PA)

Guests were always stopping by the Barracks. Some were local men and boys who became Howard's models. One older man transformed himself into Blizzard, the legless villain of the story *The Penalty*, by placing buckets on his knees and hobbling with great difficulty on a pair of sawed-off crutches. Raymond, the young boy whom Howard and I met on our first trip together to Duncan Falls, became the model for Bubbles, a young street urchin from the same story.[7]

One day, Howard set up an easel in the springhouse and painted Raymond pulling himself out of the cold pool. He wanted to replicate a scene where Bubbles, entirely nude, propels himself upon a pier following a swim in the East River, just as poor boys often did at that time in the sweltering summer heat of New York City. When Raymond emerged from the icy coldness, I wrapped him in warm blankets.

For scenes where Howard wanted Raymond to look angry, Natalie would slyly pester the young boy. Being full of humor and a little mischief, she might unexpectedly fire off the brass cannon, causing everyone to leap to their feet in great surprise, except for Howard who undoubtedly put her up to the task.

Raymond! Stay just like that! Don't move!

And with this, he would achieve the precise look he wanted.

None of Howard's immediate family members ever became his models, except for his father, who would sometimes appear as an aging Civil War veteran. And one is left to wonder whether his mother became the inspiration for many of his illustrations depicting charming elderly ladies. Howard's nephews, Howard Paul and Donald Christy, the sons of Bernard, would occasionally stop by the home of their "Uncle Hall," as they called him, and would quickly be recruited, if he was in need of a boyish subject.

Howard often posed models in various costumes and positions to transform them into different characters for the same illustration. As such, Noel might become two or three different men, and I might become six different women, as was the case with my appearance in *The Seven Darlings*. Raymond could easily

Natalie Christy stands on the rustic bridge leading to the tennis court at the Barracks. She is described as being modest and quiet but with "a keen sense of humor." (Special Collections, Lafayette College, Easton, PA)

Natalie Christy and her grandmother, Mary Christy, read Howard's 1907 best-seller, Our Girls: Poems in Praise of the American Girl, *in front of one of his illustrations. (Courtesy of Maxine Christy Peters)*

resemble several boys, and Eleanor Foster multiple girls in various stages of youth. Slight variations in physical features could make each character appear seemingly unique, but if studied closely, all would look vaguely familiar. Like a magician, only Howard and his models knew the true secrets behind his seamless magic.

Howard (back left) and Noel Talbot (back right), in sailor hats, pose on the rustic bridge spanning the ravine toward the Barracks' tennis court. In front are Howard's friends and his French model, Ghislaine Britt (center). (Special Collections, Lafayette College, Easton, PA)

The young women who posed at the Barracks were different from the rest. Only a few were bred in the Muskingum River Valley. Many came from New York City, where Howard would personally vet them. Each had her own story that drew her to become an artist's model. Noel would later confide in me the details of several of these beautiful women—my illustrious predecessors—but whatever I may have failed to discover from him, I took it upon myself to uncover on my own.

◙

IT WAS A MEMORABLE DAY when Mary Roberts Rinehart arrived at the Barracks.[8] Her crime novels and detective stories had sold in the hundreds of thousands throughout the world, transforming her into a household name. Indeed, when her novel *The Door,* in which the butler becomes the villain, became an instant best-seller, the cliché "the butler did it" was born.

With her doctor husband and her son, Stanley Junior, in tow, Mary came aboard a steamboat that stopped at the stone landing below Howard's house. From the window of my room, I could see a group of townspeople across the river and on either side of the road, waiting to see the second most popular illustrator in America greeting America's best-selling mystery author. As she stepped ashore, Mary received the same warm welcome I had received two months earlier. Howard's shiny burgundy motor car took her and her husband up the long driveway, while her baggage and young son traveled in the hay wagon behind.

When I finally met the great mystery author, she and her husband were in the billiard room, chatting with Howard near the brick fireplace. His white angora cat napped undisturbed on the seat of a nearby armchair.

And this is my arms collection. I have firearms and swords from the Spanish-American War, going all the way back to the Revolutionary War period.

Lining one wall was a vast array of weapons, each of which was secured one on top of the other and lovingly cared for. From Spanish buccaneer pistols to Indian tomahawks, it was an eclectic, if not odd, assembly of relics from military campaigns long since past.

This particular pistol was used by Jefferson Davis. And over here, we have Spanish dueling swords. Now this sword was used by Napoleon's Imperial Guard.

Mary seemed impressed, yet a bit bewildered by the assortment.

Considered to be the American Agatha Christie, she could no doubt find a place in one of her books for one or more of these dangerous weapons.

And what is this here, Howard?

Oh, those are historical artifacts from Admiral Dewey's flagship, the Olympia. *I have quite a few relics from the Spanish-American War, including several bugles. They're over there, above the fireplace mantel.*

Rising above the mantel was a sizeable metal breastplate, intersected diagonally by two swords of ancient origin. This piece of armor was likely used by some soldier from the 1600s. However, I knew it to be the breastplate worn by John Alden, just as Howard had illustrated him for Longfellow's book *The Courtship of Miles Standish*. On either side of this breastplate were brass bugles hanging by tasseled cords.

With a grin, Mary pointed to a suit of metal armor standing in the corner.

And what is this? It looks like an ancient baseball catcher's uniform.

Ah, that is the suit of armor that I used to model the knight for Alfred, Lord Tennyson's The Princess. *Noel, my caretaker, served as the knight.*

Overhearing Howard, Noel suddenly entered the room.

I say, Mrs. Rinehart! I practically lived in that sardine can for over a month. Would you care to try it on?

John Alden, as portrayed by Howard in 1903 for Longfellow's The Courtship of Miles Standish **(Private Collection)**

That's quite thoughtful, Noel, but no, thank you. It seems to be more your size than mine.

Yes, quite.

Howard turned sharply to face Noel.

I have decided that we are going to have a July Fourth party in honor of Mrs. Rinehart and her husband. I need you to put together a guest list.

Ah, how lovely. How many people do you care to invite? A hundred? Maybe two hundred?

I would say roughly 350 people.

Oh, I see, only half of Philo, half of Duncan Falls, and a quarter of Zanesville. Jolly good, Howard. I say, this should be a small soiree compared to the others. Usually, you invite the entire countryside.

Noel is kidding, of course, but I assure you that some of the parties here have been quite large. But this will be the largest of them all, as it should be.

Mrs. Rinehart and her husband nodded in agreement. Noel smiled, but I could tell he was amused by the subtlety conveyed by Howard's esteemed guests.

Howard, shall I start with last year's guest list?

"Yes, fine," Howard replied to Noel.

And whom shall I add?

"Billie and Ethel Shultz and Sarah—and of course, her beau, Harry Rhead . . . but be sure to get Frank and Baugie Durban. And be sure there's plenty to eat."

As Howard prompted his guests to join him in the dining room for dinner, I lingered behind, taking Noel's arm in mine and whispering in his ear all the way.

Who are the Durbans?

Frank is Howard's attorney, and Baugie is his wife. You know that Frank narrowly missed the Republican nomination for governor of Ohio a few years ago.

His attorney? What? No, I didn't know that. Why does he need an attorney here in the country?

Three years ago, he had a terrible spat with his wife, Maebelle. A big court battle ensued, right here in Muskingum County. It's all over now. Howard was given custody of his daughter. So she lives here.

What about his wife?

She couldn't stand the place. Not enough fancy dresses and high society. So she resides in New York City.

I see. So is he unattached?

Unattached enough.

Noel paused for a brief moment, and then completed his thought.

I can certainly tell that Mr. Christy is quite smitten with you, Miss Palmer.

Smitten? How do you know he is smitten with me?

By the way his eyes dance about you while his brush moves about his palette. You definitely can see it in his work. He truly captures you in a rare immortal splendor. Look closely . . . you will see.

Noel finished with a sly wink, just as we entered the dining room.

I did feel that Howard liked me. I could tell it in his eyes and in the smooth, charming way he spoke to me. It was a much different manner than the way he spoke to his sisters, or mother, or any other women we met together. I could also tell he thought me to be beautiful by the way he portrayed me in his work. I had never before seen another painter depict such charm and exquisiteness. But did he love me?

After we were all seated at the dining room table, Mary Roberts Rinehart, our illustrious guest, began the conversation.

Howard, you must come to our home in Pennsylvania. Stanley and I would love to have you for a weekend or even longer, if you prefer. Will you make some time at the end of July?

I'd be delighted. Nothing would give me greater pleasure.

Then we look forward to seeing you.

As do I.

Howard's father began telling another story while Bena, Howard's servant, walked around the table with a bottle of wine in hand. Passing over the children, she poured a generous amount into everyone's wine glass. When she tipped the bottle over Howard's, he quickly brushed his hand over it to suggest that he did not care for any.

"I have heard so much in the newspapers about raving beauties," Natalie said. "What is a raving beauty, Father?"

"Well, go up to your room and look in the long cheval glass, and I am sure you will see a raving beauty."

"Yes," Natalie replied, "if you stand in front of me."

As the room erupted in laughter, a great commotion came from the kitchen. Pots and pans were banging together. Bena was screaming at the top of her lungs.

Nah, git down from there! Don't you do that! Come on! Git! Git!

Howard arose from the table. *I do apologize. I have no idea what has gotten into my cook.*

Just then, Bena came bursting through the kitchen door. *That dog, Messa Christy. It's that dog of yours!*

Howard flew right past her and into the kitchen, where he found a fresh trail of paw prints. By the back door was Sargent, rolling a steaming roast of prime rib across the threshold and down the steps, gravy dripping all the way.

Howard returned shortly to explain the travesty to his guests.

That dog will steal a stick of butter if given half a chance. This time, he stole the main course.

Bena served ham and eggs that evening. And with the wine, it was delicious. Despite the minor mishap, everyone seemed satisfied, especially Sargent.

HOWARD'S FOURTH OF JULY CELEBRATION at the Barracks was one of the largest gatherings Muskingum County had ever witnessed. People were everywhere.

Arriving by steamboat, buggy, surrey, motor car, on horseback, or simply on foot, they ascended the long, winding drive in single file and swarmed the green with their summer finery—droves of gentlemen in pressed linen suits or midnight-blue blazers and downy white trousers; clusters of ladies in long, flowing dresses of ivory or pastel hues of blue, pink, and yellow.

Just as Howard had asked, Bena made sure there was plenty to eat. His sisters were busy conversing in the living room, while servants, hired just for the occasion, darted about the house carrying crystal pitchers of iced lemonade and oversized platters of warm biscuits and sliced Virginia ham.

Polly, Howard's talking green parrot, waited patiently in his cage and observed the whole affair, especially the uncommon arrival of young ladies, who, upon entering Howard's home, would scurry about, chattering and giggling throughout the first-floor rooms and up and down the double staircase leading to the second floor.

Outside, in the middle of the lawn, a brass band from Duncan Falls played on. Wearing white uniforms with blue piping, each musician held a shiny new instrument that glistened in the sun like gold. Howard had financed all of their equipment and clothes, even their well-shined shoes. On many Sundays, they would spend the afternoon practicing here, and Howard, along with his family and guests, would enjoy the energetic and inspiring melodies that would fill the air. But this day was different. This was not a practice session or a dress rehearsal but a major performance. It was said that, across the river, farmers and townspeople standing in their fields and front yards could hear the music flowing down from the high cliff of Howard's home. And they smiled.

The band had just finished John Philip Sousa's "National Emblem March" when Howard crossed the lawn to greet his eager guests. The aging bandleader called out, *Mr. Christy! Do you have any particular request?*

Yes, play Sousa's "National Emblem March"!

The band members shook their heads, wiped the sweat off their brows, and uttered a muffled protest. Then, they played the same song yet again.

By midafternoon, cake and ice cream were served. It was after this time that I caught the attention of Noel, who was providing additional orders to the exhausted servants.

I say, Miss Palmer, I trust you are having a splendid afternoon.

Indeed, I am.

Howard enjoys giving these celebrations every year. As I am not a native of the States, I cannot appreciate fully your Independence Day. It was only after I attended my first celebration here at the Barracks that I began to understand your charming customs.

Where are you from, Noel? England?

Aberdeen, Scotland, to be precise. I immigrated here in 1897.

What brought you here?

I was a newspaperman in New York—a special writer for The New York Times—*and had a bit of bad luck with my health. A fellow by the name of Crittenden—an actor and friend of mine—came here from England for the same reason. He recommended the place to me; said I should go on holiday and see it.*

Why?

He said it was like the Garden of Eden. Absolutely beautiful. No one would believe such a place could ever exist.

Do you believe?

Not until I arrived. Then, after what I saw, I most surely believed. He said this place would cure my poor health.

Did it?

Indeed, it did, and I have been here ever since. Perhaps against my better judgment, I shall never leave this place, or, if I do, I surely wish to be buried here, as there is no finer place I have ever known.

As Noel finished, a young woman, about the same age as I, walked toward us. She was wearing a long white dress with a broad-brimmed hat bearing flowers. He recognized her.

That, Miss Palmer, is Mrs. Tanner. You might learn a good deal about this place from her and, of course, Howard's former models, if you are so interested.

As she approached, his voice quickly softened.

Ah, Mrs. Tanner, how lovely it is to see you again.

She extended her hand to him, and as he kissed it, his voice became animated.

Please allow me to introduce you to Miss Nancy Palmer. She is Mr. Christy's model. Miss Palmer, this is Mrs. J. Ray Tanner.

As Noel made the introduction, I noticed that Mrs. Tanner was looking around like a socialite at a party full of politicians. This was not her first time here, I suspected.

Mrs. Tanner lives in Duncan Falls, Miss Palmer, and is often called upon to act as a hostess when one of Mr. Christy's famous guests comes to pay a visit, or he has a grand celebration such as this. And this is quite a special occasion in honor of Mary Roberts Rinehart, the famous mystery author.

Aw, Noel, you are such a dear. Such a dear! Thank you so very much for the cordial introduction. I am so pleased to meet Miss Palmer. I think we will get along quite nicely. Please call me Gertrude, Miss Palmer.

Noel quickly excused himself. *Well, so much to do, so little time to do it in. I must be off.*

Now, by the side of the lawn, Mrs. Tanner and I were standing alone.

So, Miss Palmer, are you new to the modeling business?

Yes, I arrived here in May.

I do hope you will stay.

I intend to.

Well, you know most of Howard's female models only stay a few months. He has had so many in the past four years that I can barely recall them all. One woman committed suicide right here at the Barracks.

Suicide! My goodness, why would she do that?

Because she could never have him. He's married, you know.

Married? No, I didn't know. I had no idea. I thought he was divorced, and his daughter lives with him.

Oh, my dear, sweet child! Haven't you seen the headlines?

What headlines?

The newspapers! You must have seen them. Two years ago, the Christys were in every newspaper in the country, on the front page with a huge headline. I can even still recall a few of them: "Artist Christy's New York Studio a Den of Vice."

Mrs. Tanner drew her right hand across the sky, much like the words were already written there, and she was simply reading them. *A den of vice! Isn't that just scandalous, Miss Palmer? Then, when it was his turn to dish the dirt, the headlines were even much more brazen: "Christy Rattles Family Skeleton: Artist Springs Secret Chapters in Wife's Life." So sensational, isn't it? Christy rattles family skeleton! Secret chapters! I mean, really; their indiscretions were all so riveting.*

I don't understand, Mrs. Tanner—I mean, Gertrude. His turn to dish the dirt? Why was it his turn?

My dear, two years ago in the winter, Howard went through a bitter child custody battle in Zanesville with his wife, Maebelle. She was living in New York and brought suit here to get her daughter back. The trial lasted many days. You know how trials go . . . one side goes first, then the other. Everything comes out—all the dirty laundry—all under oath. And so you see, every day was something new, and each witness told something more tantalizing than the next. Someone did this; someone said that; so-and-so had too much to drink. Howard was hugging and kissing his young lady models; Maebelle was having an affair with the chauffeur. The accounts drew everyone in, my dear. Everyone! The public couldn't get enough. They loved the drama and the unseemly details, but above all, they wanted to know who would get custody of little Natalie. Would it be Howard, or would it be Maebelle? As one headline read, "Model Husband or Tipsy Wife?" Isn't that so clever, my dear? Model husband!

Gertrude Tanner laughed as if she had just finished her third cocktail, but there was no alcohol served at this July Fourth fête, only lemonade. When she spoke, her lips moved off to the side and then back again in an unnatural way, like that of the young socialite she was.

So Howard never divorced her?

No, he's still married. My dear, how could you have missed all that? Don't you read the papers?

I suppose I was just busy working. I just didn't know.

It was true that I had no knowledge of Howard's past. Mrs. Tanner caught me entirely off guard. All I knew was that Howard Chandler Christy was once married and had a little girl. In five days from that celebration, she would become thirteen years of age in a world so different from when she was born. Little Natalie had proven to be a bit shy, but in the few weeks of our acquaintance, I saw that she was full of humor and good spirit. As for Howard, Noel had confirmed that he was entirely unattached, and I believed him. I was not disappointed at Mrs. Tanner's words, only a bit confused. The question was not so much whether Howard was married but was he happily married. Only the future would reveal that truth. And I would stay long enough to discover it.

Of course you didn't know, Miss Palmer. Of course you didn't know. This is all too new . . . for you. I perfectly understand and empathize. There are so many secrets with this Christy family. I am sure you are just uncovering some of them . . . now.

What was she like? I mean, Howard's wife, Maebelle. Do you know her?

Mrs. Tanner came closer to me, as if she were about to whisper in my ear. "She was so beautiful," she said, "that you could not believe any girl was that beautiful." Then she added, "She never drank a drop until she met Christy."

Her voice began to trail off, just as other young girls began to move in closer until they had completely surrounded us with their sophomoric gossip and idle talk, like bees buzzing around a hive. Soon, the queen bee was enveloped entirely and discussing someone else.

With the unwanted company, I was never able to determine the true extent of Howard's past. So I politely extended my sincere appreciation for her time and began mingling with the rest of the crowd.

Half past seven in the evening, the sun set over the west bank of the river, and the crowd had barely thinned. For some reason, many people wished to remain. And I was more than pleased that I did as well. Under the twinkling stars, the Barracks became a carnival of lights and swirling colors.

Howard hoisted a burning lantern up the flagpole. Strings of Chinese globe lanterns of crimson, emerald, and amber illuminated the lawn and the columns of the pergola. Near the south portico, a group of teenagers huddled around a little campfire kindled on the ground. One young couple held a rice-paper balloon the size of a small tree, while a young boy lit a piece of wax cloth at the opening at the bottom. The immense sky lantern inflated and slowly rose, with its bottom twitching and flickering in the night

Howard's 1914 illustration for the July 1916 edition of Scribner's magazine: "A Fourth of July Lawn Fête—Inflating the Paper Balloon." Depicted are two young women and a man igniting a Chinese sky lantern, while guests enjoy the night air on the lawn by the columned veranda. Nancy Palmer is featured in different poses along with Noel Talbot. The model of the young girl to the left, with back turned, is likely Eleanor Foster.

air, until it resembled that of a distant harvest moon. Another was lit, then another, and so on, until the purple heavens bounced and shimmered with the glow of two dozen moons.

To commemorate the occasion, a speech was given but not by Howard. He detested giving speeches. The guest of honor, Mary Roberts Rinehart, was appropriately praised, and the old brass cannon was ceremoniously fired.

By the side of the commanding bluff, a volley of rockets and fireworks burst forth high above trees and over the river, illuminating the faces of the awestruck crowd with a shower of red, blue, and gold. Near the end, while Howard was just staring across the lawn, lost in thought and with a lit cigar in hand, Noel caught sight of me. Once again, he engaged me in conversation.

Quite a show! Eh, Miss Palmer?

I have never seen anything quite like it. Howard has given a spectacular performance. And I so enjoyed meeting Mrs. Tanner. Thank you for the introduction. Noel, please tell me, if you will, about Howard's other models. What were they like?

I have been only acquainted with the models from New York City. That's where he selects his young ladies, you know. When there, he would often go to a reputable boarding house operated by a lady known as Mrs. Brown. She had a new boarder—a very beautiful French woman of about twenty years of age, with a great bushel of chestnut hair crowning her head. Her name was Ghislaine Britt. She had such an exquisite porcelain face, and in the sunlight, she looked like a marble statue one might see in a museum of antiquities. And the way in which she moved her hands was graceful and delicate, like that of a Russian ballerina. Naturally, Mr. Christy took an instant fancy to this young lady, and she to him. A few moments had passed after their introduction when Mr. Christy's spontaneity got the best of him, and he invited Miss Britt to come to Ohio to become his model. She readily accepted. Eager at the prospect, he requested that she be ready to depart the next day at six o'clock. To this, she sighed heavily. He sensed that she was not quite ready for the sudden journey.

She needed dresses, hats, and other apparel, as young beautiful women often do. So he commanded her to come with him. And he bought her everything she needed or ever wanted—steamer trunks full of clothes. They arrived here by steamboat. I'll never forget that day. Mademoiselle Britt was the first model I ever met here, and I found her to be quite agreeable and very alluring in her appearance. Come to think of it, Miss Palmer, you probably have seen her likeness in one of Mr. Christy's books, perhaps The Princess *or* The Lady of the Lake.

I have. I especially remember the pictures depicting her with long, luxurious hair and flowing dresses of embroidered silk.

Those dresses you saw were all real, I assure you, as Howard only paints what he sees. The wardrobe is an added expense that he pays for out of his own pocket.

Was it difficult conversing with Mademoiselle Britt?

She spoke in French or, on occasion, L'Anglais *in a broken fashion, but quite attractively. When Mademoiselle Britt first settled here, she would walk down the drive each day at four o'clock, which is precisely when the steamboat would arrive. Mr. Christy was quite curious about this odd ritual and inquired. She replied in her native language that she had sent away to Montgomery Ward for something that cost two dollars. Mr. Christy understood her French and responded in English. He told her that she should be patient, as the item would certainly have been shipped from Chicago. When she eventually received her purchase, Mr. Christy was amused to find that it was only a pair of sandals. She told him that she would look like a Greek goddess in them. And she was right.*

What was her personality like, Noel? Was she completely vapid, as I imagine some artists' models may be?

No, Miss Palmer, quite the contrary. Miss Britt was a sensitive soul. As you already have observed, Mr. Christy would often buy canaries and set them free. I remember the joy and wonder in her face as the canaries fluttered around the rose bushes here. She would summon them one by one with affectionate names. They

*Ghislaine Britt, Howard's French model, poses for this dramatic illustra-
tion from 1909. (Private Collection)*

would fly about her in circles and then alight on her hand. Moments later, when a few flew away, never to return, she would cry as if she had just lost a newborn child. I also recall that she was quite frugal. One evening, when she was upstairs getting dressed, her perfume bottle fell to the floor and the liquor leaked out, seeping through the floorboards and to the ceiling below. She quickly ran downstairs, only to find Mr. Christy catching the drops with his hands and rubbing them on his face. Stunned, she demanded that he pay her exactly one dollar ninety-eight cents, for that is precisely what the perfume cost. Mr. Christy just laughed. He derived so much fun from her girlish sentiments.

It sounds like she was quite intriguing, if not eccentric.

Indeed she was, Miss Palmer. Mr. Christy's father adored her, but his sister, Rose, did not care much for her.

Did Howard care much about his French model?

He most certainly did. He found her to be quite artistic and imaginative. I recall one occasion when he and his family were scaling a hill with her. It was twilight, and the moon was rising. The mood captivated Howard and he continued on about how beautiful the glow was and how the night sky was layered in various shades of lavender and silver. Mademoiselle Britt cut him short saying, "Sh-sh-sh—your family—they think you is cra-a-zy."

I laughed at Noel's description, but inside, I began to wonder this same thought. Howard seems so lost in his love of beauty. Perhaps he's mad, like those bohemian artists one often reads about—men tortured by their own unbridled passions and creative longings; men who destroy themselves in their quest to immortalize their fantastic visions.

Is Howard crazy, Noel? Or do you think he's sane?

Most assuredly the latter, Miss Palmer. Only Howard sees things that you and I do not. In his world, everything is beautiful, as it should be. Is it wrong to see things that way?

No, Noel. No, it isn't.

With true beauty, there is no illusion.

Just as it should be.

Indeed, Miss Palmer, just as it should be.

Whatever became of Ghislaine Britt?

No one knows for certain. She left the Barracks suddenly after an ultimatum was made.

By whom?

Mr. Christy's wife. It was either her or Mademoiselle Britt. One woman could stay; the other had to go. The choice was Mr. Christy's.

I take it Miss Britt left, and Maebelle stayed?

No, they both left . . . all quite suddenly. First, his wife. One September, she had been here for five days. Then, on a Sunday morning, her bags were all packed and placed on the drive outside the home. She summoned a taxicab to take her to the train station, alone. None of Mr. Christy's family accompanied her or even bid her farewell when she departed. Mr. Christy was certainly not there. At that point, any reconciliation looked hopeless. Then, two days later, Mademoiselle Britt packed her bags too and departed without warning. Mr. Christy's chauffeur took her to the Zanesville train station. Newspaper men followed her there and questioned her until she gave them the scoop they had all wanted, confirming the rumor that everyone wanted to know: after many months, Mr. and Mrs. Christy had finally reconciled. Mademoiselle Britt was quoted as saying, "Mrs. Christy is now in New York arranging her affairs to make Zanesville her future home." And as for Mademoiselle Britt, she told the reporters that she was commanded to leave this place forever so that Mr. Christy's wife would eventually come back. She said that she would never again return here. This was the last thing she said to them before traveling on to New York and then to Paris by steamer. That was almost two years ago. No one here has heard from her since.

Were they reconciled?

To this day, it remains to be seen. Shortly after his wife's departure, Mr. Christy announced, during lunch among his family, that an understanding had been reached between him and his wife. They were finally reconciled, he declared, and Mrs. Christy returned that October. That October, all was fine for everyone. But the following year, when she appeared again, it was much of the same drama as before. At first, it would look like things would be smoothed over and then, just days after her arrival, she would all of sudden leave in a huff.

Why? What was really the issue that separated them from each other?

Noel paused for a moment, then continued. "Well, you know, it's the old question," he said. "Mrs. Christy says she will not live back here at Duncan Falls, and Howard does not care to return to New York and possibly to his old habits of living."

Noel hesitated as he said the last few words. It was then that I had wondered what Howard's old habits of living were like. Did he resemble those other bohemian artists, or was he someone much different? From what I had seen thus far, he exemplified a glorious knight of chivalry—a prince—like those he had painted. He was a true and kind gentleman to me, not a rogue or a cad. I couldn't imagine him being any different with another woman.

Noel continued. *His sister Rose tried to be helpful to her brother's plight. She crafted a peace plan of sorts: Mr. Christy would reside in New York in the fall and winter months, and Mrs. Christy would reside here in the spring and summer months. With that, Natalie could live with both of her parents.*

Did it work?

No, Miss Palmer. It could never work between those two. Perhaps one of these days, you will meet Mr. Christy's wife. She does pop by now and again . . . all unannounced . . . about twice a year. And when she is here, everyone is so much different . . . more alert, one might say, or perhaps a bit beside themselves.

Noel, tell me of Howard's other models, my predecessors.

Ah, well, that might prove to be another long story. However, I suspect you know their days here were rather numbered. Once Mademoiselle Britt left in September 1910, there was a girl named Brita Dybergh. She was of Swedish descent and a famous beauty. Then, Daisy Adamy, one of Gibson's models, arrived. Later, she became a stage actress. Of course, Nell Sibree followed, and after her came Beryl Morris, the child actress who later became a noted New York model. Then, Miss Palmer, you arrived. What's your fate?

I intend to stay.

If I may be so bold, Miss Palmer, I would like to tell you something that I have been sensing ever since you arrived.

Please do.

I feel that someday you and Mr. Christy will marry.

That's precisely what Mr. Gibson said just before I met Howard. I suppose you and he may prove to be visionaries.

In this world, there are those who sense things that others do not and just know things that others cannot. It is a blessing and a burden, as it can allow one to see into the future, but it can also permit one to see right through another to his very soul . . . . Sometimes, it can be frightening, as what one sees on the outside as beauty is truly not that which is within but merely a deception.

An illusion.

Precisely. I must go, Miss Palmer. I bid you a good evening.

Thank you, Noel. I shall remember that. Good evening as well.

I turned over in my mind Noel's words. He confirmed what Mr. Gibson had stated earlier. It was all still too fantastic to be true. And what did he mean when he said that what one sees as beauty on the outside is just an illusion? Were these prophetic words or more of a warning? In time, I would discover the truth.

As the lawn began to hum with the din of idling motor cars, I returned to the Barracks, only to find that the crowd, once milling inside, was trickling out the door and spilling over the porch landing. Howard stood on the porch stairs and bid each person farewell.

Goodbye, Miss Shultz. Harry, so good to see you—good-bye. Ray—goodbye. Goodbye.

The guests departed, and the house fell silent once again, except for the faint rattle of dishes in the kitchen. In the dining room, several ladies sat sipping tea, unaware that the party had ended. No one seemed to notice them except for Polly, who sat in his cage patiently, desperately wanting to sleep. A shrill whistle followed, which startled the ladies, causing them to jump up. Just then, Howard's voice boomed throughout the room: *good-bye, good-bye, good-bye.* But he was outside on the porch. The ladies darted for the door all at once, brushed past Howard, and ran across the lawn to their awaiting motor cars. I had never seen anyone move as quickly as those women did—and probably never will.

回

DAYS LATER, A STRANGE AND FOREBODING SENSE FILLED MY HEART. Howard had excused me from my modeling duties. He didn't tell me why.

By midday, Noel and I were standing on the porch and talking. In the distance, I spotted Howard's burgundy motor car through the cow pasture, climbing the long drive. As it rounded the spring house, I could see, sitting next to the chauffeur, a woman in a long yellow dress—the kind that was quite fashionable a few years earlier. She wore a dark blue hat with a heavy white lace veil that shrouded her hair and face.

Who's that, Noel?

Oh, I say, that's Mrs. Christy!

Howard's sister?

No, his wife.

Is she coming to visit?

Undoubtedly.

Eleanor and Raymond stood by watching as the motor car pulled up to the side of the house. Out of thin air, Howard and Natalie seemed to appear magically at the precise time. I took hold of Noel's arm and looked into his blue eyes.

How long will she stay?

Can't say for certain. But if things play out as they usually do, I suspect her visit will last about a week . . . maybe less. You

are in for a real treat, Miss Palmer, especially if you fancy the
drama of the theater.

The chauffeur opened the car door, and Maebelle's long dress cascaded down over the running board and onto the gravel path. She lifted her veil. Her brown eyes were the first thing I noticed. Then, I could see her dark chestnut hair, carefully curled and piled atop her head. Mrs. Tanner was right; she was more beautiful than I could have ever imagined.

Howard and Maebelle greeted each other with kind words, but no expressions of affection were exchanged. Natalie ran forward and gave her mother a brief embrace. Maebelle looked unmoved.

Although first published in the August 1905 edition of Century *magazine, Howard's* Speeding the Coming Guest *ironically reflects a scene common from Howard's life during 1908–1915, a time when he lived in Ohio, and his then-wife, Maebelle, who lived in New York City, traveled twice a year to visit their daughter, Natalie, at his home.*

Howard introduced us, and her first words to me were simply, *I am Mrs. Christy.*

Noel and the chauffeur lifted the steamer trunk from the motor car and transported it inside the house, which is where the Christy family and servants were scurrying about; for that afternoon, Mrs. Christy was an unexpected visitor.

That evening, as the last rays of sunlight sparkled across the river below, Howard, Maebelle, and Natalie were together once again, high above on the bluff, playing tennis on the court to the south of the house.

The skiffs, johnboats, and canoes seemed to linger on the water, their occupants trying to catch a glimpse of the family that had intrigued an entire nation. Across the river, the Philo townspeople could see the Christy family as well—or so the newspapers said.

After a couple of days, when it looked like Mrs. Christy had settled in, a group of ambitious newspaper reporters boldly scaled the drive and knocked on the door. They wanted to interview the new celebrity guest.

Why do you wish to stay in New York, Mrs. Christy, and not live with your husband?

"I am Southern woman," she aggressively asserted to the first reporter. "I am the daughter of an army officer, and accustomed more or less to a life of excitement and entertainment. There's much of it on Broadway, and Howard Chandler Christy, my husband, led me to like such a life at times. It is to be decided now whether we can reach an agreement."

The reporter persisted.

What agreement is that, Mrs. Christy?

"Will he live part of the year in New York? If he will, I think we can agree," she responded with a grin. "Come here, Natalie."

The young girl came running up to her mother, who took her under her arm.

Within hours, another reporter knocked on the door. The tone was different this time.

"I do not know how long I shall stay," Maebelle said. "That depends entirely on future events. I came out here to see my daughter, Natalie, and have been made so welcome by everyone that I might prolong my visit indefinitely."

The issue of reconciliation arose.

"Oh no. Mr. Christy and I have not talked reconciliation yet."

That evening, the dinner was short. Few of Howard's family members spoke. Howard announced that he and Maebelle would leave the following morning to go to Sewickley Valley in Pennsylvania to visit Mary Roberts Rinehart's new home, a large estate, twelve miles from Pittsburgh, on a bluff overlooking the Ohio River.

In this original 1915 illustration published in the March 1916 edition of The Cosmopolitan *magazine for Owen Johnston's story, "The Woman Gives," Nancy presses her ear to the wall to eavesdrop. This is one of the last illustrations that Howard painted at the Barracks. (Private Collection)*

They were gone for less than a week, yet it seemed like an eternity. When they returned, Maebelle appeared despondent. Howard looked exhausted. That same night, I could hear them talking. They were in a room next to mine. Against the wall, I pressed my ear. Then, I heard them quarrel.

Howard did not want to return to New York; she did not want to stay in Ohio. Maebelle cursed and used vulgar language. Howard did not. A door slammed shut, and I could hear heavy footsteps walking down the hall until another door slammed shut.

The next morning, before breakfast, Howard stood by himself on the porch landing with his luggage by his side as his chauffeur pulled the motor car to the front of the house. I instinctively knew something was wrong.

What's the matter?

I'm leaving today.

How long will you be gone?

Two weeks, maybe less.

Is everything all right?

It is. It will be. Please forgive me.

He left before I could say good-bye and never said where he was going.

When I returned to the house, the servants were in the kitchen making breakfast. Maebelle came downstairs and said very little. She did much of the same for the remainder of the day and each of the days that followed. Her time and attention were spent only with Natalie. She simply ignored the rest of the family unless, of course, she wanted something.

Visitors and friends would often stop by the house and deliver to Maebelle small packages, which I suspected concealed liquor. She did not think anyone knew the contents of these little gifts and certainly did not want anyone to discover them. So she discretely hid them in the recesses of the house and, when the time was right, politely excused herself from company. Minutes later, she would return, dreamy-eyed and aloof. By evening, she could often be found in an unfit condition, distressing Natalie all the more.

One day, Maebelle had an incessant toothache. Promptly, she was dispatched to Zanesville aboard Howard's motorboat. The dentist rectified the problem, but Maebelle was still in much discomfort. While she was in town, a young man named Roy Dodd bought her some liquor to help numb the pain. Apparently, it failed to remedy the situation. Inconsolable, if not irascible, she returned home. By nightfall, her disposition became even more foul. From her bedroom, doleful cries could be heard, alarming the other occupants of the house. They could hardly tolerate it and moved outside. For the rest of that night, all of us sat in wicker chairs on the front lawn.

The following morning, Howard's chauffeur and motor car were dutifully waiting at the foot of the pillared side entrance. Maebelle's steamer trunk had been placed in the car, along with the rest of her luggage. Minutes passed with no sign of her. Noel was there, as was I.

I say, Miss Palmer, I trust you failed to have a restful sleep last night.

Yes, Noel. I am sorry to say that I did not sleep at all.

Mrs. Christy lays it on a bit thick, doesn't she?

She is not quite what I had expected.

Nor I, when I first made her acquaintance. Hard to believe anyone who looks so ravishing can have such a temperament.

Why is she that way?

I sense she is not pleased with herself and therefore not pleased with anyone else.

The illustrious Mrs. Christy finally emerged from the side entrance in a lavish morning dress and veiled hat. She strutted to the car without so much as even a backward glance. The chauffeur tipped his canvas cap.

I take it you had a pleasant stay, Mrs. Christy.

As she seated herself, her head tilted and then slowly rose, until her dark brown eyes met his. She replied, "Too much hayseed style to suit me."

The door shut, and the motor car rumbled along the gravel

path until it disappeared over the gently sloping hill beyond the cow pasture. Along with Maebelle went my deepest worries and darkest fears.

At last, I felt a sense of peace, much like a great weight had been lifted from my shoulders, for what I had once perceived to be true beauty was nothing more than a trick of the eye—an illusion.

Gray squared his shoulders with a look that would have been recognized in several parts of the world. "If I'm to have you, I've got to run away with you!" he said

157

Nancy Palmer and Noel Talbot model for Howard's 1913 illustration for a Cosmopolitan *magazine serial titled "The Best Man."*

CHAPTER EIGHT
The Gift of Immortality

*Y*OUTH—THAT SILVER-WINGED SPRITE—how lovely her aura makes us feel; so quickly she soars over us. Her vitality confers so much joy; her wonderment and innocence refresh and inspire. One wishes she would never leave. Only she does . . . in time.

As for me, Youth was quite present during those languid months I spent at the Barracks, as was her twin sister, Beauty. She was always by Howard's side.

A GLOWING FIRE CRACKLED in the hearth of the living room. Howard's easel was propped up in front to the left. And, next to that, was just me, standing in a long navy blue skirt and white blouse.

Please turn a little to the left. Just like that. Fine.

His brush moved vigorously, and I moved ever so slowly toward it. When he asked me to turn, I did so in measured movements, as I never wanted to overestimate his careful instructions. Sargent lay at Howard's feet, while his white cat purred on the couch.

Outside, the leaves were changing to red, gold, and purple. It was growing cold.

In the fall and early winter months, during daybreak, a gray fog would roll in that would engulf the river and rise up to the heights of the bluff until it shrouded everything in sight. In the half light of the early day, Howard's mansion and the studio barn appeared like a ghostly vision, surrounded by trees that would move and sway, playing tricks with the shadows. By mid-morning, the mist would lift, leaving the branches dripping in a silvery dew. I once asked Howard to explain to me how the trees could appear like silver candelabra. He would simply smile, as if I were a grade-school girl, and reply, *Isn't it simply beautiful? I only wish I had the time to paint those trees in the changing light.*

It was nearly noon when the scent of pecan pie began to fill the house. Beyond the living room, I could hear the tapping of hammers and wood being sawed. Howard had made good on his promise to enclose the pergola. A group of workmen was busy constructing a roof and framing the stone columns with glass windows.

Time to rest.

Howard, I don't think you've been quite straight with me.

What do you mean?

From the nearby table, I took a copy of the September 1912 edition of *Cosmopolitan* magazine.

It's all here.

I am not sure I understand, Nancy.

The secret to immortality! It's in an article I found in this magazine with your illustrations of me.

Oh, good! So you have seen the prints. Did the Cosmopolitan *do you justice?*

You captured me perfectly! What I'm more interested in is this article I found a few pages before your pictures of me.

What article?

This one: "Why Not Live Forever?"

He took the magazine in his hand and perused it. I'm sure he had read it before. Only then, he acted coy. I snapped the magazine back.

That's right. It also says, "The lower organisms are proved to be 'potentially immortal.' Why not man?" Then, it goes on to say, "Perhaps the conquest of death itself may be among the achievements of scientists of tomorrow." So, there is hope, isn't there?

Ah, well, the scientists are right on top of it. Aren't they?

Not just the scientists. It also says this: "Then there are men of another cast of mind who believed that the special elixir of life must be a product of nature herself rather than of the laboratory, and who sought after the beneficent fountain of eternal youth in far-off regions of the world. Foremost among these adventurers . . . was Ponce de Leon."

Howard's eyes lit up.

Ah, the Spanish explorer. He was on a quest for the fountain of youth. Never found it though.

Howard, it says that Dr. Metchnikoff of the Pasteur Institute is the Ponce de Leon of our day. While some may think living forever is as much a myth as the legendary philosopher's stone, Dr. Metchnikoff does not. He thinks it's all very real.

Metchnikoff. Sounds Russian. I have no doubt he knows what he's talking about; most Russian scientists do.

Dr. Metchnikoff possesses a great deal of knowledge about living forever. Four years ago, he won the Nobel Prize in medicine.

Nobel Prize! I rest my case, then.

He thinks that aging is caused by toxic bacteria that live in the intestines. According to this, Howard, "If just the right conditions are found, man need not die except by accident." So please answer my question. Is there hope?

Hope for what?

For us to live forever. Everlasting life!

There's something I would like to show you, Nancy. I think that it may answer your question, but it must wait for now. Soon, the Valley Gem *will be entering the narrows and will be passing. I must tend to the cannon before she arrives.*

Howard rose from his chair and left the living room.

He opened the front door, and as he was just over the threshold, I called out, *What your neighbors must think of you!*

He turned back with a winsome smile.

They'd say, "Reckon as how 'Hard' Christy is just up to his monkey shines again."

Through the window, I could barely see Howard on the bluff by his treasured cannon. He lit the fuse and walked to the ledge. The cannon fired with an explosion of earth-shattering force.

Oh, my goodness!

My heart raced.

I ran quickly outside to see if Howard was hurt. Still on his feet, he looked stunned but was entirely unscathed. The collapsed gun carriage appeared like a pile of broken matchsticks. Smoke poured from the cannon barrel; its severed end splayed open like a budding black-eyed Susan. Howard took a moment to survey the wreck and then walked toward me. *Nothing in this world lasts forever, Nancy. Nothing.*

The next day, the local junkman arrived. He placed the shattered pieces in the back of his wagon and then drove off, disappearing down the hill's crest. The cannon was never replaced.

◙

"THERE IS ONE PICTURE," Howard's mother said to me, "I would like to show you, for it is dearer than anything else in the world."

As Mrs. Christy and I meandered through the rooms of the Christy farmhouse one late afternoon, she pointed out Howard's work hanging on the walls. They were his early efforts and, to her, they mattered much more than anything he had done of late or any medal he ever received. We entered the old-fashioned parlor where, on the wall, a crudely made, little framed painting hung.

"It is a copy of a picture of Lake George and was made by my boy when he was nine years old," she said. "He painted it in secret, and on Christmas morning, he came and gave it to me for my Christmas present."

Mrs. Christy, it's not like anything I had seen before of Howard's work.

No. That was well before he went off to New York City to study at the Art Students League. Has he told you about his schooling there?

No, not yet.

You should ask him. Those were some of his happiest days. William Merritt Chase said that Howard was his favorite pupil.

I most certainly will.

Howard was a dreamer. An idealist. On many nights, when every-one was fast asleep, he would lie awake in bed, his head overflowing with thoughts and visions. Often, I spotted him sneaking downstairs, where he would sit in front of the fireplace, focusing his attention solely on the flames. He was lost in thought and didn't notice I was there. When I eventually spoke to him, he would tell me all about the magical visions he saw among the burning embers. He might write about these fantasies, but more often he would paint them. In his works, I could see ideas and a strange symbolism that went well beyond the realm of a young boy's imagination.

Mrs. Christy and I continued to roam through the old-fashioned rooms of the Christy homestead until I noticed the time. I had to go. I was needed for the next illustration that Howard was prepar-ing. When I returned to the living room of the Barracks, Howard was mixing the watercolors in front of the fireplace.

So, how was your visit with Mother?

Quite delightful.

I'm so glad. Mother and Father find you to be absolutely re-freshing—much different from the other models I have had here. Noel may have told you about them.

He did mention a story or two. And from what he said, each of them was quite beautiful, if not stunning, in appearance.

That's the magic of Youth. When we're young, we tend to see the outside of a person and ignore that which is within. With Age comes wisdom, but by then, Youth has left us.

So what's left after that?

Howard hesitated and then looked down, but then his blue eyes returned to meet mine.

Beauty.

Your mother mentioned to me about your days at the Art Students League. She told me that you had your happiest days there.

Howard put his brush down and looked into the crackling fire as he spoke of those memorable years from long ago.

[Howard's Voice]

THE EDUCATION OF AN ARTIST BEGINS from within. Talent is essential, for no amount of training can ever transform a mediocre pupil into a genius. Yet talent alone is never enough to turn a novice into a master. Just as a great poet must first learn the basic rules of grammar, an artist who wishes to find success must first obtain proper training. It was at the Art Students League where I first obtained mine.

At that time, the school occupied the former Sohmer piano factory, a long, red-brick building at 143–147 East Twenty-Third Street, with row over row of tall windows. The place was surrounded by horse stables and immersed in the constant foul odors that such places produce. But inside, under the pine rafters, the soft scent of turpentine and paint permeated the air, arousing the inner spirits of those learning within. To me, this structure was much grander than all of the finest palaces in Europe.

From its front steps, few could guess to what purpose this building would descend until viewing the humble sign adorning its modest entrance, the only indication that it was simply an art school.

Up the first flight of steps and through a set of partition doors was an ordinary office and a rather spartan library, containing tables, chairs, bookcases, and photographs of Old Master portraits. The library often doubled as a reception room, and it was here where students would congregate and talk of the realm of all things beautiful. Impressive discussions occurred about how everything should be painted, including ordinary objects, such as brass pots and onions. They spoke of how certain artists influenced them, how they would paint what they saw, and how the world would be completely changed by it all. Within that room, a great generation of painters repaired.

The building hummed with nine hundred students strong, instructed in nineteen various classes, provided either during the day or in the evening. They seemed to gravitate to the traditional and the conventional, but somehow I sensed they were deviating. Revolution was on the horizon. Artistic styles and preferences would eventually grow and become their own; but for now, they were mere pupils, hungry for the knowledge of the great masters. And to this end, perhaps subconsciously, they submitted to their learned instructors . . . at least then.

Across the hall from the library was the Antique Preparatory class. With few exceptions, every new student entered here. The room was long and rectangular, with a row of tall windows on either side. A high partition of black bagging fabric traversed the room's length. Screens made of the same black fabric partitioned the area around each window so that the long room was divided into a dozen smaller working areas, each twelve feet square and illuminated by the light of a single window.

In each of these little workshops, a handful of men and women of all ages sat on stools and, with charcoal, scratched out drawings of white plaster hands, feet, and other geometrical forms that dangled from strings tacked to the partitions. These shapes and forms are called blocks. One had to master the blocks first before moving on to the next class.

John Henry Twachtman, the American impressionist painter, taught this class. He gave each student a separate task to achieve for that week. For some, it was to outline the object and establish the proportions. For those who had accomplished this, it was to capture the lights and darks of the object. And for others, it was to blend the two together, seamlessly. Mr. Twachtman would glide from room to room and stand behind the students as they drew, chastising them if they would use their thumb or the stump of the charcoal to darken or blur the lines.

"Achieve it knowingly with the point; do not stumble upon it with the stump," he would say.

The day would finally arrive when the students' work was reviewed and critiqued. If a task was satisfactorily completed, Mr. Twachtman instructed the successful candidate to move on to the

Taught by John Henry Twachtman, the Antique Preparatory Class of the Art Students League is where beginning students first learn classical drawing techniques, using models called "blocks"—plaster casts of geometrical forms, hands, feet, and heads. Engraving by two unknown artists. Harper's New Monthly Magazine, **October 1891.**

next in order to learn and demonstrate new skills. Some weeks or months later, once the student excelled at drawing the most difficult block—a head or torso of Greek or Roman origin—he or she would simply disappear. Yet everyone knew this was a good thing. The student had excelled and was going upstairs, where he would attend one of the three Antique Classes taught by Kenyon Cox, James Carroll Beckwith, and Willard Metcalf.

The Antique Class derives its name from the plaster casts that serve as the artists' models. Under diffused light, casts of body parts from Greek, Roman, and Renaissance times become the center of attention. Students would gather around the subject, standing in front of an easel or squatting on a low stool before an upturned chair, and would sketch with charcoal or conté crayon on paper or artist board. The critique of their work would be more rigorous than the evaluations of the Preparatory Class. The instructor might say that the shade is entirely too dark, prompting the student to pull out a thin paper pipe to blow off the excess charcoal. Or he might say that a line needs to be removed entirely. A small lump of bread easily becomes an eraser.

After mastering the Antique Class, the student moves to a side room for the Concours Antique Class. Here, the models are life-size plaster casts of Greek and Roman marble statues. Students work for a week to capture the essence of the subject. The drawings are then submitted to the instructor, and the one that is judged to be the best entitles the winner to move up and onward to the next

James Carroll Beckwith's Concours Antique Class at The Art Students League. Engraving by an unknown artist. Harper's New Monthly Magazine, *October 1891.*

floor, where the Life Classes are provided. This is where one first learns to draw the living figure.

Four teachers—Kenyon Cox, Willard Metcalf, Benjamin Fitz, and H. Siddons Mowbray—presided over the Life Classes. And the four classes were divided and segregated so that there were two classes for men and two for women.

The class for men occupied a large attic on the building's top floor, where, upon first entering, the uninitiated would smell the pungent scent of paint and sweet pipe tobacco. A large skylight illuminates the studio by day, and by night, glass-domed gaslight fixtures brighten the room. Wooden beams bear the sentiments of earlier students: "Draw firm and be jolly." Here, there are no stools, no upturned chairs, and no partitions with black bagging. This is the class to which all artists aspire. Plaster casts and Grecian friezes line the walls, along with images of great master painters and sketches of notable alumni. To me, this was home; this is where great artists are born.

Around the center of the room, the students cluster with their tall easels, gazing intensely at what stands before them. Their hands move quickly and confidently over artist board and canvas. They glance upward; what is there on a platform is not a plaster statue but a live young woman.

She is entirely nude.

She is posing.

Her body holds fast.

Her eyes are fixed. She is completely immobile.

The students' hands move freely and confidently. They draw what they see.

The task at hand is daunting. The level of concentration is unfathomable. Now, one has to look at color, motion, and the subtleties that permeate life itself. It is here where amateurs are distinguished from true artists and where true artists become living legends.

Once a drawing is conceived and then accepted, the student graduates to paint and brush. With it, there is much more freedom. Yet much more is expected.

"Your line is too hard," the instructor says. "Look at the model and note how the edges melt into atmosphere."

"The color of the face is violent," he barks to another student. "Your man looks as though he were suffering from an attack of apoplexy."

The instructor may comment on the shadow on a neck. "It is too dark," he says, "and besides, it is opaque. A shadow should be transparent and show the flesh beneath it."

What is a student to do?

"Try it over again, and get the value right to begin with," he commands sternly.

For a half hour, the model stands. Then, there is a rest. When the model resumes, the painter paints. And the instructor criticizes again. To the uninitiated, the admonishment is harsh.

The figure is too wooden.

Stop worrying about the eyebrows and fingernails; get the proportions right first.

There is mass, solidity, and depth. Look at that. Capture the weight, the thickness. Details later.

The more one advances, the slower one succeeds. The constant criticism builds humility. The student's own skin becomes toughened by it, and he becomes more aware, more confident, and much more self-assured. It is only through sheer perseverance and hard work that the task at hand is eventually accomplished and victory seized. Many months continue before that occurs.

Next is the Still-Life Class taught by William Merritt Chase.

Mr. Chase became my mentor. He taught me much of what I know about painting.

Men and women crowd into his room. Easels stand next to each other, with one behind the other. A skylight and side window illuminate the subject matter on a central table: a brass pot, a carrot, two split lemons, a knife, and several bottles.

Mr. Chase peers over the students' easels. *Quickly, quickly, but firmly. Yes! Just like that. Yes. Now, scrape it off. Assume another vantage point and start over.*

Chase taught the students to paint with rapidity and confidence. Paintings would be done within a few hours. These were not finished works. Canvases would be reused and painted over a dozen times or more. This was only practice.

The League had many other classes as well.

Three Sketch Classes were taught three times a week. A Costume Class was taught six times every week. There, students cluster around a central platform, on top of which is usually seated a young girl reading a book. Easels would be in front and, behind them, students working in a variety of media.

Augustus Saint-Gaudens, a brilliant sculptor who was known for his Civil War memorials and later for designing US coins, trained some of the finest sculptors of the era. Twice a day in his Sculpture Class, he would instruct with wet clay.

The Sketch Class. Sketch by an unknown artist. Harper's New Monthly Magazine*, October 1891.*

The Modeling Class of Augustus Saint-Gaudens. Sketch by an unknown artist. Harper's New Monthly Magazine, October 1891.

When one had achieved a certain degree of accuracy and adeptness in painting, the highest and most respected department in the school was entered—the Portrait Class. William Merritt Chase, J. Alden Weir, and Benjamin Fitz were the instructors.

With painting portraits, the objective is clear yet challenging. One must seize with paint and brush a person's likeness—the flesh, the subtleties, and much more, including dress, accessories, and background. A model might pose in the same way each day for a month or more. Astute observation is required. Individuality becomes more encouraged. Criticism is everywhere.

Portrait painting proved to be the most formidable area of the arts and required the most amount of time. A painter was not simply applying color and line to canvas but immortalizing a human being with character. With a portrait, the face was primary,

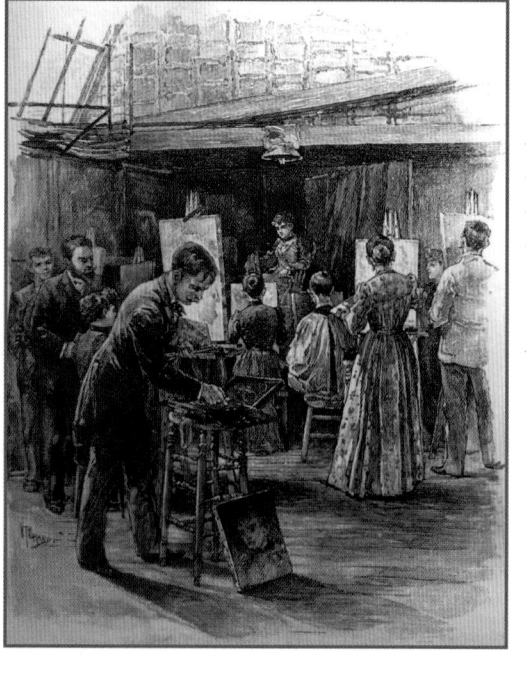

William Merritt Chase's Portrait Class. Chase is at the far left, with mustache and trimmed beard. Engraving by an unknown artist from the October 1891 edition of Harper's New Monthly

everything else became secondary. The artist is not so concerned with reproducing every thread of a piece of lace, every vane of a feather, or every facet of a jewel. Those would come later and would be painted simply as mere suggestions. The instructor would admonish, *Concentrate on the face. Observe the shadow. Focus on the tones.*

A fellow pupil would light up and criticize the student standing next to him in an effort to best his counterpart. *That's a false color. How do you see that? There is no line there. The shadow falls over there, not where you paint it. Look closely, my good friend. Look closely . . . .*

Observation is everything. If one looks closely, one will truly see.

In portrait painting, character is the essential ingredient and yet the most difficult to reproduce. The young woman posing for the portrait may be a lady of culture who attends fancy dress balls, lavish debutante cotillions, or operas. She may be a musician, a writer, or a simple worker in a garment factory. Humble or vain, whoever she is, her face will subtly reveal her true character. One might glimpse at a person's inner self, but to capture it is truly rare. Some painters can do it. The very best can seize one's soul.

Students at the League stayed for as long as they wanted. There was no established time for graduation. In fact, there was no graduation or even grades. Some had been there for more than six years, even though the average time was between two and five years. The age of students varied, as did their level of expertise. The school prepares the student and provides the skills needed and an understanding of the methods and tools that a great artist would use.

Some students, upon leaving, would go on to become designers, engravers, teachers of art—and, of course, well-known artists. A few, however, never aspired to any of these occupations and merely joined to enhance their understanding of the field. And yet many others who sought out greatness often failed to find it. They are completely forgotten and are nowhere to be found in the annals of history. But so is life. . . .

It is up to the student to become successful. Talent and perseverance are everything. To become great, one must want it more than anything.

[Nancy's Voice]

But what about you, Howard? You have told me so much about the school that you attended but nothing about your time there. Please tell me.

The glow of the dancing firelight turned Howard's face pink. His eyes sparkled in the reddish flicker of the darkness.

I will, only another day. It's getting late.

I know it is, and I am sorry kept you from your work.

No, not at all. I like reminiscing about those early years.

And I enjoy hearing about them. Please tell me more.

I will, but I think it's time that I take you to that place I mentioned—the one that might give you the answer to your earlier question.

About living forever?
Yes.
When?
Tomorrow . . . in the morning. We'll ride there on horseback.
It's not too far from here.

THE NEXT DAY, following breakfast, Howard and I gathered our long duster coats and walked across the lawn to the lower floor of the barn, where the horses were stabled. A thick fog had rolled in. The sun pierced the diffused air, making it appear like the rays of heaven were shining down around us.

We led two horses out of their stalls, bridled and saddled them, and walked them into the pasture, where we mounted and traveled north. The fog was just lifting, and the trees shimmered once again like silver candelabra.

Howard, why do the trees always look like silver when the fog rolls out. Is this more of your seamless magic?

No. Something much greater.

Tell me the secret.

Then it will spoil the magic, won't it?

No, please. Just tell me one of your secrets at least.

All right. In the night, small spiders climb up the trees and spin their silken webs on the bows and branches. The lacework survives through morning and is nearly invisible . . . until, of course, the fog sets in. That changes everything. The mist and morning dew stick to the gossamer, making it sparkle in the bright sun until the fog rolls out. Then, the magic vanishes.

I never noticed the spider webs.

You probably wouldn't. You have to look closely. Then, you will see.

But they are not there in the afternoon.

No. By then, they are gone, carried away by the wind. But at night, the spiders will return once again and spin their webs as they always do. Because that is what they do.

He smiled and said, *It's their special talent.*

We rode through the pasture and over several hills until we approached an embankment leading to a great sandstone ridge rising over the valley.

What a view!

Quite lovely, isn't it? We'll stop here.

Howard dismounted and then assisted me.

It is only a short distance on foot now.

We slowly descended the sloping embankment, until we arrived at a steep ledge at the ridge's summit. Below us was nothing but rocks and trees and the air above. To the ledge's side was a harrowing footpath leading to the north face.

Here—take my hand. It's a bit narrow and very treacherous.

As we carefully sidestepped our way along, a large, flat sandstone slab came into view.

Here it is, Nancy. This is what I wanted to show you.

The names of people were carved on its smooth surface, forming a list:

M. Geges

E. M. Porter

F. Holcomb

C. Huteins

N. Wyatt

H. Christy

B. Soubers

S. Dennis

R. Christy

Of all of the names, Howard's name was carved the deepest. Next to it was the date: December 30, 1891.

I looked at the darkened slab and was completely amazed and puzzled.

It's a rock!

Not just any rock. Look closely.

Well, I see it has your name on it, your sister Rose's name too, and the names of others. You did this in your youth. Didn't you?

The sandstone slab on the side of a ridge where Howard and others chiseled their names in 1891. (Collection of author)

In the winter '91, when I returned here from New York.

Whatever inspired you to carve your name on it?

A man by the name of Lewis Wetzel. He was a famous Indian hunter. When he was thirteen, Indians kidnapped him from his family. He escaped and then committed the rest of his life to hunting down and killing them. He was skilled at the Bowie knife, an expert with a tomahawk, and could even load, prime, and fire a long rifle while running through the woods at full speed.

An Indian hunter?

Yes, he was dark and swarthy with penetrating eyes and long black hair that reached down to his calves. Sometime when he was in the Muskingum Valley, tracking and hunting Indians in 1787, he carved his name on a stone, which bears his name today. It's in the northwest corner of Morgan County, about a mile from the Muskingum River, at a place called Wetzel's Rock.

What does it look like?

It's a slanted stone, much like this but much larger, and on its face is that of an Indian, along with a gun and the words "Enjoy the peace I have prepared for you. Engraved by me Lewis Whetzle."

With a smile on my face, I shot back, *Just the sort of thing that would make a nice painting. You painted him! Didn't you?*

Of course I did! And the stone and a dead Indian as well . . . all in one painting. For several weeks, it was exhibited in the show window of the Bauer Brothers Jewelry Store at the Clarendon Hotel in Zanesville. Then, it went straight to Chicago. Took first prize at the Columbian Exposition of '93.

What do you think Wetzel meant by "Enjoy the peace that I have prepared for you."

I would like to think he was referring to something sublime, but I think he just meant that he had cleared the area of Indians, and he wanted everyone who passed by to know it.

So he chose to carve his name on a rock, much like you did here?

Yes. I simply chiseled my name. There were no Indians to worry about when I was here in 1891.

Howard's 1892 painting of Lewis Wetzel (1763–1808), considered to be West Virginia's greatest early frontiersmen and one of the most fearless and skillful Indian fighters of the American post-colonial period. In this work, Wetzel has just shot an Indian and is carving his name on what is now called "Wetzel's Rock." (Private collection)

I paused for a moment, as I then realized the real reason Howard had written his name there.

You don't want to be forgotten. You want to be remembered.

His blue eyes turned from that moss-covered stone to mine.

We all do.

I kept pushing him to tell me the truth. *For as long as the world moves, you want people to know your name: Howard Chandler Christy. That's what you want, don't you?*

There is a part of all of us that wants to span the ages, to let others know that we once lived . . . we were once here, if only but for a brief moment.

"We are remembered by what we give," he said.

He then continued.

A painter paints. A sculptor sculpts. Some may carve their names on a rock or etch a signature on a pane of glass or a wooden beam. This is all simply done to let future generations know that they existed; that they lived then as much as you and I do now. You see, every artist wants his work to last forever, but it doesn't. It can't. Over time, it will only crack, fade or crumble.

Even a marble statue by Michelangelo?

Yes. Look around you! Those trees, this land, that river. Even the Barracks! Everything you see is really an illusion. Nothing in this world lasts forever, not even this old, weathered rock. All of it will be gone someday.

I understood what he said completely. Yet I still needed to know the answer to the question that burned within my heart.

But if you could, would you want to live forever?

He looked away and acted as if he didn't hear me, but I knew he did. Only he did not want to answer me, at least not at first, so I asked again. *Howard, do you want to live forever?*

His voice became a pensive whisper. *The gift of immortality. Everyone wants it.*

His face slowly turned to me. Although serious at first, he reflected a hint of a smile, as if I had asked a silly question that a young schoolgirl might pose to her sage and worldly teacher.

But this matter wasn't silly after all. It was real. He knew it was real, and he knew the truth.

But can we truly have it, Howard? Can we possibly live forever?

Of course we can. This was the promise that was made.

That was all he said.

My heart was put at ease, and I asked nothing more, for I put my trust in him.

We quietly climbed back up the side of the embankment, mounted our horses that had been grazing nearby, and, in the mid-morning light, returned home.

Howard never told me the secret to the gift of immortality, and I never pressed him any more about it. Eventually, I would learn what he had meant that day, but over half a century would come to pass before I did.

END OF BOOK ONE: THE MAGIC OF YOUTH

Howard and Nancy's romance continues in . . .

Romantic Illusions

the next book in the epic trilogy

An Affair with Beauty
The Mystique of Howard Chandler Christy

In *Romantic Illusions,* Nancy spends Christmas 1912 at the Barracks, where she learns of Howard's early years studying in near-poverty as an impoverished art student in New York City and his sudden ascent to stardom as the top pupil of William Merritt Chase, the premier portrait painter in America.

During the Great Flood of 1913—the worst tragedy the Midwest had ever experienced—Howard and Nancy sequester themselves high above the Muskingum River, as Howard tells her of his daring experiences with Teddy Roosevelt during the Spanish-American War in Cuba and his brush with near-certain death, no less than three times. The effects of the war profoundly transform Howard and his vision of beauty, inspiring an idea that becomes a dream made real—the Christy Girl—catapulting him to fame and fortune.

As Nancy's love for Howard deepens, he unexpectedly becomes distant, undoubtedly distracted by the unseemly press of his then-wife, Maebelle, but also troubled by the war looming in Europe. A divorce seems almost inevitable, yet Howard is slow to move. Curious about his past, Nancy is compelled to search deeper into his troubled marriage until she uncovers the shocking truth: his bout with alcoholism, his commitment to an insane asylum, his miraculous recovery from blindness, and his bitter child-custody battle with Maebelle over their little daughter, Natalie.

When World War I breaks out in Europe, Howard announces that he will return to New York City to live. Nancy remains undeterred, choosing to fight to remain by his side, even though it may mean losing her newfound home, a paradise she has come to love and consider as the legendary Fountain of Youth.

A List of Selected Books Illustrated By Howard Chandler Christy

1895   Rose Blanche Woodyear, *In Camphor*, New York, New York: G. P. Putnam's Sons, 1895.

Washington Irving, *Bracebridge Hall or the Humorists*, New York, New York: G. P. Putnam's Sons, 1895 (chapter head initial designs by Christy).

1896   Martha Finley, *Elsie Dinsmore*, New York, New York: Dodd, Mead & Co., 1896.

George Lansing Raymond, *A Poet's Cabinet*, New York, New York: G. P. Putnam, 1896.

1897   Richard Harding Davis, *Soldiers of Fortune*, New York, New York: Charles Scribner's Sons, 1897.

William Shakespeare, *The Tragedy of Hamlet, Prince of Denmark*, New York, New York: Dodd, Mead & Co., 1897.

1898   Richard Harding Davis, *The Cuban and Porto Rican Campaigns,* New York, New York: Charles Scribner's Sons, 1898.

W. Nephew King, *The Story of the Spanish-American War and the Revolt in the Philippines*, New York, New York: Peter Fenelon Collier & Son, 1898.

1899   Howard Chandler Christy, *Men of the Army and Navy; Characteristic Types of Our Fighting Men; Six Pastels in Colors*, New York, New York: Charles Scribner's Sons, 1899.

Howard Chandler Christy, *Pastel Portraits from the Romantic Drama; Pictures in Colors Drawn from Life*, New York, New York: Charles Scribner's Sons, 1899.

Richard Harding Davis, *The Lion and the Unicorn*, New York, New York: Charles Scribner's Sons, 1899.

1900   Howard Chandler Christy, *Types of the American Girl*, New York, New York: Charles Scribner's Sons, 1900.

Paul Leicester Ford, *Wanted—A Matchmaker*, New York, New York: Dodd, Mead & Co., 1900.

Thomas Nelson Page, *The Old Gentleman of the Black Stock*, New York, New York: Charles Scribner's Sons, 1900.

Maurice Thompson, *Alice of Old Vincennes*, Indianapolis, Indiana: Bowen-Merrill Co., 1900 (frontispiece by Christy).

Marcus J. Wright, *Official History of the Spanish-American War*, Washington, DC: War Records Office, 1900.

1901   George W. Cable, *The Cavalier*, New York, New York: Charles Scribner's Sons, 1901.

Winston Churchill, *The Crisis*, New York, New York: The MacMillan Co., 1901.

Evalyn Emerson, *Sylvia: The Story of an American Countess*, Boston, Massachusetts: Small, Maynard & Co. 1901.

Anthony Hope, *The Dolly Dialogues*, New York, New York, R. H. Russell, 1901.

William Dean Howells, *The Heroines of Fiction*, New York, New York, Harper & Brothers, 1901.

Frederick Palmer, *The Ways of the Service*, New York, New York: Charles Scribner's Sons, 1901.

1902   Cyrus Townsend Brady, *Woven with the Ship*, Philadelphia & London: J. B. Lippincott Company, 1902.

Robert W. Chambers, *The Maid-at-Arms*, New York, New York: Harper & Brothers, 1902.

Paul Leicester Ford, *Wanted—A Chaperon*, New York, New York: Dodd, Mead & Co., 1902.

Charles Major, *Dorothy Vernon of Haddon Hall*, New York, New York: The MacMillan Co., 1902.

Martha Morton, *Her Lord and Master*, Philadelphia, Pennsylvania: Drexel Biddle, 1902 (frontispiece by Christy).

Clara Morris, *A Pasteboard Crown*, New York, New York: Charles Scribner's Sons, 1902 (frontispiece by Christy).

James Whitcomb Riley, *An Old Sweetheart of Mine*, Indianapolis, Indiana: The Bobbs-Merrill Co., 1902.

John Philip Sousa, *The 5ᵗʰ String*, Indianapolis, Indiana: Bowen-Merrill Co., 1902.

1903   Frederic Stewart Isham, *Under the Rose*, Indianapolis, Indiana: The Bobbs-Merrill Co., 1903.

Henry Wadsworth Longfellow, *The Courtship of Miles Standish*, Indianapolis, Indiana: The Bobbs-Merrill Co., 1903.

F. Hopkinson Smith, *The Underdog*, New York, New York: Charles Scribner's Sons, 1903 (frontispiece by Christy).

Mrs. Humphry Ward, *Lady Rose's Daughter*, New York and London: Harper & Brothers, 1903.

1904   Howard Chandler Christy, *Music and Life: A Series of Drawings*, New York, New York: Charles Scribner's Sons, 1904.

James Whitcomb Riley, *Out to Old Aunt Mary's*, Indianapolis, Indiana: The Bobbs-Merrill Co., 1904.

Hallie Erminie Rives, *The Castaway*, Indianapolis, Indiana: The Bobbs-Merrill Co., 1904.

Brand Whitlock, *Her Infinite Variety*, Indianapolis, Indiana: The Bobbs-Merrill Co., 1904.

Brand Whitlock, *The Happy Average*, New York, New York: A. L. Burt Co., 1904.

1905   Howard Chandler Christy, *Drawings by Howard Chandler Christy, Reproductions in Black and White*, New York, New York: Moffat, Yard & Co., 1905.

Henry Wadsworth Longfellow, *Evangeline*, Indianapolis, Indiana: The Bobbs-Merrill Co., 1905..

Edward Sandford Martin, *The Courtship of a Careful Man*, New York, New York: Harper & Brothers, 1905.

Emma Dorothy Eliza Nevitte Southworth, *Ismael, or In the Depths*, New York, New York: A. L. Burt Co., 1905.

Emma Dorothy Eliza Nevitte Southworth, *Self-Raised*, New York, New York: A. L. Burt Co., 1905.

1906   Richard Harding Davis, *Ranson's Folly*, New York, New York: Charles Scribner's Sons, 1906.

Howard Chandler Christy, *The American Girl as Seen and Portrayed by Howard Chandler Christy*, New York, New York: Moffat, Yard & Co., 1906.

Howard Chandler Christy, *The Christy Girl*, Indianapolis, Indiana: The Bobbs-Merrill Co., 1906.

Arthur Ruhl, *A Break of Training and Other Athletic Stories*, New York, New York: The Outing Publishing Co., 1906 (frontispiece by Christy).

1907   Robert W. Chambers, *The Tree of Heaven*, New York, New York: D. Appleton & Co., 1907 (illustrated page 174).

Howard Chandler Christy, *Our Girls; Poems in Praise of the American Girl*, New York, New York: Moffat, Yard & Co., 1907.

Herbert Kaufman & May Isabel Fisk, *The Stolen Throne*, New York, New York: Moffat, Yard & Company, 1907.

Meredith Nicholson, *House of a Thousand Candles*, New York, New York: A. Wessels Co., 1907.

E. Phillips Oppenheim, *Berenice*, Boston, Massachusetts: Little, Brown & Co., 1907 (frontispiece by Christy).

1908   Howard Chandler Christy, *The Christy Book of Drawings*, New York, New York: Moffat, Yard & Co., 1908.

Winston Churchill, *A Modern Chronicle*, New York, New York: The MacMillan Co., 1908.

Edward Peple, *The Spitfire*, New York, New York: Moffat, Yard & Co., 1908.

James Whitcomb Riley, *Home Again with Me*, Indianapolis, Indiana: The Bobbs-Merrill Co., 1908.

Mrs. Wilson Woodrow [Nancy Mann Waddel Woodrow], *The Silver Butterfly*, Indianapolis, Indiana: The Bobbs-Merrill Co., 1908.

Various illustrators, *A Book of Sweethearts: Pictures by Famous American Artists*, New York, New York: Grosset & Dunlap, 1908.

1909   Ross Beeckman, *The Last Woman*, New York, New York: W. J. Watt & Co., 1909 (frontispiece by Christy).

George Eliot, *Two Lovers*, New York, New York: Moffat, Yard & Co., 1909.

Hudson Douglas, *The Lantern of Luck*, New York, New York: W. J. Wyatt, 1909.

Edith Macvane, *The Black Flier*, New York, New York: Moffat, Yard & Co., 1909.

James Whitcomb Riley, *Riley Roses*, Indianapolis, Indiana: The Bobbs-Merrill Co., 1909.

Mary Roberts Rinehart, *The Man in Lower Ten*, Indianapolis, Indiana: The Bobbs-Merrill Co., 1909.

Charles Somerville and Thompson Buchanan, *A Woman's Way*, New York, New York: Grosset & Dunlap, 1909.

Louis Tracy, *A Son of the Immortals*, New York, New York: E. J. Clode, 1909.

Grace Miller White, *Tess of the Storm County*, New York, New York: Grosset & Dunlap, 1909.

1910 Frederick Orin Bartlett, *The Prodigal Pro Tem*, Boston, Massachusetts: Small, Maynard & Co., 1910.

Stephen Chalmers, *When Love Calls Men to Arms*, Boston, Massachusetts: Small, Maynard & Co., 1910.

Howard Chandler Christy, *Songs of Sentiment*, New York, New York: Moffat, Yard and Co., 1910.

Gordon Holmes, *The de Bercy Affair*, New York, New York: Grosset & Dunlap, 1910.

Harold MacGrath, *A Splendid Hazard*, Indianapolis, Indiana: The Bobbs-Merrill Co., 1910.

E. Phillips Oppenheim, *The Lost Ambassador*, Boston, Massachusetts: Little, Brown & Co., 1910.

Ralph Pulitzer, *New York Society on Parade*. New York, New York: Harper and Brothers, 1910.

James Whitcomb Riley, *The Girl I Loved*, Indianapolis, Indiana: The Bobbs-Merrill Co., 1910.

James Whitcomb Riley*, A Hoosier Romance*, Indianapolis, Indiana: The Bobbs-Merrill Co., 1910 (cover illustration by Christy).

Louis Tracy, *Cynthia's Chauffer*, New York, New York: Edward J. Clode, 1910.

Sir Walter Scott, *The Lady of the Lake*, Indianapolis, Indiana: The Bobbs-Merrill Co., 1910.

1911 Rex Beach, *The Ne'er Do Well*, New York, New York: A. L. Burt Co., 1911.

E. Phillips Oppenheim, *Havoc*, New York, New York: A. L. Burt Co., 1911.

James Whitcomb Riley, *When She Was About Sixteen*, Indianapolis, Indiana: The Bobbs-Merrill Co., 1911.

Mary Roberts Rinehart, *The Amazing Adventures of Letitia Carberry*, Indianapolis, Indiana: The Bobbs-Merrill Co., 1911.

Alfred Lord Tennyson, *The Princess*, Indianapolis, Indiana: The Bobbs-Merrill Co., 1911.

1912 John A. Sleicher, ed., *At the Front with the Army and Navy*, New York, New York: Leslie-Judge Co., 1912.

Howard Chandler Christy, *Liberty Belles: Eight Epochs in the Making of the American Girl*, Indianapolis, Indiana: The Bobbs-Merrill Co., 1912.

Juliet Wilbor Thompkins, *Pleasures and Places*, New York, New York: A. L. Burt Co., 1912.

1913 Gouveneur Morris, *The Penalty*, New York, New York: Charles Scribner's Sons, 1913.

James Whitcomb Riley, *Good-bye, Jim*, Indianapolis, Indiana: The Bobbs-Merrill Co., 1913.

Marie Van Vorst, *His Love Story*, Indianapolis, Indiana: The Bobbs-Merrill Co., 1913.

1914 George Lansing Raymond, *A Poet's Cabinet*, New York, New York: G. P. Putnam's Sons, 1914.

James Whitcomb Riley, *A Discouraging Model*, Indianapolis, Indiana: The Bobbs-Merrill Co., 1914.

James Whitcomb Riley, *Old Fashioned Roses*, Indianapolis, Indiana: The Bobbs-Merrill Co., 1914.

Various authors and artists, *King Albert's Book, A Tribute to the Belgian King and People from Representative Men and Women throughout the World*, London, United Kingdom: the *Daily Telegraph* in conjunction with the *Daily Sketch*, the *Glasgow Herald*, and Hodder and Stoughton,

Christmas, 1914.

1915 Gouveneur Morris, *The Seven Darlings*, New York, New York: Charles Scribner's Sons, 1915.

1916 Richard Harding Davis, *Van Bibber and Others (The Novels and Stories of Richard Harding Davis)*, New York, New York: Charles Scribner's Sons, 1916.

Owen Johnson, *The Woman Gives*, Boston, Massachusetts: Little, Brown & Co., 1916.

James Whitcomb Riley, *The Complete Works of James Whitcomb Riley*, New York, New York: Harper & Brothers, 1916.

1918 Grace Miller White, *Judy of Rogues' Harbor*, New York, New York: Grosset & Dunlap, 1918.

1923 Samuel G. Blythe, *A Calm Review of a Calm Man (Warren G. Harding)*, New York, New York: Cosmopolitan Book Corporation, 1923 (frontispiece is Christy's portrait of Harding).

1924 Mrs. Wilson Woodrow [Nancy Mann Waddel Woodrow], *The Second Chance*, New York, New York: W. J. Watt & Co., 1924 (frontispiece by Christy).

1937 Sol Bloom, *The Story of the Constitution*, US Constitution Sesquicentennial Commission, House Office Building, Washington, DC, 1937 (cover illustration only).

Author's Note

A QUARTER CENTURY AGO, when I became enchanted with the life of Howard Chandler Christy, I slowly learned that his epic story was very much alive in America, only it had yet to be unearthed and told. In the years following, I uncovered thousands of newspaper articles featuring him and his wife, Nancy—many celebrating the then-famous couple as "connoisseurs of beauty"— but there was not one single book about either of them. This intrigued me, but what I eventually encountered inspired me all the more.

At the US Capitol in Washington, DC, no fewer than six of Christy's portraits of senators and representatives of Congress adorn its walls, as does *The Scene at the Signing of the US Constitution*, the largest painting on canvas there. In the White House, two of three portraits by his hand are prominently displayed, one of First Lady Grace Goodhue Coolidge, which defines the executive mansion's "China Room," and another of former First Lady Rachel Jackson, wife of President Andrew Jackson. In the US Department of State, Christy's rendering of Secretary of State Charles Evans Hughes catches the eyes of all who pass through its richly decorated diplomatic rooms. His colorful World War I posters still line the walls of many American military recruiting offices, nearly a century after those images were created. And his nude paintings—as risqué by today's standards as they were decades ago when he painted them—continue to draw throngs of patrons to New York City's famed Café des Artistes restaurant and its successor, the Leopard—a testament to the longevity of the artist's incomparable art and a reminder of the public's continued admiration of his distinctive style and talent. These are but a few examples of Christy's artistic legacy. There are a host of state capitols, museums, governors' houses, and other places throughout America where Christy's works are prominently displayed.

Although many decades had passed since he departed from this earth, Christy's achievements were never truly forgotten. They just lay dormant, locked within the American subconscious but waiting for just the right moment to be rediscovered and appreciated once more. With this, I longed to know more about the incomparable life of Howard Chandler Christy, as I did his model, muse, and wife, Nancy. For who could ever dare to write about a great man without describing the true inspiration behind him—a great woman?

If one looks closely, there was not just one great woman behind Christy's success but several—the Christy Girls. They, along with this extraordinary artist, made his epic tale truly unfold. Yet there was something even more striking, more powerful that compelled me to dedicate over a decade of my life to writing the story.

回

IN 2006, WHEN I BEGAN WORK on the introduction to *The Magic of Youth*, the first book in this trilogy, I quickly realized that Christy's life exemplified the quintessential American story—the American dream—which, over time, had transformed itself into one giant jigsaw puzzle, the pieces of which were dispersed and lay scattered throughout the United States in the most unlikely of places.

From Maine to Hawaii and from Illinois to Florida, the faded and sometimes tattered bits of this puzzle could still be found. Many pieces—such as the archive of his personal correspondence now housed in the Skillman Library at Lafayette College in Easton, Pennsylvania—had once been stuffed in trash bags and left to molder in the musty Wayne Township root cellar of Nancy Christy's sister-in-law, Jane Conneen. In 1999, while visiting

Jane, Lafayette College archivist Diane Shaw discovered them "by chance" and, with Jane's permission, saved them.

Other pieces had been utterly forgotten, such as the artist's memoirs, as transcribed and typed by Christy's favorite model, Elise Ford. By pure luck, Elise's daughter, Holly, found her mother's work abandoned in the corner shadow of a dilapidated garage near her aunt Doris's farmhouse in the Berkshire Hills of Massachusetts. The ream of paper was entombed in a battered tin box and sat undisturbed below the entangled vines swallowing the garage's crumbling walls. Holly rescued the fragile pages and preserved them.

Some pieces had not seen the light of day in almost a century, as they were buried underneath the towers of files in the dusty attic of Zanesville, Ohio's Muskingum County Courthouse. And a few were brought to light after much searching in nondescript boxes matching thousands of others, lining the massive rows of shelves in the bowels of the United States Archives in Washington, DC.

Still others turned up only after my discovery of two photos at the Smithsonian American Art Museum, seemingly identical 1938 portraits of a glamorous woman but each with a different hairstyle and hair color. One was titled *Mrs. Hobart Ramsey* and the other, *Collette Ramsey*. This prompted further investigation, and a letter, with the two photographs enclosed, was sent to the New York City address of the Deafness Research Foundation. The elusive Mrs. Ramsey founded the charity in 1958, and it had since grown to become America's leading source of private funding for hearing research. My letter was a long shot, to be sure, but it paid off. Weeks later, I received a phone call from the mysterious woman in those portraits, Collette Ramsey Baker. She was Christy's close friend and model—a true Christy Girl. Collette later invited me to her home in Vero Beach, Florida, to interview her and view her collection of Christy paintings, including the finished portrait Christy had painted of her. When I asked her why he had repainted her head to reflect a different hairstyle and hair color, she simply said, "Well, you know how women are."

A remarkable quantity of information came to me unsolicited and, quite eerily, at the right time. Whenever I seemed to be missing a piece to the puzzle, I would invariably receive a phone call, a letter in the mail, or a package containing the precise information for which I had been searching. In a few cases, original photos, newspaper clippings, and even Christy's handwritten correspondence were generously given. At one point, I received custody of a life-size oil painting of Christy's favorite model, Elise Ford. The handsomely framed 1935 Christy painting came into my possession just days after I developed writer's block on a passage I was completing about Elise for a subsequent book about the artist's models. The owner, Sean West, whom I had met by happenstance two years earlier through a random Internet query, asked me to take care of his treasured artwork. Once the painting was delivered to my office, the writer's block magically disappeared. And not long after, newspaper columnist John Kelly of the *Washington Post* arrived at my doorstep to take photos of the painting because he wanted to do a story about its missing history. Ironically, when Sean acquired the

Howard, painting Collette Ramsey, in his studio in 1938 (Collection of Collette Ramsey Baker)

work in 1985, it had been forgotten and neglected. Someone had slathered garish yellow paint over the entire canvas, yet left the faces of Elise and the children standing next to her still visible. Sean salvaged the work and had it expertly restored.

In the end, despite the many years and the possibilities of what might have been, the Christy story was never truly lost. The pieces of this grand puzzle were miraculously still there, saved from harm's way, waiting to be rediscovered and resurrected like some ancient statue reemerging from centuries of earth and rubble.

Howard's finished portrait of Collette Ramsey, also known as "Mrs. Hobart Ramsey" (Collection of Collette Ramsey Baker)

Sean West (left) and Howard's painting of Elise Ford, warning against the dangers of railroad crossings. Sean's quest to learn the mysterious 50-year gap in its provenance prompted an article in the December 28, 2013 edition of The Washington Post. (Collection of author)

◻

SADLY, SEVERAL CHRISTY GIRLS who greatly contributed to this book passed away before they could see it published. Collette Ramsey Baker left us on May 9, 2010, as did her devoted husband, Maurice, on August 15, 2012. On one Sunday afternoon in the summer of 2007, Collette kept me spellbound with her intimate knowledge and "affectionate friendship" of Howard, Nancy, and Elise during the 1930s and 1940s. She also graciously supplied me with nearly three decades of the artist's correspondence to her. When my eyes first saw Collette, I could immediately see why Christy was so fond of her. She was just as beautiful, vivacious, and fine as he had described her exactly seventy years earlier in one of his many letters.

One of the greatest joys of writing this work was becoming great friends with Jocelyn Johnston Green, a Christy Girl model from the late 1940s and a close acquaintance of the artist; his wife, Nancy; daughter, Natalie; and granddaughter, Carolyn. She also knew Elise Ford and Elise's daughter, Holly, quite well. As Jocelyn's mother, Ruth, was once Nancy's confidant, Jocelyn soon became mine, as we corresponded with each other weekly, if not daily, by phone, letter, or e-mail. On two occasions, she traveled by herself over eight hundred miles by car to my home, every time bringing another piece of the Christy legacy and expressing confidence that I would find a new place for each. From the Christy's 1920s mahjong set to Nancy's silk nightgown, purchased in Italy in 1927 when Howard painted the portraits of Prince Umberto I and Mussolini, Jocelyn's gifts from the Christys became gifts to me. They are now a part of the Christy archive at Lafayette College and preserved in her honor. Aside from her steadfast friendship, Jocelyn's greatest gift to me was her living memory. Through her vivid stories and colorful anecdotes, she became my eyes and ears for Nancy during the last days of Howard's life, his star-studded funeral, and those long, dark months when the widowed Nancy secluded herself in the studio apartment, only to find happiness once again when former horse show jockey Bobby Conneen entered her life. Jocelyn helped me find Nancy's "worldly wise" voice, reviewing and editing the chapters of *The Magic of Youth* to ensure that each detail was correct. Surrounded by her family, Jocelyn peacefully passed away on Labor Day 2013.

I will be forever indebted to Maxine Christy Peters, Howard's grandniece, who regaled me with colorful family stories and personal recollections of her uncle Howard and his brother (her grandfather) Bernard Christy. She also entrusted me with Christy family treasures—original photographs, cards, letters, personal notes, and clippings—which her daughter, Mollie Hedges, and son, Tracie Peters, graciously transmitted to me over the course of three years. After a long life, Maxine passed away on May 15, 2010. Her children told me how proud she was to be a Christy, and it showed every time we talked or corresponded.

回

NUMEROUS OTHER PEOPLE helped to fulfill my dream of writing Christy's biography. Many of those people will be thanked in the subsequent books in the trilogy, where their assistance proved to be invaluable. However, it is impossible to complete this first book without giving my heartfelt thanks and appreciation to those who not only provided significant information but extended to me great encouragement and inspiration, along with love and support.

Words alone are not enough to express my gratitude to Jaye and Melodie Hayes, the owners of the Barracks and the keepers of the Christy flame. They invited me to give the keynote address at the Christy Centennial Celebration in June 2009 and then opened their home to me (and my wife and daughter) many times, over many seasons so that I could walk in the footsteps of Howard and Nancy and absorb the beauty of the land and river, just as they did a century before. Their kindness and generosity will never be forgotten.

Marilyn Schafer, Howard's grandniece, entertained me one warm October afternoon in 2009 at the Barracks with stories of her uncle Howard, father Howard Paul Christy, and grandfather and grandmother, Bernard and Maud Christy. From that, a lasting friendship was forged and many more personal recollections from her followed. Marilyn's keen interest in her uncle Howard's story is truly an inspiration, as is she.

Spirited, witty, and intelligent, Christy Girl Olga Steckler recounted for me her years as a stunning model, not just for Christy but for the "dean of calendar girls" Rolf Armstrong, illustrator and portrait painter Bradshaw Crandell, and iconic photographer Philippe Halsman. Like many other Christy Girls I had interviewed, Olga considered Howard one of the greatest men she ever knew.

I cannot find enough words to thank Jane Conneen and her family for protecting Christy's papers and generously donating them to Lafayette College. The Conneen family, which includes Joseph Conneen Sr., Joseph Conneen Jr., Barney and Olga Conneen, and Anne Conneen Thompson, provided me with many entertaining anecdotes and numerous photos of Nancy later in life, along with her husband, Bobby. I am only sorry that Jane and Joe Sr. did not live long enough to see the fruits of their efforts.

I am also especially grateful to Maebelle Christy's grandnieces, Elsie Thompson Johnson, Jennie Madden Craig, and Joyce Rammel, as well as her grandnephew, Bill Madden, noted sports writer for the *New York Daily News*. Each of them, in some way, provided greater insight into Maebelle's life and character.

Fred Grant shared stories of his "Uncle Smitty" (Walter Smith, one of Christy's male models) and confirmed the story that what few Christy illustrations remained at the Barracks were later used to patch up the Christy barn and chicken coop. Vibeke Lichten and Joel Assouline granted me the rare opportunity to spend a memorable December morning in Christy's once-famous Hotel des Artistes studio apartment. Charlie Stebbins and his sister, Jane Riddle, provided files and photos from their father, the late

Zanesville editor Claire Stebbins, and shed light on Howard's mysterious farm manager, Noel Talbot, while filling in the gap as to the identities of his female models at the time he lived at the Barracks. Dale Meyers Cooper, a much-beloved instructor at the Arts Students League and the historian of the Hotel des Artistes, provided me with the rich history of the cooperative apartment building and the missing Café des Artistes murals.

Various institutions, both public and private, opened their doors to my research requests, and numerous people helped track down information and sources, the importance of which gave this story its depth and authenticity. Diane Shaw and Elaine Stomber of Lafayette College were absolutely invaluable. Not only did they graciously permit me free rein of the Christy archives for a period of three weeks over the span of eight years, but they and their support staff promptly answered my numerous research requests and copied and scanned many documents and photos. Thanks also goes to Mitzi Shook, former archivist of the Muskingum County Court of Common Pleas, Zanesville, Ohio, who trudged though the dark and dusty attic of the court in search of long-forgotten pleading files, merely because I knew they had to be there, somewhere; Julianne Lothes, deputy clerk of the Muskingum County Court of Common Pleas, Probate Division, for tracking down the death certificates and probate records of Christy's family; Cindy Schaad, deputy clerk of the Morgan County Circuit Court, who helped solve a mystery that has baffled me since I began researching Christy's life—the artist was actually born in 1872 rather than 1873, as previously thought; Susan Tell of the Surrogate's Court for New York County, New York, who provided the probate documents for Howard, Nancy, and others; Elbert Yurian, who gave me Mary Christy's family genealogy and invited me to photograph his family scrapbooks; Dr. Gordon Lloyd of Pepperdine University; Bill Davis, legislative archivist of the

National Archives, Washington, DC, who guided me through the maze of metal-shelved tunnels that form the largest repository of information ever assembled in the world and, in doing so, became my good friend; Rob Hudson, associate archivist at the Carnegie Hall Archives, who provided invaluable information about Charles Dana Gibson's once-famous studio perched high above the legendary music hall; Andrew Thomas and the Smithsonian Institution's American Art Museum, who permitted me to review the huge number of Christy painting photographs in the Peter Juley and Son Collection; Amy Kesting, registrar of the Zanesville Art Museum; Melanie Knapp of the Columbus Art Museum; Mike Pintauro of the Parrish Art Museum; Jan Alexander of Widener University; Jane Marsek of Ferncliff Cemetery; Randy Sowell, archivist of the Harry S. Truman Library; Cathy Coburn Ives O'Brien and Marguerite Ives Beavers, granddaughters of James Montgomery Flagg, who instilled great insight into the life of their illustrious grandfather and close friend of Christy; Dr. Barbara Wolanin, curator of the Office of the Architect of the US Capitol; Bob Hudovernik, the author of *Jazz Age Beauties* and an expert on Christy contemporary photographer, Alfred Cheney Johnston, who photographed many of the models Christy painted; Sybil Light, philanthropy coordinator of the Guideposts Foundation and the editor of its inspirational magazine, *Daily Guideposts*; George Hart, archivist of the Peale Center for Christian Living and historian for the Peale organizations who, through his kind efforts, provided invaluable information about Christy's strong religious convictions; the Peale Family for allowing me access to the papers of Dr. and Mrs. Norman Vincent Peale housed at Syracuse University; Nicollette Dobrowolski of Syracuse University, who marshaled numerous boxes of correspondence for my hardworking assistant, Debbie Olson, to wade through; the Ohio Historical Society; Donald Handelman, financial adviser and good friend to Marjorie Merriweather Post, who was, in turn, good friends with Howard and Nancy; Gerald Green; Randy Green; Barb Schafer; the Miss America Organization; and Holly Berman and Jordan

Berman of the Illustrated Gallery, Fort Washington, Pennsylvania, who permitted me the use of Christy's drawing of Dorothy Dianne.

I extend a special thanks to Holly Longuski for her longstanding friendship, knowledge, patience, and perseverance. Many of the details in this trilogy about Elise Ford, Howard, Nancy, and the Christy studio were obtained through her kindness and magnanimity. Her words have lifted my spirits and given me courage to sail forward through the ever-changing tide, and through her, I discovered an enchanting, glamorous world I never knew existed and many untold stories waiting to be written.

THERE WERE QUITE A FEW INDIVIDUALS who spurred me on and, with their gentle words and kind endeavors, encouraged me to capture Christy's life. Vits Knuble, a brilliant Maine painter and portraitist, infused within me many years ago a deep passion for portraiture and a keen understanding that American illustrators produced some of the best art that the world has ever seen. T. A. D. Tharpe, Director of Fine Arts for Sloans and Kenyon Auctions, sold to me my first Christy painting and pushed me to keep writing. Helen Copley, who through her book, *The Christy Quest*, and our e-mail correspondence, inspired me to dig further in my research. She promised that many miracles would happen, and indeed they have. The late Walt Reed was always willing to "pull out the Christys" for me when I visited his gallery, Illustration House, in New York City. The late Charles Martignette, whose astounding collection of Christy works decorated the pages of art magazines in the 1990s and early 2000s, fueled my passion for Christy. Judy Goffman Cutler and her husband, Lawrence, who have written several books on the illustrators of the Golden Age of Illustration, have won my deep admiration and respect as they tirelessly strive to preserve the legacy of the American illustrators at their grand museum in Newport, Rhode Island. Author and muralist Glenn Palmer-Smith, Christy collector Jeff Rich, illustration collector

Richard Kelly, and philanthropist Susan Gottlieb forged important connections for me, for which I will always be thankful. Paula Conway provided invaluable assistance in the publication of my book. If I were going to write a bible on beauty, she would be in the book of Genesis.

I am deeply indebted to those who assisted with editing the book, especially to my former English and journalism teacher, the award-winning Kevin N. Keegan, whose insights have polished the narrative to a brilliant sheen. Had it not been for Kevin and his profound influence upon me since the young age of sixteen, I would never have been able to write this series. Laura Atkinson's sage advice as editor, research assistant, and public-relations expert extraordinaire lifted my work to new heights. My loving parents, James and Phyllis Head, pored through many rough drafts of this book, and their comments advanced the book's structure and ease of reading. Best of all, they ingrained within me a love of art, architecture, history, and the English language. Forever, I am grateful to them.

Countless individuals read the book's introduction and listened to the many stories and anecdotes I had to tell. I, therefore, wish to acknowledge the efforts and comments of Learetta Parrett, Linda Rigsby, Paul Caron, Melody Rosenberry, Dr. Alan Dayhoff, Charles and Theresa Hoyt, Lisa Waller, Paul Hartley, Elizabeth Baldwin, Desi Sedgewick, Anh Lee, Tanya Harvey, Larry Salans, Connie Benesh, Paul McConnell, Tressie Tucker, Paul Hartley, Gil and Marcia Siegert, and Robert and Bette Finkelmeier. They were my benevolent critics and my encouraging supporters. By their kind and helpful comments, they persuaded me to continue writing about the life of this extraordinary man and his wife.

Thanks also goes to Jane Lahr and Lyn Delliquadri, with Lahr & Partners Literary Agents, whose dutiful effort to refine my book proposal and manuscript resulted in a tighter, more focused product. My sincere appreciation goes to my fantastic graphics designer Iman Jordan, and to Aaron McMenamy, Kate Ankofski, and all of the other folks at North Loop Books and Hillcrest Media for bringing this story to life.

My daughter, Christianna, often warned me that when she reads my book, she will skip to the end because she wants to learn how Christy truly died. Well, she will have to wait until the third book in the trilogy. For now, perhaps she will read this acknowledgment and know how dearly thankful I am for her and for her love and unfailing understanding for the long journey I had to complete.

My greatest thanks is saved for my loving wife and muse, Rita. Her boundless love and continuing support, patience, and wisdom—along with her rare beauty, both inside and out—makes her my very own "Christy Girl." If I am dreaming, please don't ever wake me up.

My final thanks go to Howard and Nancy Christy, for it is in their extraordinary lives that I first began to understand the meaning and power of true beauty.

Jim Head
February 2016

Notes

ABBREVIATIONS

A   unpublished autobiographic journal of Howard Chandler Christy

AAA   Smithsonian Institution Archives of American Art

B   Nancy Palmer Christy's unpublished journal manuscript on Howard Chandler Christy (1st carbon draft)

CA   collection of the author

CS   Charles Stebbins

CRB   Collette Ramsey Baker

EFM   Elise Ford's Howard Chandler Christy Memoirs (unpublished dictated memoirs)

HCC   Howard Chandler Christy

HL   Holly Longuski

JWC   Jane Conneen

JJG   Jocelyn Johnston Green

JMH   Jaye and Melodie Hayes, the Barracks, Blue Rock, Ohio

MS   Marilyn Christy Schafer

NPC   Nancy Palmer Christy

NFS   Norris F. Schneider Collection, Ohio Historical Society, Columbus, Ohio

OS   Olga Steckler

SB   scrapbooks created by Nancy Palmer Christy

SI   Smithsonian Institution, Washington, DC

SL   Howard Chandler Christy Archives, Special Collections, Skillman Library, Lafayette College, Easton, Pennsylvania

W   Widener University

◻

INTRODUCTION

"The Barefoot Boy from the Blue Muskingum": A, p. 1, SL.

"the most commercially successful U.S. artist": "Congress Critics," *Time*, June 20, 1938.

"It is undoubtedly Mr. Christy's ability": "A Painter of Presidents," *Wardman Park Vista*, Vol. 2, No. 28, April 1924, p. 1, SL.

"paint big pictures of big things": B, p. 4, SL.

"The Christy Girl": Susan E. Meyer, *America's Greatest Illustrators* (New York, New York: Harry N. Abrams, Inc., 1978), pp. 232–255.

Shoes, hats, dresses: B, p. 68, SL; *see also* Miley, Mimi C., *Howard Chandler Christy—Artist/Illustrator of Style: September 25–November 6, 1977, Allentown Art Museum* (Kutztown, Pennsylvania: Kutztown Publishing, Inc., 1977).

"Howard Chandler Christy has been painting": B. F. Wilson, "Who Are the Beauties of Today?" *Movie Classic*, June 1935, pp. 28–30, 65.

Yet, he continued his usual daily pace: Eleanor Bailey Johnson, "Howard Chandler Christy's Fame Continues to Bring New Renown to Zanesville Area," unknown newspaper, November 16, 1947, NFS; *see also* L. B. Sisson, "Few of Famed Artist's Originals Remain Here," unknown newspaper, March 9, 1952, NFS.

"You can learn a good deal": "A Painter of Presidents," *Wardman Park Vista*, Vol. 2, No. 28, April 1924, p. 14, SL.

"the softest of real golden-blonde": Ibid.

PROLOGUE: AN AFFAIR WITH BEAUTY

Sigmund Freud/fame, fortune, and beautiful lovers: Tom Wolfe, "Golden Age: America's Greatest Illustrators," *The New York Times,* June 4,

1978; *see also* Joshua Zeitz, "Flapper," (New York, New York: Three Rivers Press, 2006), p. 56.

1923 gallery exhibition: "Art Exhibitions of the Week Portrait and Landscapes," *The New York Times,* October 26, 1923.

Emil Fuchs' accent: "Art," *Time*, February 21, 1927.

Some say he could capture: JJG, e-mail, February 23, 2008.

Something was uniquely different: *See, e.g.,* Eleanor Bailey Johnson, letter to NPC, October 27, 1947, SL ("Everyone here is still talking about you both [Nancy and Howard] and full of praises for your sweet cordiality and charm and amazed at the youthful <u>verve</u> of your handsome 'Poppy'." (emphasis in original)); Eleanor Bailey Johnson, letter to NPC, March 5, 1952, SL ("He was so <u>ageless</u>, so <u>vital</u>, it did not seem possible not that he would live and work and <u>create</u> <u>beauty</u> for many more years to come." (emphasis in original)).

Perhaps that is because: *See generally* NPC, "My Beauty Recipe: By Mrs. Howard C. Christy, as Told to Diana Dare," *The* [Atlanta, Georgia] *Constitution*, November 5, 1924, p. 15 (Nancy's conception of looking outside to others, and not at herself, for beauty).

CHAPTER ONE: HOMEWARD BOUND

As I PREPARED TO DEPART: B, p. 343, SL; JJG, telephone interview and various e-mails, January–February 2008; *see* "Weekend Snow Turns to Slush, But City Prepares for a New Storm," *The New York Times,* March 3, 1952, p. 23; "Snow Lays Stripe of White from Nevada to Indiana," [Harlingen, Texas] *Valley Morning Star*, March 3, 1952, p. 1.

Just before dawn: JJG, telephone interview and e-mails, January–February 2008; *see* EFM, p. 82, SL; S. J. Woolf, "Creator of the Christy Girl," *The New York Times,* January 18, 1948; Vibeke Lichten, various e-mails, October 2008.

New York City population: "1950 Fast Facts," online article (US Census Bureau, accessed July 5, 2015) www.census.gov/history/www/through_the_decades/fast_facts/1950_fast_facts.

"City of New York and Burroughs: Population and Population Density from 1790," online article (Demographia, accessed July 5, 2015) www. demographia.com/dm-nyc.htm.

Everyone came from different backgrounds: Frederick Lewis Allen, *Look at America: New York City* (Boston, Massachusetts: Houghton Mifflin Co., 1948), p. 195.

Within minutes, the cavernous space: Vibeke Lichten, various e-mails, October 2008 (relating to the sunlight streaming through the north window at sunrise and the studio ceiling rising twenty-two feet in height); *but see* Norris F. Schneider, "Howard Chandler Christy Turns to Portraits," *The* [Zanesville, Ohio] *Times Recorder*, May 18, 1975, p. 7-A (stating that the Christy studio is twenty-five feet in height).

On that particular Monday: HL, telephone interview, January 15, 2008; OS, telephone interview, March 8, 2008; JJG, telephone interview and e-mails, January–February 2008; CRB, telephone and in-person interviews, Jan. 20, 2007 and July 15, 2007; S. J. Woolf, "Creator of the Christy Girl," *The New York Times,* January 18, 1948; *see* HCC passport and photographs, SL.

It was within this soft light: "Famed Ohio Artist Dies in New York," *The Coshocton* [Ohio] *Tribune*, March 4, 1952, p. 10; "New York Rites for Mr. Christy," *The* [Zanesville, Ohio] *Times Recorder,* March 5, 1952, p. 2; B, p. 343, SL.

HOWARD WAS EIGHTY / Nancy's conception of Beauty: *See generally,* NPC, "My Beauty Recipe: By Mrs. Howard C. Christy, as Told to Diana Dare," *The* [Atlanta, Georgia] *Constitution*, November 5, 1924, p. 15.

Howard considered himself just a plain, "A Great Personality," *The Zanesville* [Ohio] *Signal*, March 5, 1952, p. 4.

Douglas MacArthur portrait: B, p. 340, SL.

Douglas MacArthur history: "Douglas MacArthur," online article (Wikipedia, accessed July 5, 2015): http://en.wikipedia.org/wiki/ Douglas_MacArthur.

Douglas MacArthur portrait: "Douglas MacArthur," online article (National Portrait Gallery, accessed July 5, 2015) http://www.npg.si.edu/exh/marshall/macarth.htm.

"old soldiers never die": "Old Soldiers Never Die (They Just Fade Away)," *The Racine* [Wisconsin] *Journal Times*, April 23, 1951, p. 6.

The next day, he received: "N.Y. Give M'Arthur Biggest Mass Tribute in American History," *The Springfield* [Massachusetts] *Union*, April 21, 1951, p. 1.

"the most stupendous mass tribute in American history": Ibid.

He never used photographs: L. B. Sisson, "Few of Famed Artist's Originals Remain Here," unknown newspaper, March 9, 1952, NFS.

"Christ at the Peace Table": B, p. 340, SL.

Over another table, preparatory drawings: Ibid.

"Hiawatha's Wooing": B, p. 337, SL; Margaret Teague, "Christy Treasures in Tulsa Museum," *Daily Oklahoman*, March 9, 1952, p. 24.

"Don't be alarmed": B, p. 340, SL.

"A bed with too many pillows": Ibid., p. 341.

"I'll be painting before long": Ibid., p. 342.

"He was in the middle of portrait painting": Ibid.

"Smiley": Ibid., pp. 5–6.

He did not resemble: "A Painter of Presidents," *Wardman Park Vista*, Vol. 2, No. 28, April 1924, p. 14, SL.

"Just a note to extend": Norman Vincent Peale, letter to HCC, Jan. 8, 1952, SL.

"Also I congratulate you": Ibid.

By late February: B, pp. 337–343, SL.

It is this name: OS, telephone interview, March 8, 2008; JJG, telephone interview, January 26, 2008.

Those short hours: B, pp. 305, 342, 343, SL.

As Howard worked at his desk: "Howard Christy, Illustrator, Dies," *The [Long Beach] Independent*, March 4, 1952, p. 4.

Central Park West: Frederick Lewis Allen, *Look at America New York City* (Boston, Massachusetts: Houghton Mifflin Co., 1948), pp. 150-152.

Turning homeward: B, p. 343, SL.

"It's almost spring, Nancy": Ibid.

heart attack: City of New York Department of Health, Death Certificate for HCC, No. 156-52-1051.77, filed on March 5, 1952 (immediate cause of death was a coronary occlusion due to generalized arteriosclerosis).

Chapter Two: Fanfare for a Common Man

At first I refused: JJG, telephone interview and various e-mails, January–February 2008.

"It doesn't look good": Ibid.

an old friend, Mrs. William P. Timmon: "Howard Christy, Illustrator Dies," *Long Beach* [California] *Independent,* March 4, 1952, p. 4.

While writing checks at his desk: Ibid.; "Famed Ohio Artist Dies in New York," *The Coshocton,* [Ohio] *Tribune*, March 4, 1952, p. 10; "Howard Chandler Christy Rites Thursday in N. York," *The Zanesville* [Ohio] *Signal*, March 4, 1952, p. 1; "Ohio-Born Artist is Dead; Painted Presidents, Pinups,*"* Chronicle-Telegram* [Elyria, Ohio], March 4, 1952, p. 2; *see* B, p. 343, SL.

I purposely delivered this brief account: JJG, telephone interview and various e-mails, January–February 2008.

Only later did I discover: Ibid.

Within hours of Howard's passing: Ibid.

Howard loved his trusty pipe: "Candidettes . . Camera Study of the Famous Artist . . Howard Chandler Christy," *New York Evening Journal,*

April 4, 1936, p. 10.

"I take too much time out": Ibid.

"[s]alon, equal of year ago": EFM, p. 82, SL.

"relics": HCC, letter to Paul Eldridge, January 26, 1914, CA.

Favorite breakfast: HL, e-mail, February 22, 2008 (bacon and eggs with a cup of hot coffee laced with modest amounts of cream and sugar); *but see* Eleanor Bailey Johnson, "Howard Chandler Christy's Fame Continues to Bring New Renown to Zanesville Area," unknown newspaper, November 16, 1947, NFS (NPC declares that HCC also likes pork chops, bacon, or pork tenderloin with fried mush for breakfast).

"an artist of tireless energy": "Howard C. Christy, Noted Artist Dies," *The New York Times,* March 4, 1952, p. 27.

"If popularity is a hallmark of artistic success": "Howard Chandler Christy," *New York Herald Tribune*, March 6, 1952.

From New York to New Mexico: "Illustrator Dies," *The Daily Messenger* [Canandaigua, New York], March 4, 1952, p. 1.; "Howard Christy, Illustrator, Dies," *Alburquerque* [New Mexico] *Journal*, March 4, 1952, p. 1; "Howard Christy Dies," *Florence* [South Carolina] *Morning News,* March 4, 1952, p.1; "Portrait Artist Dies," *Council Bluffs* [Iowa] *Nonpareil,* March 5, 1952.

"right for each other": Norman Rockwell, *My Adventures as an Illustrator* (New York, New York: Harry N. Abrams, Inc.), 1988, p. 176.

"the Ohio artist": "Howard Chandler Christy Rites Thursday in N. York," *The Zanesville* [Ohio] *Signal*, March 4, 1952, p. 1.

"[f]rom a barefoot boy": "New York Rites for Mr. Christy," *The* [Zanesville, Ohio] *Times Recorder*, March 5, 1952, p. 2.

"honest, straight-forward personality": "A Great Personality," *The Zanesville* [Ohio] *Signal,* March 4, 1952, p. 4.

"seldom equaled": "Christy's Art Seldom Equaled," *The* [Helena, Montana] *Independent Record,* March 19, 1952, p. 4.

"influenced and reflected the customs and tastes of the changing decades": Ibid.

"some of them nudes": "Howard Chandler Christy Passes," *The Lethbridge* [Alberta, Canada] *Herald*, March 6, 1952, p. 15.

"If it were given to all men to see": Howard Chandler Christy," *The Salisbury* [Maryland] *Times*, March 6, 1952, p. 6.

THE FUNERAL SERVICE: JJG, various e-mails, January–February 2008.

Early that morning: Ibid.

The day before, Jocelyn: Ibid.

Mrs. Babe Ruth: Mrs. Babe Ruth, "Ex-Teen Age Bride Meets the King of Swat," *The Oakland* [California] *Tribune,* March 11, 1959, Sports Section; Mrs. Babe Ruth, "Claire Neither Liked Nor Disliked Babe Ruth the First Time They Met," *Appleton* [Wisconsin] *Post-Crescent*, March 11, 1959, p. D1-4.

Wearing a long, ebony wool coat: JJG, various e-mails, January–February 2008.

IT WAS A SOLEMN: JJG, interview and various e-mails, January–February 2008; HL, various e-mails, January–March 2008; *see generally* Funeral Guest List and Honorary List of Pallbearers at HCC's Funeral, SL; *see also* Chuck Martin, "Remembering Howard Chandler Christy," *The* [Zanesville, Ohio] *Times Recorder*, April 28, 2001, p. C1 (Gen. Douglas MacArthur and Cong. Bob Secrest could not attend).

Honnie: Letters from Bernice Brennan to Col. Frank K. Hyatt, dated January 10, 17, and February 11, 1935, W; Letter from Frank K. Hyatt to Mrs. Thomas Brennan, February 28, 1935, W.

The honorable judge so loved: Smith Davis letter to Charles Sawyer, February 2, 1950, SL.

As a young boy, Roger: Norman Vincent Peale, "'Imaging' Can Make Dreams Come True," *Syracuse* [New York] *Herald Journal*, September 10, 1983, p. A-4; *see* Norman Vincent Peale, "Former Newsboy Has

Tales," *Findlay* [Ohio] *Republican Courier*, June 16, 1973, p. A6.

Thomas Yawkey: Harry Grayson, "Tom Yawkey Has Open Purse, Gets More Out of Baseball Than Any Other Owner," *The Laredo* [Texas] *Times*, March 11, 1940, p. 4.

Roger Lee Humber: Letter from HCC to Thomas Gilcrease, June 16, 1949, AAA.

Thomas J. Watson: "Name Business Machines Firm in Trust Suit," *The* [Madison, Wisconsin] *Capital Times*, January 22, 1952, p. 12.

"I am looking forward to sitting": Telegram from Thomas J. Watson to HCC, January 10, 1952, SL.

W. Alton Jones: "W. Alton Jones," online article (Harvard Business School accessed July 5, 2015) www.hbs.edu/leadership/database/leaders/w_alton_jones.html.

Albert V. Moore: "Hog Islanders," *Time,* November 6, 1939.

Hobart Ramsey: Interviews with CRB, January 20, 2007, July 15, 2007.

ELISE WAS A MODERN DAY VENUS: HL, e-mails, January 22, 2008, March 6, 2008.

Elise became Howard's favorite model: "Girl of the Future," *The* [Hagerstown, Maryland] *Daily Mail*, April 9, 1934, p. 6.

Elise never disclosed to anyone: Ibid. *See* HL, *Rattling Eden's Gate*, unpublished manuscript.

That afternoon, Elise's twelve-year-old: HL, e-mail, March 14, 2008.

People pushed through: JJG, e-mails, March 11, 2008, April 28, 2008.

Will Hays: Miles E. Connolly, "Will Hays Wants Public Help Clean Up Movies," *Boston Sunday Post*, July 9, 1922, p. 1.

Eddie Rickenbacker: "Portrait of Rickenbacker by Christy Unveiled Today," The *Zanesville* [Ohio] *Signal,* December 8, 1943, p. 6 (portrait was finished in March 1943 and unveiled at the Columbus Gallery of Fine Art; it hangs at the Columbus Museum of Art in Columbus, Ohio);

see "Capt. Rickenbacker Dies at 82," *Nevada State Journal*, July 24, 1973, p. 1.

John D. Bulkeley: Letter regarding John D. Bulkeley, June 24, 1942, SL.

"Pop": "Howard Chandler Christy, at 70, Doing Best Work of His Career," *The* [Zanesville, Ohio] *Sunday Times-Signal*, November 1, 1942, p. 8.

"I shall return.": "Mac Reflects Brave Action" *The Lima* [Ohio] *News*, April 6, 1964, p. 14.

"I have known Howard Chandler Christy": Memo from Douglas MacArthur, March 3, 1952, SL.

Rube Goldberg: "Rube Goldberg," online article (Wikipedia, accessed July 5, 2015) http://en.wikipedia.org/wiki/Rube_Goldberg.

Dean Cornwell: Ernest W. Watson, *Forty Illustrators and How They Work* (New York, New York: Watson-Gupthill, 1946), pp. 74–81.

James Montgomery Flagg: *See generally* Susan E. Meyer, *America's Greatest Illustrators* (New York, New York: Harry N. Abrams, Inc., 1978), pp. 256–279; Walt Reed, *The Illustrator's America 1860–2000* (New York, New York: Society of Illustrators, 2000), p. 143.

He used his own face: Marguerite Ives Beavers, telephone interview, August 11, 2008; but see Cathleen Coburn O'Brien, e-mail, May 28, 2010 (stating that Flagg obtained the notion for the poster from the face of a 17 year-old Marine he met on a train trip to Paris Island, South Carolina).

Monty started his career: James Montgomery Flagg, *Roses and Buckshot* (New York, New York: G. Putnam's Sons, 1946), pp. 39–40.

"The only difference between a fine artist": Susan Meyer, *America's Greatest Illustrators* (New York, New York: Watson-Gupthill, 1978), p. 264.

"Draw continually from life": James Montgomery Flagg, letter to Miss Laul, Sept. 30, 1931, CA.

Monty would often make: *See* James Montgomery Flagg, *The Well-Knowns as Seen By James Montgomery Flagg* (New York, New York: George H. Doran Company, 1914); *see also* James Montgomery Flagg, *Celebrities: A Half-Century of Caricature and Portraiture* (Watkins Glen, New York: Century House, 1951).

Arthur William Brown: James Montgomery Flagg, *Roses and Buckshot* (New York, New York: G. Putnam's Sons, 1946), p.146.

William Oberhardt: Walt Reed, *The Illustrator's America 1860-2000* (New York: New York: Society of Illustrators, 2000), p. 143; William Oberhardt, "Obie—The Modern Headhunter," *American Artist*, September 1953, pp. 38–39.

WHEN THE PROMENADE: JJG, e-mail, February 16, 2008.

where Howard was to be laid: Jane Marsek, e-mail regarding Ferncliff Cemetery, August 28, 2006.

"Again and again": "Tribute is Paid to Noted Artist," *Zanesville Signal*, March 10, 1952, p. 12.

CHAPTER THREE: MOMENTS OF PLEASURE

MY FRIEND RUTH JOHNSTON: JJG, e-mails, June 1–18, 20–24, 2008; JJG, telephone interview, January 26, 2008.

As I stood there: JJG, e-mail, April 28, 2008 (affirming that HCC's painting *The Signing of the United Nations Charter* was in front of the Christy fireplace in March 1952 as reflected in photo #J0067484, Peter A. Juley & Son Collection, SI); *but see* S. J. Woolf, "Creator of the Christy Girl," *The New York Times*, January 18, 1948 (stating that this painting was in front of the Christy balcony in 1948); Sol Bloom, letter to HCC (mentioning that HCC had begun *The Signing of the United Nations Charter*), September 28, 1946, SL.

However, the commission was not yet paid: Kathleen McLaughlin, "Painting of Charter-Signing Embarrasses U.N.," *The New York Times*, June 26, 1954 (commission for painting was not yet paid until 1954).

COMPLETED IN 1947: *See* "Signing of United Nations Charter," SL.

Howard's painting depicts: "The Ceremony of the Signing of the Charter of the United Nations," U.S. Government Printing Office, n.d., SL; "U.N. Charter Signing," *The New York Times,* July 2, 1995.

Democratic Congressman: Sol Bloom, letter to HCC, September 28, 1946, SL.

He also negotiated: Sol Bloom, letter to HCC, July 16, 1947, SL.

"I know it is going": Sol Bloom, letter to HCC, September 28, 1946, SL.

On an early February morning: Calendar of daily appointments for Harry S. Truman on February 6, 1947, online entry (Harry S. Truman Library, Independence, Missouri, accessed July 19, 2015) *www.trumanlibrary. org*; Sol Bloom, letter to HCC, Feb. 4, 1947, SL (Sol Bloom arranges an appointment for HCC to meet President Truman at 8:45am).

"certainly you would not": Sol Bloom, letter to HCC, July 16,1947, SL.

"OH, R-u-uth": JJG, e-mails, June 20, 24, 2008.

Her first husband, Milton: Ibid.; JJG, e-mail, March 25, 2012.

"You have had enough": JJG, e-mails, June 20, 24, 2008.

She was right. Howard's financial affairs: Estate of HCC, Surrogate's Court for the County of New York (A-1224–1952).

Through the years: Claire Stebbins, "Speech before the Art Institute," September 25, 1952, CS.

I too was once a Christy Girl: "Christy Sticks to The Christy Girl," *New York Evening Post*, August 21, 1921.

Among the bundles: Dorothy Dianne, letter to HCC, May 17, 1932, SL.

She later starred: "Dorothy Dianne," online entry (Internet Broadway Database, accessed July 5, 2015) http://www.ibdb.com/person. php?id=38014.

She called Howard "Dearest": Dorothy Dianne, letter to HCC, May 17, 1932, SL.

"A little girl": Ibid.

"Merry Christmas": Dorothy Dianne, cards to HCC, n.d., SL.

It was a cold spot: JJG, e-mails, May 27–28, 2008.

Unraveling the Estate: *see generally* SL.

It was in this formidable tower: "14 Wall Street," Online article (Wikipedia, accessed July 5, 2015): https://en.wikipedia.org/wiki/14_Wall_Street.

Despite the imposing exterior: *See* Charles Reich, "The Way We Were," *The American Lawyer*, December 2007, pp. 108–111 (describing the office of law firm of New York City's Cravath, Swaine & Moore in 1952).

Edmund Beecroft: Edmund Beecroft, letter to NPC, September 24, 1952, SL; *see* "Interview of Ambassador Robert M. Beecroft," Foreign Affairs Oral History Project, September 17, 2004, pp. 5-7, online article (Association for Diplomatic Training and Studies, accessed July 5, 2015) http://www.adst.org/OH%20TOCs/Beecroft,%20Robert%20M.toc.pdf.

Howard believed that: "Blames Men for Making Flappers Out of the Girls: Howard Chandler Christy, Noted Artist, Describes Emancipation of Women," *Appleton* [Wisconsin] *Post-Crescent,* March 15, 1922, p. 11; "Only 37 Jobs That Women Don't Hold Today," The *Sandusky-Star* [Sandusky, Ohio] *Star Journal*, September 2, 1926, p. 4.

By my count: Inventory of the Estate of HCC, Surrogate's Court for the County of New York (A-1224-1952).

Howard's only child: JJG, e-mail, December 20, 2011.

Howard had left: Last Will and Testament of Howard Chandler Christy dated April 29, 1927, SL.

Weeks after that meeting: Accounting of the Estate of HCC, Surrogate's Court for the County of New York (A-1224-1952).

As for the enormous painting: Kathleen McLaughlin, "Painting of Charter-Signing Embarrasses U.N.," *The New York Times,* June 26 1954.

"Prince of Hearts": inscription in NPC's *The Seven Darlings* from NPC to Bobby Conneen dated October 12, 1964, SL.

We met one night: "Zanesville Isn't Alone Applauding Christy Talents," *The* [Zanesville] *Times Recorder*, December 4, 1977, p. 8-B; JWC e-mail, September 1, 2007.

He said he was a former: "Conneen, at 68, Reflects on His Life with Horses," *The New York Times*, February 26, 1978; Robert Conneen Obituary, *New York Globe Times*, March 14, 1980.

a gentleman jockey: Amory L. Haskell, letter to Robert F. Conneen, June 9, 1949, Collection of Joseph Conneen.

After that fateful night: Robert F. Conneen, "Tuesday, 9:00 pm," letter to NPC, n.d., SL.

Eventually, I received: Robert F. Conneen, various letters to NPC, circa summer 1957, SL.

It was in that same year: "Studio Fire Kills Stanlaws, Artist," *The New York Times*, May 20, 1957, p. 20; "Famed Portrait Painter Penhryn Stanlaws, Dies," *Lebanon* [Pennsylvania] *Daily News*, May 20, 1957, p. 2.

"Artists don't die": James Montgomery Flagg, *Roses and Buckshot* (New York, New York, G. Putnam's Sons, 1946), p. 53.

Harrison Fisher: "Harrison Fisher, Dead," *The New York Times*, January 20, 1934, p 15; "Harrison Fisher," *Bluefield* [West Virginia] *Daily Telegraph*, January 26, 1934, p. 6.

"the king of magazine-cover illustrators": "Harrison Fisher, Dead," *The New York Times*, January 20, 1934, p. 15.

He went to the hospital: Naomi Welch, *The Complete Works of Harrison Fisher* (Images of the Past, 1999), pp. 23–24.

Next was N.C. Wyeth: "N.C. Wyeth, 63, Famous Artist, Grandson, Die," *Chester* [Pennsylvania] *Times*, October 19, 1945, p .1; "Newell C. Wyeth Killed by Train," *Somerset* [Pennsylvania] *Daily American*, October 20, 1945, p. 6.

Then, there was Haskell Coffin: "Haskell Coffin, Famed Artist, Leaps to Death," *Los Angeles Evening Herald and Express*, May 12, 1941; "Haskell Coffin, Artist, Killed in 3 Story Plunge," *Chicago Daily Tribune,* May 13, 1941, p. 14.

Nationally known illustrator: "Frances Starr Gets Divorce from Coffin," *The New York Times*, May 13, 1930, p. 24; Dallas MacDonnell, "Couple's Heart Experience Told as Famed Artist Plans Exhibit, unknown newspaper, n.d., SI; "McClelland Barclay, Artist, Missing in South Pacific War," *The Washington Post*, July 25, 1943.

So, in those lonely: JJG e-mails, 2008; JGG, *Memoirs of Howard Chandler Christy* (unpublished), p. 8, SL; Robert F. Conneen, letter to NPC, "Tuesday, 8:30 pm," n.d., SL (Bobby reiterates a quote from Nancy's earlier letter to him stating, "the most difficult thing is realizing days and weeks are going by—never to return—so much is lost, but one must accept things as they come.").

In the corner of the studio: B, p. 86, SL; *see* Bobby Conneen, "Saturday, 2:00 pm" letter to NPC, n.d., SL (stating that Bobby could not find time to look at the scrapbooks because he was "completely engaged" with Nancy).

It was Howard's former home: Jaye Hayes, "National Register of Historic Places Registration Form—Howard Chandler Christy Art Studio," Collection of Jaye and Melodie Hayes; *see* B, p. 84, SL.

CHAPTER FOUR: A LOVELY PLACE TO BE

It was the spring of 1912: B, pp. 93, 96, SL (Nancy claims to have been sixteen years of age when she met Howard, but she was actually just a couple months shy of her twenty-first birthday).

There was nothing left: "Personal and Social," *Poughkeepsie Eagle–News,* September 5, 1919, p. 6; 1910 Census records for Poughkeepsie, New York (Anna M. Coon, 11 Bellevue Avenue, Poughkeepsie, New York).

For me, the only means: "Christy to Wed Po'Keepsie Girl," *Poughkeepsie Eagle–News*, April 18, 1916, p. 5, "Society Notes," *The Kingston* [New

York] *Daily Freeman*, April 18, 1916, p. 10; "H.C. Christy to Wed Model," *The Carbondale* [Illinois] *Daily Free Press*, April 19, 1916, p.1 (Nancy worked for John Schwartz & Sons which operated a cigar factory at 313 Main Street in Poughkeepsie).

Full of ambition: *See* B, pp. 95, 98, SL.

Charles Dana Gibson: *See generally* Fairfax Downey, *Portrait of an Era as Drawn by C.D. Gibson* (New York, New York: Charles Scribner's Sons, 1936); *see also* William Griffith, "'Gibson's Girl' Creator and American Girl Types, *The New York Times,* April 30, 1905, p. 4.

"Come in again": "Charles Dana Gibson—Illustrator," *The Illustrated American*, October 20, 1894, p. 487.

"unconscious throwback of New England heritage": "Charles Dana Gibson, Artist Who Created Gay 90s Model, Dies," *The Washington Star*, December 24, 1944.

Young women regularly imitated: John Rice, "The Man Who Sold A Dream," *The Sunday* [Kingston, Jamaica] *Gleaner Magazine*, July 5, 1970, p. 9.

"I have hundreds of girls": "Types of New Gibson Girl," *The* [New York] *Sun*, March 30, 1913, p. 11.

Dana did have hundreds: Fairfax Downey, *Portrait of an Era as Drawn by C.D. Gibson* (New York, New York: Charles Scribner's Sons, 1936), pp. 126–129.

"Gibson Man": Ibid., pp. 102, 128.

The Gibson man was clean: L. M. Boyd, [no title], *The Daily Sitka* [Alaska] *Sentinel*, May 13, 1986, p. 7; John Rice, "The Man Who Sold A Dream," *The Sunday* [Kingston, Jamaica] *Gleaner Magazine*, July 5, 1970, p. 9.

Dana drew what he saw: Fairfax Downey, *Portrait of an Era as Drawn by C.D. Gibson* (New York, New York: Charles Scribner's Sons, 1936), pp. 104–105.

Years earlier: Langhorne Gibson, Jr., *The Gibson Girl: Portrait of a Southern Belle* (Richmond, Virginia: Commodore Press 1997), p. 96.

Undoubtedly, it was the Gibson Girl's: John Rice, "The Man Who Sold A Dream," *The Sunday* [Kingston, Jamaica] *Gleaner Magazine*, July 5, 1970, p. 9.

I WOULD BE THE NEXT GIBSON GIRL: *See* B, p. 95, SL.

Ah, Miss Palmer: Ibid.

IN THOSE DAYS, MANHATTAN: Ibid.

Carnegie Hall: William Griffith, "'Gibson's Girl' Creator and American Girl Types," *New York Times,* April 30, 1905, p. 4.

The studio of Charles Dana Gibson: Rob Hudson, e-mail, March 12, 2012.

"Now, as curious": William Griffith, "'Gibson's Girl' Creator and American Girl Types, *New York Times,* April 30, 1905, p. 4.

You know, there are some: "Woman is Woman Still Declares Gibson," *Syracuse Journal,* October 30, 1910, p. 6.

"When the sun becomes": Ibid.

Well, you know he is presently: *See* B, p. 96, SL.

"You're a beautiful girl": Ibid.

The old Waldorf-Astoria: James Remington McCarthy, *Peacock Alley* (New York, New York: Harper Brothers, 1931), pp. 60–62.

I looked up: *See* B, p. 98, SL.

"I know you must": Ibid.

"I am Howard Christy": Ibid.

That particular night was stormy: James Remington McCarthy, *Peacock Alley* (New York, New York: Harper Brothers, 1931) pp. 87–93.

The event occurred: "Opening the Astoria Hotel, *Leslie's Weekly,* November 18, 1897, pp. 328–329.

"Her hair was white": HCC, "The American Woman of To-Day," *Metropolitan* magazine, March 1901, p. 346.

We strolled down: *See* B, pp. 98–99, SL.

Miss Palmer, I'd like: *See* Ibid.

Street & Smith specializes: "Street & Smith Dime Store Covers," online article (Syracuse University Library, accessed July 5, 2015): http://library.syr.edu/find/scrc/collections/diglib/streetsmith.php.

"I think I know": B, p. 100, SL.

"You would like this place": HCC, Letter to Paul Eldridge, January 26, 1914, CA.

I want you to see: *See* B, p. 100, SL.

As DAWN BROKE: *See* B, p. 101, SL.

Trinway Station: "Trinway Station," online page (Ohio Railroad Stations Past & Present, accessed July 5, 2015): www.west2k.com/ohpix/trinway.jpg.

Steam arose from the platform: *See* B, pp. 101-102, SL.

"Thought I would meet you": Ibid. p. 102.

Christy's Knob: "Canoeists at an Artist's Home," *The* [Massillon, Ohio] *Evening Independent*, September 21, 1908, p. 6.

Its name comes: HCC, Letter to Paul Eldridge, CA, January 26, 1914.

I receive all sorts of guests: Norris Schneider, "Talent Awakens in Christy When He Saw Artist at Work in Zanesville," *The [Zanesville] Times Recorder,* September 29, 1963, p. 6-B.

Evelyn Nesbit: Ibid.

One might say my home: "Canoeists at an Artist's Home," *The* [Massillon, Ohio] *Evening Independent*, September 21, 1908, p. 6.

The boat launch: Jaye Hayes, e-mails, May 5, 16, 2012.

Noel Talbot: Claire Stebbins, "Howard Chandler Christy," unpublished and undated article, p. 1, CS.

For that, Howard: EFM, p. 52.

billows of pink and white lilac blooms: Norris F, Schneider, "75th Anniversary Observed by Authors Club," *The* [Zanesville] *Times Recorder*, October 10, 1971; *see* Letter of S. B. Bowman to HCC dated June 11, 1934, SL.

Directly across from his home: "Canoeists at an Artist's Home," *The* [Massillon, Ohio] *Evening Independent*, September 21, 1908, p. 6.

On the hillside: Melodie Hayes, e-mail, May 7, 2009.

Heliotrope bloomed: *The* [Marshall, Michigan] *Evening Chronicle*, September 24, 1912.

Peacock!: SB, photo no. 373, SL.

Nancy, this is Sargent: Norris Schneider, "Talent Awakens in Christy When He Saw Artist at Work in Zanesville," *The* [Zanesville] *Times Recorder,* September 29, 1963, p. 6-B.

Nipping at Howard's: Ibid.

From the front veranda: *See* B, p. 103, SL.

"I think she's thinner": Ibid., p. 106.

Natalie: JJG, e-mail, May 31, 2012.

Father can't hear: *See* B, p. 15, SL; EFM, p. 10, SL.

Ah, yes, I did: Francis M. Christy's Civil War Remembrances, undated, Morgan County Historical Society, McConnelsville, Ohio; *see* "62nd Ohio Infantry," online article (Ohio Civil War, accessed July 5, 2015): www.ohiocivilwar.com/cw62.html.

The Union only wanted men: Francis M. Christy's Civil War Remembrances, undated, Morgan County Historical Society, McConnelsville, Ohio; EFM, p. 3, SL; "Francis M. Christy," American Civil War Soldiers: www.ancestrylibrary.com.

"[A]nd pretty soon Custer": EFM, p. 10, SL.

Muskingum River: *See generally* "Muskingum River," online article (Wikipedia, accessed July 15, 2015) https://en.wikipedia.org/wiki/Muskingum_River.

Duncan Falls: Dana Allen Dilley, *The History and Development of Duncan Falls, Ohio*, (Columbus, Ohio: Avonelle Associates, Ltd., 1982), pp. 2–5; *see also* Norris F. Schneider, Muskingum River Offers Recreation and History to Touring Americans," *The Zanesville* [Ohio] *Times Recorder,* March 10, 1968, p. 4-B.

I returned to my room: B, p. 104, SL.

Chapter Five: Of Youth and the Magnificent River

At 7 o'clock the next morning: B, p. 104, SL.

He was completely naked: *See* Nancy Keeley, "Rankin Drive Man One-Time Model for Christy," *The Zanesville* [Ohio] *Times Recorder*, July 18, 1971, D Section.

A half hour later: B, p. 104, SL.

"You do that every morning": B, p. 105, SL.

No, that's just Polly: *See* EFM, pp. 48–49, SL.

"Howard, telephone": Ibid., p. 48.

It took eight carpenters: Ibid., p. 46.

A short time later: B, p. 105, SL.

Swamp Angel: Ibid., p. 15; *see* Stephen R. Wise, *Gate of Hell, Campaign for Charleston Harbor*, 1863 (South Carolina: University of South Carolina Press, 1994), p. 148.

Howard, where's Bill?: B, p. 116, SL.

Virginia brought out: *See* Eleanor Bailey Johnson, "Howard Chandler Christy's Fame Continues to Bring New Renown to Zanesville Area," unknown newspaper, November 16, 1947, NFS.

Each week, I receive: EFM, p. 53, SL.

"He never could have": Ibid.

It's a grand story: Gouverneur Morris, "The Penalty," *Cosmopolitan*, Vol. LIV, No.2, January 1913, p. 236.

The summer of 1876: EFM, p. 3-5, SL; Michel Mok, "Just Lots of Good Clean Fun at 63: Howard Chandler Christy Finds Life Good," *New York Post*, January 9, 1936. (Howard refers to being three years of age at the time of the Battle of Little Big Horn and also at the time his family moved to their Muskingum County farm. However, he was actually four years of age. This misconception is preserved in the text.)

I wanted to know more: *See* Letter from Elizabeth B. Custer to Howard Chandler Christy, n.d. SL; *see also* Claire Stebbins, "Howard Chandler Christy," unpublished and undated article, CS. (Early in his art career, Howard maintained a correspondence with General Custer's wife, Elizabeth.)

A sharp whistle: *See* B, p. 108, SL.

A glass of cream?: Ibid.

When Howard was a boy . . . Russ Bethel: B, p. 13–14, SL; EFM, p. 7–8, SL; Mary A. Livermore, *My Story of the War: A Woman's Narrative of Four Years of Personal Experience As Nurse in the Union Army* (Hartford, Connecticut: A. D. Worthington and Co., 1892), pp. 63–64.

Fearlessness—Howard always: Grace B. Robinson, "H.C. Christy Poses for his Mental Photo," unknown newspaper, SB, SL.

"Now I'll try to answer": HCC, letter to Paul Eldridge, January 26, 1914, CA.

"They—the book publisher—": Ibid.

For some reason: See Wilson, B.F., "Who Are the Beauties of Today?" *Movie Classic*, June 1935, p. 30.

"Perfection of feature is not enough": Jane Dixon, "At What Age Are Women Most Interesting? When They're Beautiful Says Howard C.

Christy," *Oakland Tribune*, January 5, 1920, p. 1.

"Beauty—but with character to back it up": Grace B. Robinson, "H.C. Christy Poses for his Mental Photo," unknown newspaper, SB, SL.

"That he be a reliable friend": Ibid.

And I detest insincerity: Ibid.

When I was but a young boy: EFM, pp. 7–8, SL.

"The truth": Ibid.

"I can close my eyes": Michel Mok, "Just Lots of Good Clean Fun at 63: Howard Chandler Christy Finds Life Good," *New York Post*, January 9, 1936.

I HAD AN IDEAL: B, pp. 1–9, SL; EFM, pp. 5–6, 16, SL.

"Backward, turn backward": EFM, p. 10, SL.

"'Tis a lesson you should heed": Ibid.

"Do you see that smoke": B, p. 4, SL.

I COULD NEVER BE CONTENT: *See* B, p. 5, SL.

"Well," I said daringly: EFM, p. 7, SL.

"Never, as long as you live": B, p. 8, SL.

Now, if you excuse me: *See* B, p. 109, SL.

CHAPTER SIX: A GLIMPSE OF HEAVEN

IN THE STUDIO BARN: *See* B, p. 113, SL.

First, there was one: Gouverneur Morris, "The Penalty," *Cosmopolitan*, Vol. LIII, No.3, August 1912, pp. 292, 297, 300-301; Gouverneur Morris, "The Penalty," *Cosmopolitan*, Vol. LIII, No.4, September 1912, pp. 802 (embroidered dress), 807, 813, 816.

"wonderfully young and beautiful": Ibid., p. 802.

The road to Duncan Falls: Mary Edith Christy, "Howard Chandler Christy—The Story of an Ohioan," 1957 speech, p. 7, MS.

Charlie Craig: "Howard Chandler Christy, at 70, Doing Best Work of His Career, *The* [Zanesville, Ohio] *Times-Signal*, November 1, 1942, Section 1, p. 8; Norris Schneider, "Talent Awakened in Christy When He Saw Artist at Work in Zanesville," *The* [Zanesville, Ohio] *Times Recorder*, September 29, 1963; "Zanesville Artist Later Became Famous," *The* [Zanesville, Ohio] *Times-Signal*, April, 1940, Section 1, p. 2.

IT WAS THE WINTER: B, p. 9–11, SL.

Father listened: Ibid., p. 10.

First, I painted some ears: EFM, p. 14, SL.

After that, I wanted: Ibid., p. 13.

As the drawings and paintings: Ibid., p. 17; B, p. 12, SL.

Your middle name is Clifton: EFM, p. 27, SL (states HCC's original middle name was "Clifton" after a blockade runner in the Civil War, likely the USS *Clifton*); *but see* Mary Edith Christy, "Howard Chandler Christy—The Story of an Ohioan," 1957 speech, p. 1, 5, MS (states HCC's original middle name was "Clifford").

And perhaps you might: *See* 1910 Census records for Poughkeepsie, New York (Anna M. Coon, 11 Bellevue Avenue, Poughkeepsie, New York).

"Birthday fight!": EFM, p. 11, SL.

The teachers did not like the fact: "Howard Chandler Christy, at 70, Doing Best Work of His Career," *The* [Zanesville, Ohio] *Times-Signal*, November 1, 1942, Section 1, p. 8.

I would keep a tablet: "L. E. Baughman Taught Howard Chandler Christy, *Coshocton* [Ohio] *Daily Age*, January 29, 1905, pp. 1, 5.

I became popular: EFM, p. 15, SL.

The boy screamed: Ibid.

Day afterward, my teacher: "L.E. Baughman Taught Howard Chandler Christy, *Coshocton* [Ohio] *Daily Age*, January 29, 1905, pp. 1, 5.

The town butcher: EFM, p. 15, SL; "Howard Chandler Christy, at 70, Doing Best Work of His Career," *The* [Zanesville, Ohio] *Times-Signal*, November 1, 1942, Section 1, p. 8.

"It was a beautiful job." Ibid.

ONE DAY, DURING A HISTORY LECTURE: Ibid.; B, SL, p. 19; "L.E. Baughman Taught Howard Chandler Christy, *Coshocton* [Ohio] *Daily Age*, January 29, 1905, pp. 1, 5.; *see* Norris F. Schneider, "Muskingum Valley to Offer Fishing, Boating and Camping this Summer," *The* [Zanesville, Ohio] *Times Recorder*, March 17, 1968, p. 9-B. "The Garfield Observer," online article, (James A. Garfield National Historical Site, accessed July 5, 2015) https://garfieldnps.wordpress.com/2014/01/14/james-a-garfield-in-muskingum-county-ohio/ (This blog of the James A. Garfield National Historical Site contains additional information on the Back Run School at which President Garfield taught for several months in the spring of 1851).

The local newspapers reported: B, p. 19, SL. "Howard Chandler Christy, at 70, Doing Best Work of His Career," *The* [Zanesville, Ohio] *Times-Signal*, November 1, 1942, Section 1, p. 8. (sources differ as to who advised HCC to decline the position of staff artist for *The Toledo Blade*); *see* Norris F. Schneider, "Muskingum Co. Inspired Artist's Interest in Historical Subjects," unknown newspaper, date stamped January 23, 1945, NFS (states that another original drawing is held by the Ohio Historical Society); Norris F. Schneider, "Talent Awakened in Christy When He Saw Artist at Work in Zanesville," *The* [Zanesville, Ohio] *Times Recorder*, September 29, 1963, p. 6-B.

What happens to the originals of the paintings: B, p. 111, SL.

I make arrangements: Letter from HCC to Rose McCune, February 1891, JMH.

Magazines: B, p. 113, SL.

yellow canaries: *See* EFM, p. 50, SL.

We travelled to the local fruit: Ibid.

That's Eleanor Foster: Nancy Keeley, "Rankin Drive Man One-Time Model for Christy," *Zanesville* [Ohio] *Times Recorder*, July 18, 1971, D Section; "Death Comes to James Foster, 72," *The Zanesville* [Ohio] *Signal*, November 18, 1940, p. 8; "Mrs. Sophina E. Foster Dies at Age 93," *The* [Zanesville, Ohio] *Times Recorder*, March 13, 1970, p. 8-A.

CHAPTER SEVEN: AN UNEXPECTED VISITOR

I'm trying, but it's hotter: JJG e-mail, November 17, 2012.

The yellow canaries: *See* EF's journal, p. 50, SL.

Everything must be authentic: L. B. Sisson, "Few of Famed Artist's Originals Remain Here," unknown newspaper, March 9, 1952, NFS; Paul R. Martin, "At Home with Howard Chandler Christy," *The Indianapolis Sunday Star*, December 17, 1911 ("He is a stickler for accuracy of detail . . . .").

This is how I shall remember: B, pp. 110–112, SL; *see* Norris Schneider, "Ohio Sketches," unknown newspaper, November 1, 1949, NFS (refers to an article from the *Courier* dated October 9, 1888, in which HCC and his brother are described excavating an Indian mound).

Guests were always stopping by: Nancy Keeley, "Rankin Drive Man One-Time Model for Christy," *Zanesville* [Ohio] *Times Recorder*, July 18, 1971, D Section; Gouverneur Morris, "The Penalty," *Cosmopolitan*, Vol. LIV, No.2, January 1913, p. 239.

One day, Howard set up: Ibid.

For scenes where Howard: Nancy Keeley, "Rankin Drive Man One-Time Model for Christy," *Zanesville* [Ohio] *Times Recorder*, July 18, 1971, D Section.

None of Howard's: L. B. Sisson, "Few of Famed Artist's Originals Remain Here," unknown newspaper, March 9, 1952, NFS.

Howard's nephews: Robert Wingett, "County Engineer is Nephew of Late Famous Artist, Illustrator," unknown newspaper, February 27, 1966, MS.

Howard often posed: Nancy Keeley, "Rankin Drive Man One-Time Model for Christy," *Zanesville* [Ohio] *Times Recorder*, July 18, 1971, D Section; B, pp. 106–107, SL.

The young women who posed: *See* "Exhibit of Christy's Work Opens Today at Art Institute," unknown newspaper, September 14, 1952, NFS (one such local female model of HCC was Marguerite Bailey McCoy, the sister of journalist and feature writer Eleanor Bailey Johnson).

It was a memorable day: Mary Roberts Rinehart: "Mary Roberts Rinehart," online article (Wikipedia, accessed July 5, 2015) https://en.wikipedia.org/wiki/Mary_Roberts_Rinehart; "Why Do We Think the Butler Did It?" online article (*The Guardian*, accessed July 5, 2015) http://www.theguardian.com/books/booksblog/2010/dec/09/why-we-think-the-butler-did-it.

And this is my arms collection: Paul R. Martin, "At Home with Howard Chandler Christy," *The Indianapolis Sunday Star*, December 17, 1911.

"Yes, fine": Letter of David Noel Maitland Talbot, September 12, 1933, NFS.

Frank is Howard's attorney: L. B. Sisson, "Few of Famed Artist's Originals Remain Here," unknown newspaper, March 9, 1952, NFS ("Among the most regular guests were Attorney and Mrs. Frank Durban"); Norris F. Schneider, "Durban Served as General Counsel for B&O in Ohio and Indiana," *The* [Zanesville, Ohio] *Sunday Times Signal*, April 22, 1951, p. 2, section 4.

Howard's father began telling: Paul R. Martin, "At Home with Howard Chandler Christy," *The Indianapolis Sunday Star*, December 17, 1911; L. B. Sisson, "Few of Famed Artist's Originals Remain Here," unknown newspaper, March 9, 1952, NFS ("The guests could have a glass of wine if they so desired, but Christy touched no liquor at the Barracks.").

"I have heard so much": "At Home with Howard Chandler Christy," *The Indianapolis* [Indiana] *Sunday Star*, December 17, 1911.

As the room erupted: B, pp. 116–117, SL.

HOWARD'S FOURTH OF JULY: Mary Edith Christy, *Howard Chandler Christy—The Story of an Ohioan,* 1957 Speech, p. 7, MS.

Outside, in the middle of the lawn: "Few of Famed Artist's Originals Remain Here," unknown newspaper, March 9, 1952, NFS ("The artist financed these [brass bands].").

It was said that, across the river: B, p. 86, SL.

The band had just finished: Ibid.

Aberdeen, Scotland: U.S. Military Registration Card and Registrar's Report for David Noel Maitland Talbot, World War II; 1910 U.S. Census records for Muskingum County, Ohio.

I was a newspaperman: Clair C. Stebbins, "Howard Chandler Christy," undated, p. 1, CS.

A fellow by the name of Crittenden: Ibid.

That, Miss Palmer, is Mrs. Tanner: Norris F. Schneider interview with Mrs. J. Ray Tanner, October 5, 1975, NFS.

One woman committed suicide: Letter from Marilyn Schafer to author, February 16, 2011.

"Artist Christy's New York Studio": "Artist Christy's New York Studio Den of Vice," *The Zanesville* [Ohio] *Weekly Courier,* January 20, 1910, p. 5.

"Christy Rattles Family Skeleton": "Christy Rattles Family Skeleton," *The* [Massillon, Ohio] *Evening Independent*, January 18, 1910.

"'Model' Husband and Tipsy Wife": "'Model' Husband and Tipsy Wife," *The Fort Wayne* [Indiana] *News*, January 19, 1910, p. 1.

"She was so beautiful": Norris F. Schneider interview with Mrs. J. Ray Tanner, October 5, 1975, NFS.

"She never drank a drop": Ibid.

Howard hoisted a burning: Edith Christy, *HCC The Story of an Ohioan,* MS, p. 7.

I have been only: EF's journal, SL, p. 49.

Her name was Ghislaine: Harold S. Hoover, "A Day at the 'Barracks'," *The* [Massillon, Ohio] *Evening Independent*, September 17, 1909, p. 1, 5; 1910 U.S. Census records for Muskingum County, Ohio.

A few moments: EF's journal, SL, p. 49.

She spoke in French: Ibid., p. 50; "A Day at the 'Barracks'," *The* [Massillon, Ohio] *Evening Independent*, September 17, 1909, p. 5; B, SL, p. 93.

"Sh-sh-sh--your family": EF's Journal, SL, p. 51.

She left the Barracks suddenly: "Model Leaves Christy Home," *The Elyria* [Ohio] *Evening Signal*, September 25, 1910, p. 5.

No, they both left: Ibid.; "Child Reconciles Artist and Wife," *Oakland* [California] *Tribune*, September 21, 1910, p. 11; "Doings in Ohio," *The* [Maryville, Ohio] *Evening Tribune*, September 22, 1910, p. 1; "Snapshots at Social Leaders," *The Washington Post*, September 22, 1910, p. 7; "Mrs. Christy Leaves Home," *New York Times*, September 27, 1910, p. 1; "Christys at Outs, Artist is Silent," *The Newark* [Ohio] *Advocate*, September 27, 1910, p. 1.

"Mrs. Christy is now in New York": "Off Again, On Again," The *Fort Wayne* [Indiana] *Daily News*, September 28, 1910, p. 4; "Christys are Reconciled Says Miss Britt," *New Castle* [Pennsylvania] *News*, September 28, 1910, p. 8.

And as for Mademoiselle Britt: "Model Leaves Christy Home," *The* [Elyria, Ohio] *Evening Telegram*, September 29, 1910, p. 5. "The Gay French Model," *The Bradford* [Pennsylvania] *Era*, September 29, 1910, p. 1.

To this day: "Mrs. Christy Gives Up," *The Van Wert* [Ohio] *Daily Bulletin*, September 26, 1910, p. 1; "The Christy's Make Up," *The* [Massillon, Ohio] *Evening Independent*, September 26, 1910, p. 2.

"Well, you know": "Mrs. Christy Welcome at Ex-Husband's Home," *The Lincoln* [Nebraska] *Evening News*, September 22, 1910; "Old Obstacle is

Still in the Way," *Coshocton* [Ohio] *Daily Tribune,* September 24, 1910.

His sister Rose: "Mr. and Mrs. Christy: Christy Peace Plan," *Warren* [Pennsylvania] *Mirror,* September 24, 1910, p. 7.

Ah, well that might prove: Clair C. Stebbins, "Howard Chandler Christy," CS, undated, p. 1.

The guests departed: EF's journal, pp. 48—49, SL.

DAYS LATER, A STRANGE: "Christys To Be Reconciled?" *The* [New York] *Sun*, July 30, 1912, p. 1.

That evening: *See* "Snapshots at Social Leaders," *The Washington Post*, September 22, 1910, p. 7.

"I am a Southern woman": "Social Sets of Other Cities," *The Washington Post*, September 23, 1910, p. 7.

"Will he live part": Ibid.

"I do not know how long": "Social Sets and Other Cities," *The Washington Post*, June 7, 1911.

"Oh no": Ibid.

That evening, the dinner: "Christys To Be Reconciled?" *The* [New York] *Sun*, July 30, 1912, p. 1.

Maebelle cursed: Interview with Mrs. J. Ray Tanner, October 5, 1975, NFS.

I'm leaving today: *See* "Doings in Ohio," *The* [Maryville, Ohio] *Evening Tribune*, September 22, 1910, p. 1.

Visitors and friends: Interview with Mrs. J. Ray Tanner, October 5, 1975, NFS (friends brought Mrs. Christy liquor at the Barracks, causing Natalie distress).

One day, Maebelle: Ibid.

"To much hay seed": Clair Stebbins, Speech before the Art Institute, September 25, 1952, p. 4, CS.

CHAPTER EIGHT: THE GIFT OF IMMORTALITY

In the fall and early winter: Author's observations of the Barracks and surrounding landscape during a visit, October 10–11, 2009.

Howard had made good: B, SL, p. 112.

This one: *"Why Not Live Forever?"*: Professor Elie Metchnikoff and Dr. Henry Smith Williams, "Why Not Live Forever?" *Cosmopolitan*, Vol. LIII, No.4, September 1912, pp. 436–446.

"Then there are men": Ibid., p. 440.

Dr. Metchnikoff . . . is the Ponce de Leon: Ibid.

"Reckon as how 'Hard'": Paul R. Martin, "At Home with Howard Chandler Christy," *The Indianapolis Sunday Star*, December 17, 1911.

I ran quickly: B, SL, pp. 118-119.

"THERE IS ONE PICTURE": Paul R. Martin, "At Home with Howard Chandler Christy," *The Indianapolis Sunday Star*, December 17, 1911.

"It is a copy": Ibid.

Howard was a dreamer: Ibid.

THE EDUCATION OF AN ARTIST: John C. Van Dyke, "The Art Students' League of New York," *Harper's New Monthly Magazine*, October 1891, pp. 688-700; *see* "The Art-Schools of New York," *Scribner's Monthly*, October 1878, pp. 775-781; *see also* Raymond J. Steiner, The Art Students League of New York: A History (CSS Publications, Inc., Saugerties, NY, 1999).

"Achieve it knowingly": John C. Van Dyke, "The Art Students' League of New York," *Harper's New Monthly Magazine*, October 1891, p. 692.

"Draw firm": Ibid.

"Your line": Ibid.

"The color of the face": Ibid., p. 694.

"It is too dark": Ibid.

"Try is over again": Ibid.

The names of people: "Christy's Rock" at "The Barracks," Blue Rock, Ohio.

A man by the name of Wetzel: *See* "Whetzel Rock," unknown newspaper, MS; "The Sunday News: An Historical picture by a Muskingum County Artist," unknown newspaper; MS; Norris Schneider, "Talent Awakened in Christy When He Saw Artist at Work in Zanesville," The [Zanesville, Ohio] *Times Recorder*, September 29, 1963, p. 6-B.

Lewis Wetzel: James D. Pierce, "Lewis Wetzel, Dark Hero of Ohio," online article (Archiving Early America, accessed July 5, 2015) http://www.earlyamerica.com/review/spring97/wetzel.html.

Took first prize: EF's journal, p. 26; MS, telephone interview, January 21, 2013.

"We are remembered": "Spirit of Americanism," *GRIT Family Section*, September 10, 1950, MS.

Of course we can: A strong Christian, HCC believed that a person's soul was immortal.

Endnotes

1 Despite its unfinished state, General MacArthur's portrait would hang in the National Portrait Gallery in Washington, DC, when it reopened on July 1, 2006, after undergoing extensive renovations. Displayed in one of four newly created galleries within the Great Hall on the museum's colossal third floor—the same floor that saw President Lincoln's inaugural ball—the portrait became one of the major highlights of "Twentieth-Century Americans," a permanent exhibition spotlighting the major political, cultural, and scientific heroes of the twentieth century.

2 According to his death certificate, Harrison Fisher died at the age of fifty-six due to cirrhosis of the liver and chronic nephritis, with edema of the lungs being a contributory factor.

3 Prone to mild exaggeration, Nancy claimed to have been sixteen years of age and a flaxen blonde when she arrived in New York City in 1912. In reality, she was a few months shy of her twentieth birthday and a brunette.

4 Until the early 1940s, Howard believed he was born in 1873, rather than in 1872, as court birth records from Morgan County, Ohio, his county of birth, so indicate. According to family accounts, Howard learned of his true birth year sometime in or around 1942. Accordingly, all references to Howard's age in the chapters occurring before 1942 preserve this misconception. Thus, to determine Howard's true age at a particular time before 1942, one year should be added to the age so stated.

5   Charles Craig eventually moved to Colorado Springs, Colorado, where he became, according to the Zanesville *Sunday Times-Signal* in April 14, 1940, "America's greatest painter of Indian and buffalo." One of Craig's most significant paintings was *Custer's Last Stand*, a subject that became Howard's first childhood memory and dear to his heart.

In February 1913, Craig stated to the *Colorado Springs Gazette* that women in the past had been inspirational but, at that time, were "so busy hiding their individuality under a bushel that they have no time left to develop their personality." Craig declared that he would rather paint Indians than women. "Every one of them," he said, "rich or poor, seems bent upon imitating one particular fashion or custom until they look exactly as similar as so many garden varieties." At that time, most women were patterning their fashions and looks upon that of fictional women found in magazines, newspapers, and books and created by the illustrators of beauty: Gibson, Fisher, Flagg, and, of course, the young artist whom Craig had inspired in the winter of 1877 — Howard Chandler Christy.

After a two-year illness, Craig died on October 20, 1931, in Colorado Springs, Colorado.

6   Raymond Crumbaker (1903–1980) was the paternal grandson of Howard's Duncan Falls doctor, O. B. Crumbaker (1846–1932), and the maternal grandson of Howard's blacksmith, Skelton S. Waxler (1851–1938). His parents, Oliver (1871–1931) and Lura Crumbaker (1874–1947), were schoolmates of the artist.

7   According to Howard's grandniece, Marilyn Schafer, her father, Howard Paul Christy (1901–1966) modeled for the character of Bubbles, prompting her uncle Donald (1898–1984) to refer to him often as "Bub." Howard's use of two different models—local boy Raymond and nephew Howard Paul—to paint the same character for a magazine serial reflects a customary practice that he continued to use throughout his career,

including his later World War I posters. In that case, various women, including Nancy Palmer, claim to have modeled for the same poster girl.

8   At the Zanesville train station, Howard's attorney, Frank Durban, a much-respected member of the Ohio Bar, met the Rineharts as "Howard's hired man." The Rineharts did not know it was Howard's attorney, but they thought it odd that he was wearing an English suit and holding a cane with chamois gloves.

About the Author

*A*s a freshman at the University of Maryland, Jim Head discovered a gilt-edged folio of Charles Dana Gibson's *The Social Ladder* in the stacks of the campus library one night, starting him on a journey to learn more about Gibson and the "Illustrators of Beauty." In turn, he became captivated by the talent, fame, and subsequent obscurity of Howard Chandler Christy and began amassing the largest private collection of documents, photographs, and other material related to the artist. Over the years, he has interviewed Christy's former models, family members, and others who knew him, and ultimately engaged research assistants throughout the country to help him uncover the true, untold story of Christy and his wife, Nancy.

A graduate of the University of Maryland, the George Washington University Law School, and Georgetown Law School, Jim is a law partner with Williams Mullen, P.C., in Tysons Corner, Virginia, where he concentrates in estate planning, business succession planning, and trust and estate litigation. Jim was selected by his peers for inclusion in *The Best Lawyers in America*© 2016 for trusts and estates. He lives in Chantilly, Virginia, with his wife, Rita, and daughter, Christianna.